C000271498

About the author

Lennie Lower was born in Dubbo and lived in Darlinghurst, Sydney, where, according to one of his colleagues, he learnt to write Australian 'as she is spoke'. After leaving the navy, he served time on a number of newspapers and his witty columns made him one of the most loved characters in Australian journalism throughout the 30s and 40s. A hard-drinking, unpredictable man, he was often the despair of sub-editors and more than a handful for proprietors. Though he died in 1947 at the age of 43, he is still remembered as a true genius of Australian humour.

Prion Humour Classics

Augustus Carp, Esq	Henry Howarth Bashford
Seven Men and Two Others	Max Beerbohm
How to Travel Incognito	Ludwig Bemelmans
The Freaks of Mayfair	E F Benson
Mapp and Lucia	E F Benson
How Steeple Sinderby Wanderers Won the FA Cup	J L Carr
*The Diary of a Provincial Lady**	E M Delafield
The Papers of A J Wentworth, BA	H F Ellis
Squire Haggard's Journal	Michael Green
The Diary of a Nobody	George and Weedon Grossmith
Three Men in a Boat	Jerome K Jerome
Mrs Caudle's Curtain Lectures	Douglas Jerrold
Sunshine Sketches of a Little Town	Stephen Leacock
No Mother to Guide Her	Anita Loos
Here's Luck	Lennie Lower
The Autobiography of a Cad	A G Macdonell
*The Serial**	Cyra McFadden
*The World of S J Perelman**	S J Perelman
*The Education of Hyman Kaplan**	Leo Rosten
*The Return of Hyman Kaplan**	Leo Rosten
The Unrest-Cure and Other Beastly Tales	Saki
The English Gentleman	Douglas Sutherland
*My Life and Hard Times**	James Thurber
Cannibalism in the Cars	Mark Twain

*For copyright reasons these titles are not available in the USA or Canada in the Prion edition.

Here's Luck

This edition published in 2001 by
Prion Books Limited,
Imperial Works,
Perren Street,
London NW5 3ED
www.prionbooks.com

First published in 1930

A catalogue record for this book is available from the British Library

ISBN 1-85375-428-5

Jacket design by Keenan
Jacket image courtesy of Getty Images
Printed and bound in Great Britain
by Creative Print & Design, Wales

Here's Luck

Lennie Lower

with a new introduction by
JAMES SCANLON

INTRODUCTION

by JAMES SCANLON

Ask a young Australian today about Lennie Lower and you'd probably get a blank look. Ask anyone outside Australia and you most certainly would. Yet to an older generation of Australians, Lennie Lower was the stuff of legend. And not just in literary circles. He was a man of the people, the authentic irreverent voice of the Australian working man. As noted newspaper man Cyril Pearl put it: 'Even the Sydney taxi-driver, hunched ape-like over his frayed cigarette, would emit an approving, almost-human grunt if you asked him to deposit you at the newspaper office where Lower worked.'

In fact, the legend came to obscure much of the real Lennie, making it difficult to tell the man from the myth. Though hard facts are hard to come by, we know he was born Leonard Waldemar Lower in Dubbo on September 3, 1903, and died in Sydney on July 10, 1947. Brought up in Darlinghurst, Sydney, he joined the navy as a young man. He then took to the road, living the hobo life, occasionally dossing in Sydney's

Domain, along with the homeless. He lumped his swag around the countryside, riding goods trains and sleeping under tarpaulins.

Lennie soon started to make a living in the most haphazard of occupations, that of the peripatetic scribbler. He was to become, for a generation, one of the best-known and best-loved voices in Australia, and certainly the top newspaper columnist of his day. Imagine Flann O'Brien, Julie Burchill and Hunter S Thompson all rolled into one. Most of his output consisted of short humorous pieces: meditations on domestic trivia and current news items, all perfectly puncturing the presumptions and snobberies of his time. Many of these items were published in the collections *Here's Another* (1932), *Life and Things* (1936) and *The Bachelor's Guide to the Care of the Young and Other Stories* (1941).

Lennie was of humble origins, and his brilliant literary career similarly kicked off with articles in a rag called *Beckett's Budget*, described by one observer as 'a sleazy scandal sheet'. While still in his twenties, his commercial appeal was recognised by editors and publishers of the top-selling papers and magazines. He went on to write for the *Daily Guardian*, *Daily Telegraph*, *Sunday Telegraph*, *Smith's Weekly* and the *Women's Weekly*, commanding what at the time was big money, writing eight columns each week. Though as a hard-drinking, unpredictable law unto himself, his employers often came to feel he was something of a mixed blessing and ultimately a thorn in their side.

His early break came when he visited the office of the *Labor Daily*, telling writer Clif Cary that he had a funny story. Having no great expectations, Cary tossed the would-be humorist a pencil and a couple of sheets of paper. When Lower returned with his copy, Cary absentmindedly tossed it into the editor's basket, quickly forgetting about it. That afternoon the editor, Quentin Spedding, sent for Cary. 'Why did you send me this?' asked Spedding, who at that moment was lying on his back, laughing until tears came. Lennie Lower was hired.

The Lower legend has him being fired too. He once courted the sack, contriving to tip a bucket of printer's ink and paste over his immediate boss. Instead of relieving Lennie of his duties, he simply laughed and laughed, unable to see a serious side to anything Lower said or did.

When another paper Lower wrote for, *The World*, collapsed in 1931, a colleague met Lennie staggering down the back stairs of the office. Lower was weighed down by a large sack. 'What have you got there?' asked the erstwhile workmate. 'You had better get up there and help yourself,' replied Lower. He had three typewriters in the bag.

Most famously, he got the sack from the *Telegraph*, a paper still in daily production, unlike so many of those forgotten mastheads of the pre-war years. There was a big reception for Noel Coward, visiting Sydney in 1940. Introduced to Lower, the English genius glanced him over and drawled patronisingly, 'I understand you're the king of Australian comedy?' Lower looked Coward square in the eye and intoned, 'And I understand you're the queen of English comedy.' Whether the exchange went beyond words depends on which version of the story you're hearing. But the upshot was that Lower had insulted the visiting star, and he was sacked on the spot. He also found that he was still sacked when he arrived at the office the next day. So he took himself to the pub, pulled up a stool, and bought himself a drink. While the story of the previous night's contretemps was already doing the rounds of the various newspaper offices, someone wandered into *Smith's Weekly* headquarters and mentioned that they'd just seen Lower propping up the bar at a nearby watering-hole. 'What are you doing here?' cried the editor. 'Go and fetch him!'

The extent of Lower's drinking is another bone of contention. Popular mythology tends to paint him as a holy drinker, crawling between benders and using pubs as his office in the manner of Flann O'Brien. Others, such as his contemporary Cyril Pearl, claim the picture of him as a drunk is largely an invention and that he drank no more than the next red-blooded Australian male.

Here's Luck was Lennie Lower's only published novel, an immediate bestseller in 1930 that has remained perennially popular. If Lennie Lower had written nothing else, this alone would have earned his place in the Western canon of humour. The story of one Jack Gudgeon, a boozy ne'er-do-well of Sydney's lower classes, *Here's Luck* has an easy conversational tone that pulls the reader in immediately, and does not relent. Jack and his son Stanley are a roguish, urban update of that 19th-century Australian comic father and son team Dad & Dave, from Steele Rudd's *On Our Selection*. Unlike their antecedents from the bush, however, the

Gudgeons have a wide streak of devious immorality. Yet it is the very faults in Jack Gudgeon's character, as well as his appalling behaviour, that so endear him to readers.

It is interesting to note that Jack Gudgeon is, as we learn in the first sentence of the book, forty-eight years old, whereas Lennie Lower was at the time of writing still under thirty. It seems that Lennie felt himself old and cynical beyond his years even then; few young writers have pulled off a first-person narrative exploiting such an age discrepancy between writer and central character. Jack has been around, and knows a thing or two, yet for all his ingrained misanthropy he cannot remain immune to even the smallest misfortune that life, and the author, can throw at him. As a victim of circumstances, Gudgeon reaches anti-heroic status. He is truly a man ahead of his time – fictional characters of the first half of the twentieth century were rarely as wicked, or as funny.

Lower's anti-hero is one of the founding fathers of what has now become the comic Australian stereotype; a character since popularised in the work of Barry Humphries, Paul Hogan and a thousand Australian lager commercials – an untameable chauvinist and slovenly reprobate who'd sell his wife for a drop of the hard stuff ('If I had to choose between my family and my pipe, I'd choose my pipe,' says Jack at one point). He has the innocence of the provincial combined with the guile of the larrikin and is always on the make, searching for the path of least resistance. He is resignedly unflappable and talks with a natural deadpan wit.

As one colleague put it, Lower learnt to write Australian 'as she is spoke' and his brazen idiomatic prose has aged nicely. Much better, for instance, than the now archaic vernacular used in C J Dennis's once equally popular *Songs of the Sentimental Bloke* (1915). Lower has no compunctions about resorting to painful puns, yet keeps up the interest and variety mixing fast-moving farce, slapstick, absurd juxtapositions and a bar-room philosopher's world-weary wisdom. Some of the humour is overt, while some of the jokes remain half buried, waiting for the more perceptive reader to uncover their depths.

A hardened professional, Lower's prose was always well-honed and occasionally even lyrical:

> A foaming pint-pot thumped wetly on the bar as I spoke and I clasped it by its big friendly handle, raised it, and the stuff swooped down my throat bearing a message of hope to my dejected internals. I replaced the pot, empty, on the bar and sighed—one of those deep, satisfactory sighs that seem to start from one's boots, gather all the little cares and troubles on the way, and from the mouth dissipate in the air.

He was also a master of the deadpan one-liner:

> The best way to tell gold is to pass a nugget around in a crowded bar. If it comes back, it's not gold.

Lennie Lower lived in difficult times: a world sunk in depression, and heading towards another senseless war.

He had no time for politicians or government officials; he thought they were all just filling up space, their sole purpose being to educate and amaze us simply by being so unutterably absurd. They are a frequent subject of Jack Gudgeon's rants which target anything that oppresses the little man. Here he is on bookmakers, landlords and double standards:

> I fully realize, as a good citizen, that private property is sacred and that no man should be robbed except by proper business methods, but somehow the sporting malefactors of this world appeal to me more than people like my rotten landlord, who goes to church on Sunday and has the damned hide to call for rent on Monday.

Lennie fought the good fight of the working man, whether of the left or the right, against the petty bureaucrats and the self-improving gentility of the Australian middle-classes (witness Jack's hilarious visit to his wife's mother's respectable suburb). His humour was always a glorious two-fingered salute to all of that.

Chapter 1

It is absolutely ridiculous to call a man of forty-eight old. A restricted vocabulary might account for such a remark, and then of course there are people whose observations are superficial and even frivolous.

Temple, however, is a man who is never frivolous and I was astounded when he said it.

"Gudgeon," he said, "you're getting old."

"I'm not old!" I protested.

"You look old!" he insisted.

That was a lie. I pride myself on my looks. I have not a grey hair in my head, and numerous acquaintances have favourably remarked on my appearance. I am perhaps, a little under medium height, but then mere height is nothing. Notice the relative importance of Napoleon and the giraffe. I have been called fat by envious persons less kindly treated by nature and there was one who at the height of his jealousy called me "Barrel".

I am not a vain man, but in my own defence I quote a remark made by the girl in Flannery's saloon bar to a friend.

"I like," she said, "his ruddy, clean-shaven, ingenuous face; and he has such a splendidly mature figure and manly bearing...."

That, I think, should be sufficient. If, however, I say *if* there is the slightest excuse for a remark such as Temple made there is only one excuse for it. It is not age. It's worry.

It's Stanley—and if there is anything within the ken of man more calculated to bring a man's grey hairs in sorrow to the grave, it, whatever it is, is not human.

Stanley is about eighteen or nineteen, I am not sure which, but looks much older than his years. He is taller and thinner than I but otherwise resembles me as closely as can be expected these days. His face can look positively cherubic on occasion, but this makes no difference to the fact that he can be a fiend from the blackest pit when he likes. I've had a lot of trouble with him. A few weeks ago he was at that stage where he had given up the idea of being a pirate, engine-driver, or chief rescuer in the fire brigade, and wanted to be a poet. He has altered greatly since, but I would much rather rear a platypus than a boy. Problems innumerable beset the conscientious father, but the greatest problem of all is to know in what trade or profession the boy will be best fitted to support his old father at a later date.

The medical profession, of course, suggests itself immediately. I have no yearning to have Stanley descend to the familiarity of listening-in to the heart-throbs of the vulgar, and punching people in the ribs and asking if it hurts. Neither do I wish to stand on one leg with my mouth open and say ninety-nine, as I would undoubtedly be compelled to do if he were training for the medical profession. His mother would see to that. Furthermore, judging by the number of divorce cases that doctors become entangled in it would seem that the only way some of them can keep their names untarnished is by the application of a little metal-polish to their brass plate. And whatever else Stanley is, I want him to be untarnished. That is to say, he'd be fool enough to get caught.

I could make a lawyer of him. He really has a talent in that direction. He comes home in the small hours of the morning with an iron-clad alibi and even the wife can find no chink in his armour of excuses. He is a fountain of fluid eloquence. I'm a bit that way myself: it runs in our family. Still, admitting that lawyers are quite all right in their place, the trouble is to find the place.

There is the Church. Somehow I don't think he is fitted for it. He hasn't heard the call, so to speak. It seems to be a weakness of his, this deafness to calls. Every morning I have to go to his room and pull the bed-clothes off him before he shows any signs of life. This despite the fact that his mother has shouted herself black in the face at the foot of the stairs and his aunt has battered the paint off his door. He did show some interest in the subject of the revision of the prayer-book. His suggestion was to insert crossword puzzles on alternate pages with blank leaves interspersed here and there for sketches and notes to be passed along to fellow sufferers during the sermon. He can be wooden-headed, dull and entirely lacking in imagination when the mood seizes him, and taking into consideration these assets, I had hopes of a brilliant career for him in the army, but unfortunately he is flat-footed, so his other qualifications go for nothing.

I could, I suppose, put a stiff collar on him, give him a pair of gold cuff-links, a cigarette-holder, and a couple of fountain-pens and incarcerate him in a warehouse; to emerge at the expiration of his sentence as a business man: a successful business man: a man who has won the right to put his thumb in the armhole of his vest and look over the top of his glasses and grunt. Or I could start him off in the Public Service. There he could remain for about forty years in a more or less comatose condition and later be dismissed from his position of Temporary Casual Supernumerary Class II clerk with a pension. The pension would not be sufficient to keep me and I could not bear the thought of filling in forms, LX2, A3, Folio 9716Q in quadruplicate, digging up birth certificates, writing out references for him and getting his finger-prints taken in order to get him on the waiting-list.

I have read of fathers cutting their sons off with a shilling and casting them into the world with a clout in one ear and a lot of invaluable advice in the other. And the sons have become celebrated Lord Mayors, bushrangers, politicians and big business men. Worked themselves up from newsboys to a position where they can sign cheques for thousands without having to flee the country immediately. I have thought over this arrangement of cutting him off with a shilling—but I cannot spare the shilling. Anyhow, he'd be bound to make a mess of things. And then there's this poet business. He's in love. He generally is, more or less.

I thought there was something wrong when he started cleaning his teeth every hour and oiling his hair and walking stiff legged about the house to preserve the crease in his trousers. I had the wife give him the onion test and when he said he didn't care for onions while his eyes glistened and his mouth watered—I knew.

"Who's this knobby-kneed, enamel-faced giggler you're going out with?" I asked him kindly.

It's always best to be tactful when a boy is like this. They're very sensitive in the moony stage.

We had a bit of a session—a "go in" as they call it. I tried to reason with him. I explained to him about women. I showed him a portrait of his mother as she was when I married her and left the rest to his imagination.

I explained to him that, if ever he found himself getting serious with a woman, if he bashed his head against a nearby wall for about ten minutes instead, he'd feel better for it in the long run. I told him that if he bought himself a hair-shirt and a loud-speaker he would be just as comfortable as if he was married.

It was useless.

"I love her, father," he said.

Just like that.

"I wish I were a poet, father, that I might describe her to you," he murmured, lying back on the bed in a kind of rapturous swoon. That's how the poet idea started.

"Her teeth are like pearls."

"I understand," I said, "mouth like an oyster."

"Her hair——"

"Clipped and stuck to her cheek-bones with saliva." He ignored me.

"I have basked in the sunshine of her smile——"

"That how you got sunburnt on the back?" I asked.

"Gazing into her eyes — eyes like two deep wells——"

"Well! Well!" I said. Rather smart, I thought, but he looked up at me, and, well, sort of looked up at me and looked down on me, if you understand what I mean.

"Knees like a retired Highland piper, I suppose," I said, just to regain my composure.

"Her lips!" he muttered, gazing rapturously at the door-knob.

"Ah! her hips. Explain about her hips, my son."

"I said lips, father, not hips," he said disdainfully.

I was a bit disappointed. Still I suppose, I couldn't expect—anyhow he's young yet, and I always was his pal and confidant, more or less. Lord knows, life is dull enough. Anyhow he insisted that it was "lips" he said, so I let it go at that.

It was then that he brought out the poem.

He got up from the bed as though in a trance, there was a glazed look about his eyes, he even forgot about the crease in his trousers as he bent to get the poem from underneath the linoleum.

"If I show you this, father, will you swear by all you hold sacred to keep it secret?" he asked.

His voice has not yet decided whether it is a tenor or a baritone, and he had to change over half-way through. It sounded very emotional. I was rather surprised at the form of the swear. When he had wanted to be a pirate he used to ask me to swear by the blood of my ancestors. Later, after he had been reading some book or other, it had to be done by the beard of the profit. What the devil the beard of the profit is, I don't know. I haven't seen so much as a whisker of a profit in the last few months. Money is close in the city and I haven't noticed its proximity in the suburbs. However, after thinking for about three seconds on all I held sacred, I swore.

Then he showed me the poem. I read it out aloud.

When I gaze into her eyes,
I see blue skies,
And mists arise;
Her lips, blood-red
From Psyche bled,
Set up a singing in my head.
Her little nose——

"I haven't finished it," he said, twisting one foot round the other.

I pondered for a while.

"Her little nose she loudly blows," I suggested.

"She doesn't!" he cried.

"Untidy little brat. Surely——"

"Father! You must not speak like that of my future wife!" he cried; something after the old pirate manner.

This knocked me. I didn't expect it. Even a man who has been married twenty years can still be surprised at things occasionally. I was astonished. He had certainly rung the bell. Mentally I gave him the choice of a kewpie doll or an aluminium saucepan.

"Wife!" I gasped.

"My wife. My mate," he whispered reverently.

"Hey!" I said. "Hold off! Finish. D'you hear me? That's enough. Wife! Pah!"

His mouth fell open a little.

"To think that I should have reared a son," I cried; "dandled him on my knees, listened to his childish burblings, bought him toffee with stripes on, let him ruin my razor shaving a lot of lather off his face; been friend, Roman, countryman to him, and then—and then—he tells me to my face, without a blush or the batting of a solitary eyelash, that he will sell his birthright for a mess of face-cream!"

I sank down on the bed, overcome.

"To leave his poor old father to push a peanut cart with a whistle on it in his old age, while *he* keeps a woman supplied with shoes, hats, grievances and pet dogs!"

I buried my face in my hands.

"Father!" said Stanley hoarsely. "Father—Ar! I say—father!"

I remained prostrate. This was the first real opportunity I'd had of trying out his mother's tactics, and I wasn't going to throw it away.

"Father!" he cried theatrically, "I will go away and try to forget! I will give her up and go away. Away—away!" and he tottered out of the room and stumbled down the stairs.

I sat up. The next thing to do to carry the experiment to a conclusion was to lie on the bed motionless and claim weakly that I had a splitting headache and that I forgave everyone, poor down-trodden creature that I was. However, there was no one to look at me so I lit my pipe instead. I could hear Stanley downstairs talking to his mother—making trouble. How much, I never guessed but knowing what a young hound he was I began to feel perturbed. Stanley *is* a hound.

I could hear his aunt's voice too. His aunt is my wife's sister I'll admit, and no doubt she would make some paralysed deaf mute a good wife—but I'll say no more. After all, blood is thicker than water. But then so is soup, and even water is of some use when you can't get anything else—but still, I will say no more.

Never let it be said that *I* ever said anything derogatory of that parrot-brained Gorgon.

Chapter 2

I smoked for a while and then went downstairs after salvaging one of my ties which Stanley had borrowed and thrown under the bed with the rest of his discarded clothing. One thing about Stanley, he is a methodical boy and pitches his clothes on the floor in symmetrical heaps where they can be easily turned over with the foot when anything is required. The two women were waiting for me at the foot of the stairs when I came down. I felt like going back. Stanley's aunt folded her arms, shot a glance at the wife, pursed her lips, and shrugged her shoulders. Without speaking she managed to say that this was the plague they had been speaking about. I knew immediately that Stanley had seized his opportunity. He's like that. And his mother will back him up in any fool thing so long as I'm made to look ridiculous.

"What have you been doing to Stanley?" snapped the wife.

"Stanley who?" I asked.

Silly, I know, but I wasn't prepared.

"What's wrong with him?" I added.

"He is going to South Africa to hunt elephants," she said slowly.

Aunt Gertrude spoke up. She has a voice like a knife that has been left stuck in a lemon too long.

"He is going to South Africa to hunt elephants," she said slowly in a hanged-by-the-neck-till-you-are-dead tone.

Elephants mind you! But I had got used to this sort of thing.

"Well, well!" I said, "I suppose he'll need to take his lunch; or perhaps he can get lunch over there. I think they do have that sort of thing. Mealies and kopjes and veldts and things. Of course, he'll find it a little different but——"

"John!" said my wife.

If there's anything I hate, it's "John".

"The poor boy is going to South Africa to try to forget. His hopes are blasted——"

"Agatha!" I said.

She blushed slightly.

"To think that the wife of my bosom——"

"Bosom your grandmother!"

There are times when the veneer of refinement peels off Agatha.

She led the way into the drawing-room. Stanley was there, standing with arms folded and a look of hopeless determination on his face—or determined hopelessness. Properly blasted. He was gazing out the window as if he already saw the elephants advancing with writhing tentacles.

Agatha sank into a chair, suddenly overcome.

"He is going to South Africa—to hunt elephants!" she whispered brokenly. "Elephants! He is going to hunt them in South Africa!" she moaned. "Elephants—Africa—South!"

"Hunt—going—to," I added, to help her out of the mess.

Aunt Gertrude sniffed.

Her sniffs remind me, somehow, of the dried husk-like skin of a snake, after it has been shed.

"Ah, Stanley!" moaned the wife, warming up to the work. "Don't go to South Africa!"

It made me mad to see her pretending to take him seriously.

"I will. I am. I shall—must!" said Stanley.

I could see that with all the encouragement he was getting he had become rather taken with the idea.

"But, Stanley—it's so far away! Couldn't you go to the zoo?"

"Zoo!" hooted Stanley. "Zoo! What zoo?"

It sounded like the war-cry of the Randwick Rovers.

His eye-balls seemed to pop out.

"I don't want those lop-eared, peanut elephants! I want elephants that are wild! That crouch ready to spring and tear one limb from limb with their claws! Elephants!" he concluded with a shout of triumph.

"But, Stan; elephants don't have claws," said Agatha.

"They'll wish they had before I'm finished with them," said Stanley fiercely.

"Ah, let him go and hunt elephants if he wants to—the poor boy," put in Gertrude. "If he's brought home mangled beyond recognition perhaps he (me) will see what a heartless brute he is!"

Agatha seemed to think this over for a while and then with an air of comparative cheerfulness straightened her dress and remarked: "Oh, well; I suppose if he wants to go, he wants to go."

This seemed to me profound, but sound. There was absolutely no argument against it.

"Elephants!" muttered Stanley, gazing at me and

licking his lips.

"Bah!" I exclaimed, turning to him, "what have elephants ever done to you that you should pick on them like this! Poor little elephants that never said a harsh word—who woke you up to this damned elephant rot, anyhow?"

"Well, Stanley, if you've made up your mind that's all there is about it," cut in Gertrude.

"Yes. Yes," sobbed Agatha.

I closed my mouth. It only needed me to object to all this rot; to put my foot down firmly and forbid it, and the pair of them would have bundled him off to South Africa immediately. I know women. That is, I know that much about them. Of course this elephant talk was all damned rot. Stanley's idea of amusement at my expense. Any unpleasantness where I was the goat could always command Agatha's and Gertrude's hearty support. I treated the matter as a joke—fool that I was.

Agatha went out of the room, presumably to cut a few sandwiches for Stanley to take to South Africa.

Gertrude walked over to Stanley and put her hand on his shoulder, "Stanley," she said, "be very careful in South Africa. Don't go rushing in among the elephants and hurting yourself——"

"That's the way. One at a time," I said heartily. "I bet they laugh their trunks off when they spot him."

I got the snake-skin sniff again.

"And always wear your goloshes," she went on, "I'm sure those jungles are not properly drained—and flannel next to your skin, and be careful crossing the roads at intersections, and *don't* speak to any strange men."

"And wash behind your ears and see if you can bring home an ant-eater," I said.

I pronounced it "aunt-eater" and, thinking that was good enough to exit on, I exited, with the honours of the last word thick upon me.

The next few hours I spent roaming about the house waiting for dinner. Stanley had gone out. I strolled into the kitchen two or three times. They were both sitting there; Agatha sobbing loudly behind her handkerchief each time I entered, and Gertrude eyeing me as she would a sick python, and saying, "Poor dear," to Agatha and patting her on the hand. It was impressed upon me that I was as welcome as a leprous gorilla at a wake, but it was some time before it dawned on me that there wasn't going to be any dinner!

This was over the odds! Even if all this tomfoolery was true, and Stanley was going to South Africa; and supposing everybody was all torn to shreds with sorrow, and that—a man's dinner is his dinner. A man must eat though the earth collapse and the heavens roll together as a scroll. There is a limit to everything. It struck me that it would be a pretty good idea to go to South Africa and take Stanley. A man could at least fry a slab of elephant to keep him going between meals. I was beginning to get a bit nasty tempered, when the front door opened and Stanley came in. He looked a bit down in the mouth.

"Look here, Stan," I said, going up to him. "Are there enough of these blasted elephants to go round? Couldn't we share them between us? We'd get on all right together, you and I. I could hold the elephants while you shot them?"

"Or," I added, as he didn't seem to be too enthusiastic, "we could take a tusk each and tear them apart. I'm sure we could make a do of it. What about it, Stan?"

"I'm not going, dad," he said mournfully.

"Not going!"

Despite the fact that I knew he hadn't the faintest hope of going, I was surprised and a little disappointed. I had been thinking the matter over and the more I thought about it the better it looked. The thought of getting away from Agatha and snake-skin and living in the decent society of wild elephants had taken hold of me. Then of course, one wouldn't be with the elephants all the time. Most likely they'd have a bar in South Africa. Very likely a billiard-table too. A rough-hewn stone affair, but still a billiard-table. Perhaps one could even teach the natives poker! And here were all my new-risen hopes dashed to the ground and trodden on.

"Is that you, Stanley?" came a shrill voice from the kitchen.

"Come upstairs, dad," whispered Stanley.

We cat-footed up to his room.

"Dad," he said, as soon as he had shut the door, "I've just been around to say good-bye to Estelle."

"Who the hell's Estelle?" I asked. The phrase struck me at the time as a good title for a Fox-Bottom or something.

"Estelle? She's that knobby-kneed, enamel-faced giggling man-eater we were talking about a while ago."

"Oh!" I said, "the one with the sky-eyes and the bleeding lips?"

"Where is that damned thing!" he snapped savagely.

I handed him the poem from the dressing-table and he tore it about in a way that must have strained him from the waist up, and threw the pieces up in the air as if he was having a Venetian carnival all to himself. I waited.

He burst out at last.

"You know that tripe-faced mug Oscar Winthrop?"

I nodded.

He paused and seemed to gather himself together; his eyes narrowed and he leered at me. Then slowly he hissed, "He's got a motor-bike and side-car!"

"Good God!" I gasped.

To say that I was stunned by this disclosure would be to put it feebly: moreover, it would be a lie.

"Got it day before yesterday," he explained, "and she's been riding out in it ever since. The mug!"

"Who?"

"Oscar," he said, sitting down on the edge of his bed.

"And little Oyster-mouth—what about her?"

"Now that I look back," he growled, "I can see that I was her ice-cream fetcher, her target, her door-mat, her picture-show ticket. Mug!"

"Who?"

"Me."

"And elephants are off?" I said regretfully.

He snorted as he wiped the dust off his boots with the quilt.

"Think I'm mad?"

We looked at each other for a while.

"There's no dinner," I said.

"No dinner!" he cried, staring at me.

"Perhaps you could go down to your mother or your aunt and——"

He stood up and put his hand affectionately on my shoulder.

"Don't be silly, dad."

"Well," I said, "there's a place down in King Street where I usually go when your mother is like this. One can get steak and eggs——"

"Come on," he said, "and we'll go to the fight after."

He looked back as he made for the door.

"Of course, I'm broke, you know."

"That's all right," I said, "I've got a pound or two your mother doesn't know about."

While I brushed my hair I thought of Stanley. He's got sense, although it's pretty well camouflaged. He gets more like me every day. It was just possible that I might get him a job at Flannery's Crown and Anchor, as a useful. I know Flannery. Stan would be useful all right. It would be pretty hard lines if he wasn't useful to his poor old father in a job like that. At least, that was what I thought.

Still thinking, I got my hat and we sneaked out and headed for steak and eggs and freedom. I said steak and eggs, and freedom. Freedom we understand. It means letting one's beard grow and going without a collar. Freedom is what we wave flags for. But steak and eggs!

Chapter 3

Where in this world will you find anything more sustaining, more inspiring, more satisfying, more invigorating, more absolutely culminating and fulfilling than steak and eggs? Nowhere.

As I said to Stanley at the Greek restaurant, after we had given our order: "Stanley, when the poor sailor returns from foreign lands, from long, lonely cruises, from sleepless nights and toil-filled days; when at last he sets foot in his home port—what does he do?"

"Gets drunk," said Stanley.

The boy was right.

"What does he do next?" I asked.

"Father, I'm surprised at you talking about that. You know very well what——"

"No," I cut in firmly, "I don't mean that; I mean, well damitall he orders steak and eggs, doesn't he?"

"Yes, of course."

"Well, why didn't you say so at first? Trying to confuse your poor old father!"

"What," I continued, "does the explorer do when he returns to civilization after long months in the jungle—what does he crave?"

"Steak and eggs."

"Right. When the starving wanderer, lost in the

desert, first starts to lose his reason, what does he see?"

"Steak and eggs."

"What does the acquitted co-respondent rush for as soon as he leaves the divorce court?"

"Steak and eggs."

I was satisfied. I leaned back in my chair and gazed around me. Two young women of the gimme type were gazing with bright, lizard eyes at our table.

"Who are those girls over there, Stan?" I asked.

"Steak and eggs," replied Stan in a flat, toneless voice.

I looked at him. He was staring straight in front of him with the rapt look of a crystal-gazer.

"Thinking of little Oyster-mouth?" I asked gently.

"Blah! Women!" he said in a tone of utter disgust. Almost I expected to see him spit on the cruet as I believe they do on the Continent. The steak and eggs arrived and I gazed at my plate. A succulent slab of steak sprawled across it. Two blonde eggs gazed back at me in a warm, friendly frizzled manner. I forked one.

"I was thinking how much it would cost to buy a motor-bike and side-car!" said Stanley, stroking his steak with his knife. "One big enough, that is to say, strong enough, to smash another motor-bike and side-car if they happened to bump into one another."

"Attend to your fodder," I said severely.

He champed at his steak for a few minutes, then waving the cruet about in front of me to attract my attention he whispered, "Eh, dad! Who are those two girls over there? They keep looking over here."

I raised my face from my plate.

"They, it would seem, are known to their intimates as Steak and Eggs. The one with the red hair I should say is Steak, and the one with the legs, is Eggs."

This seemed to puzzle him for a while, but he came at me again.

"But who are they, dad?"

"They are Gimmes," I said, "their names I do not know."

"Gimmes?"

"Gimmes. Yes, Gimmes. Gimme this and gimme that. Human leeches. They'd extract a fur coat from a marble statue of Harry Lauder. Don't smile or we're lost."

It was too late. He had smiled.

"I think I'll go over to that table, dad," he said. "Would it look funny if I took my steak and eggs with me?"

"Siddown," I growled.

"But, father——"

"Don't call me father. D'you hear? Call me Jack."

"Orright."

I looked across to the other table. They smiled.

I slightly raised one eyebrow, an accomplishment of which I have always been proud and which is, I believe, practised a great deal in diplomatic circles. I then looked back at my plate and ate on. I could see that Stanley was straining at the leash. He looked at me with bright eyes like a water spaniel waiting for his master to throw the stick into the pond. I should not have been at all surprised if he had jumped up on me and barked.

"Go on," he urged, in a hoarse whisper, "go on, Jack."

One thing about Stanley, he's swift on the intake, even if he is a bit premature on the exhaust stroke. You don't have to tell him anything twice—except when it involves physical effort on his part. I finished my meal, drank a little Worcestershire sauce and called the waiter.

"Mm-mm, mm-m-mm-mm ah mm?" I asked.

He nodded. "Two shillings a cup," he said.

It was after hours.

"We'll be over at the other table," I said.

"The ladies also mm-mm?"

I nodded and he shuffled off.

"Come on, Stanley," I said, pushing my chair back. "Come with Jacky."

He beat me to the other table by a head.

"Haven't I seen you before?" he burbled.

Of course, he is only young.

I bowed slightly, and with the courtly air for which I am renowned among my friends, said, "Pardon our intrusion, but would you ladies care for a snifter?"

"A he-man," said Steak.

"Balm of Gilead!" said Eggs, gulping. "Bring the mat in with you and shut the door."

I indicated Stanley.

"This is a young friend of mine, Stan. My name is Jack."

"Smith?" inquired Steak.

"Of course. Sit down, Stan."

"I want to sit next to Eggs," said Stan in a whisper that could be heard for leagues.

We exchanged places and remarks about the weather.

"When," asked Steak, "is le garçon coming avec les snifters?"

No one can spring that stuff on me and get off with it.

The waiter rolled up with a trayful.

"Mon homme," I said, turning to him in a confidential manner, "honi soit qui mal y pense?"

"No, sir," he replied, shaking his head, "not a drop of it left in the place."

"Mais donc," I said resignedly.

It's a pleasure to meet an intelligent waiter.

Steak was squashed, anyhow, and Stanley regarded me with additional respect.

I dawdled over my cup. At two shillings a time, it pays to dawdle.

Eggs had got one in below the belt on poor Stanley, by asking him if he had ever been a bull-fighter. He reminded her so much of a bull-fighter she used to know. Same fierce, handsome face, same dark mysterious eyes. Stanley was roped in and eating out of her hand. I remarked that I had done a bit of bulling, myself, at odd times, and she replied that she could quite believe it. I was rather taken with Steak. She was the sort of woman that grows on you. Her name was Daisy.

She had red hair and blue eyes, and a wide mouth. Not a hard mouth, but a mouth that knew its way about. Her figure was rather good, with the legs a little on the thin side. She had a lot of tiny wrinkles near her eyes. On the whole, pleasing.

Eggs was a beautiful chemist's blonde. Scientifically made up, low slung in the body, with the merest suggestion of an eyebrow on either side of an otherwise vacant forehead. Big eyes she had, and an excellent leg. Excellent. We got on well, the four of us.

"Jack," said Stanley at last, "I have just asked Maureen to come to the fight." Maureen was Eggs.

Seeing that *le garçon* had by this time recupped the party three times at my expense and I was now twenty-four shillings out, I sat down on the fight suggestion. I explained that I quite understood that the ladies would not care to be present at the brutal buffeting of poor boxers, who perhaps had fathers and managers and trainers and various other people to keep out of their meagre earnings, and had to bash each other and lie down for ten seconds, to get a living. Steak supported me. She went further. She said she would much prefer a theatre, with a quiet little supper afterwards and perhaps a little car ride out to the beach after that. It was then that I suddenly discovered that I had forgotten to lock the safe in my office. I paid the bill, apologized, and hurried out, shouting to Stanley that I supposed I would meet him some other time and to drop in any time he was passing.

I waited on the corner, two blocks away, and presently he came along, mumbling to himself.

"That was a dirty trick, Jack," he said when he came up to me. "Fancy leaving those two poor girls——"

"Never mind about the 'Jack'," I snapped. "Remember I'm your father."

He was quiet after that till we got down to the Stadium, half an hour late, and the fight all over. We walked home from there and I lectured him all the way. It was just like playing the bagpipes—sheer waste of time. In the middle of a really fine bit—I was working up to something about the Divinity that shapes our ends and a bird in the bush gathering no moss in time—he said: "Father; do you think I look like a bull-fighter?"

It's hard.

Then he wanted to know how he could become a bull-fighter. Whether there were any correspondence colleges that taught bull-fighting. Humouring him, I explained how the bull-fighters started as calf-chasers and he commenced talking about Maureen and I had to explain that I meant the leather-covered ones; and then went further and told him how they worked up from calf-chasing to cow-punching, and from cow-punching to bull-fighting; and by that time we were nearly home.

The lights were all out when we got to the house, and I guessed that the wife was in bed, fostering a headache, and Gertrude was at the police-station getting out a warrant for my arrest for abducting and murdering Stanley. I got the door open beautifully but Stanley, the fool, shut it so that it clicked.

"Who's that?"

It was Argus. Agatha. The wife.

"It's only me and Jack," said the fool Stanley.

I lifted him in the back of the neck and tramped over his body into the bedroom. Four or five hours after I got into bed I got used to the drone of Agatha's voice, and fell asleep. It doesn't sound much, just to say, "I fell asleep", but married men will understand.

What a wonderful thing is sleep! Knits up the ravelled sock of care, restores the tissues; the greatest post-jag pick-me-up ever shaken together. You never feel a dirty taste in your mouth, or a headache, when you're asleep: it's only when you wake up. It is, no doubt, Nature's greatest gift to man, only, as in most cases, Nature hasn't gone far enough. If one could only fall asleep when one liked! To be able, when "Where have you been till this hour of the night?" and "What do you mean by coming home in that condition?" are fired at you, to drop off to sleep immediately!

Ah! priceless boon—withheld.

Still, sleep is a wonderful thing.

As I have remarked to my friend Temple: If it were not for sleep, how the hell could we keep awake?

Chapter 4

Stanley has made a complete mess of things. Better that I had reared a guinea pig. I knew he was like that. I knew it right from the first. When I first saw him, bald, florid and toothless in his nurse's arms and heard them mouthing that vile, age-old slander, "Isn't he like his father?" I shuddered. When he was crawling about the floor and I was falling over him in all directions, I said, "That child is a menace."

Later, when he came home from school and said the teacher caned him because he deserved it, I remarked to his mother, "There's something wrong with that boy. He's unnatural."

I was right.

I'll admit there have been one or two occasions when my judgment was wrong. One was when Mustard Plaster won the Carrington Stakes, in 1902, and I had my metaphorical shirt on Onkus, a retired cart-horse that couldn't beat a carpet. The other was when I got married. There may have been other slips but these two stick in my mind. Usually I am occasionally invariably infallible.

To get back to Stanley.

He came downstairs the morning after our little excursion, looking as if he had put in a heavy night in the bull-ring. He was a bit annoyed too. Said he had a stiff neck and that I needn't have tramped on him in the hall.

"Let bygones be bygones," I said. "What is a biff in the neck between father and son? You need a shave."

This last remark was a pure brain-wave. Since he was sixteen he has been searching his face for a hair to shave. A few months ago he discovered one, and after gazing at it as though a new planet had swum into his ken, he hurled himself, shrieking, on my shaving gear. He has been in a more or less continual lather ever since.

"Yes," he said, tenderly rubbing the down on his cheek, "I am a bit bristly. Suppose I'll have to shave every day soon. Pity a man has to shave." He looked unutterably bored at the prospect. "Ah, well. I'll have to grow a moustache, I suppose."

A sudden thought struck him.

"Do bull-fighters—I say, dad! Do you think Maureen——"

"Shut up, you fool!"

I caught him by the arm. "You were at the fight last night," I said meaningly.

"No, father. I went to the Stadium with you last night."

"True. True. So you did. Keep it at that. No need to tell a lie."

Agatha appeared at this juncture and the usual breakfast-time procedure was gone through. She indicated by an air of resigned martyrdom that breakfast had been ready for weeks and she would not be able to keep it from going blue-mouldy much longer; so we slowly dragged ourselves to the breakfast-table. Stanley fell into his chair and said he didn't want anything. I just said, "Chops again?" and sighed heavily. Gertrude butted in, of course.

"You're too well fed; that's the trouble with some

people." ("Some people" is me.) "There's many a poor, starving Russian would be glad of half a chop, even the *bone* of a chop."

"Agatha," I said, "wrap up a few chops for Gertrude to take to Russia."

There was no answer.

I mumbled my way through a plate of porridge, got up, rinsed my mouth out and sat down again. Gertrude brought up a sniff that shook her to the fetlocks.

"Stanley," said Agatha, breaking the seal of her tomb, "you must eat something. Are you ill? You look very pale."

"I feel just a trifle wonky, as it were, mother. I think it must be the result of going without dinner last night."

I chuckled. First score to our side. Agatha closed her lips firmly and gave me the sort of look that snakes mesmerize birds with. The chops came on.

"What greyhound was done to death to make this butcher's holiday?" I asked, pointing to the chop.

No answer. It was rather disheartening. I had tried my best to make conversation and be friendly, merely to be answered with looks which, had they been articulate, would have shouted the house down. Is it any wonder marriage is a failure?

Echo answers, "No. It damn well isn't."

Stanley was nibbling at a crust like some ascetic hermit bent on mortifying himself. He was gazing at the salt-cellar, in one of his trances. Gertrude patted Agatha and said, "Poor dear," and added as if entirely ignorant of my presence, "you have a lot to put up with."

"My load is heavy," chanted Agatha in a clerical voice.

Stanley came out of his trance.

"Dad," he said, grabbing the only decent chop off my plate and falling on it like a famished wolf, "what was that one Daisy told us last night about the old man who bought the jazz-garters? Something about elastic—elastic something——"

"Who!" shrieked Gertrude. Agatha had a mouthful of bread, but her ears waggled. I looked at Stanley. Figuratively, he had sunk. Only one despairing hand showed for a moment before he was engulfed in the enormity of his folly.

Agatha had swallowed her bread.

"Who, may I ask, is—er—Daisy?"

Her voice was a chill breath from the Antarctic. The chop bones trembled on my plate like live things and Stanley, the coward, said that he felt sick, tottered from the room, dashed upstairs, and, as he told me later, crawled underneath the bed.

"Daisy?" I said nonchalantly. "Oh, he's a real decent chap. Got a wife and four kiddies. Works down a mine. Stan and I met him at the Stadium last night. His name is Day, really, but all the boys call him 'Daisy'. Funny how a nickname sticks to a fellow. I remember when we went to school, we were both in the same class. One day——"

I stopped abruptly. They were both listening like lawyers. "My God, those chops are rotten!" I said. "Surely, with me bringing home money week after week, week after week, never complaining, going about with holes in my socks and my trousers held up with nails, surely it's little enough to expect a meal from you! But, no! It's chops, chops, chops, chops, and nag, nag, nag. Chops, nag, chops, nag——" I was backing out the door, keeping time with my feet and had grabbed my hat and escaped before they knew what I was doing. I hastened up the street wondering to myself why I hadn't tramped Stanley to death the previous night when I had the opportunity. It was a good getaway I thought. They'd have had me if I'd kept on. That's the trouble with me. When I get started on a lie I must carry it on. Artistic pride, I suppose. The creative instinct. I keep on adding little adornments here and refinements there until I stand on a motley but magnificent mound of pure fiction; from which, nine times out of ten, my wife will pick the keystone, so to speak, and bring me swooping to earth with a smothered but undeniable thud. I was thinking how dexterously I had diverted the conversation and was just wheeling into the Crown and Anchor, when I remembered that Stanley was at their mercy. They had only to lay a conversational tentacle on Stanley and information would ooze from him without him being aware of it. Gertrude, especially. She could ask you what you thought of the weather, and gather from your answer your name and address, favourite poet, next of kin, and form shrewd suspicions that you were keeping two homes going. I drifted, stricken, into Flannery's.

"Well, Mister Gudgeon; how are y' this mornin'?"

"A double whisky, Flannery; closely followed by another double whisky. No. Give me a mug of whisky and have one yourself."

"Flyin' bulldogs! Wasser matter with y'?"

I proceeded to tell him, and when I had finished we gazed for the third time on empty mugs.

"Jack," he said, and the tears stood in his eyes, "if so be it you have to murder the three of 'em you can always hide in the cellar of your old pal, Bill Flannery."

I pressed his hand. Here was sympathy! Here was fellowship and a friend in time of need.

"Bill," I said, "I'm going back to the house. Leave the cellar door ajar." I had another drink and then with a final handclasp, turned away and left him sobbing on the counter. I was so overcome with emotion, so steeped in sorrow, that my poor grief-stricken brain could scarce control my legs, and I wandered from one side of the road to the other, singing mournfully.

It was pitch dark when I woke up lying on my back inside the gate. Overcome with misery and mental anguish, I must have collapsed at last beneath the strain. Somebody had been kicking my hat about the road and I noticed that the gate hung by only one hinge. I felt tired and sick and worried. I got to my feet and walked wearily toward the door and leaned against it. Stanley opened it and I fell flat on my face in the hallway. He was startled but soon regained his normal nimbleness of mind. Swinging his foot he kicked me deftly in the back of the neck.

"What," he said oracularly, "is a biff in the neck between father and son?"

He then tramped on me, shut the door, tramped on me again and so out to the kitchen. I sat up.

"Stanley," I called.

Silence.

"Stanley, bring me the axe."

No answer.

"Stanley boy, bring father the axe, there's a good boy." I listened in vain.

"Ickle Stanley bing daddy axey-paxey?"

No good. No good at all. Useless to try to murder him without an axe. I took off a boot and composed myself to slumber.

Chapter 5

It was still dark when I awoke the second time, feeling cramped and cold, but much better than before. Sorrow, like everything else, passes away and is forgotten, but it's the first time a great grief has left me so furry in the mouth. It felt late. As I groped around on the chilly floor, still only half awake, a distant clock chimed the usual preliminaries and then struck two. Almost immediately a voice welled up from somewhere in the remote darkness. It seemed to come from the wash-house. "It's two o'clock in the mo-o-orning. La da de da de do——" *Crash!*

It was Stanley.

"Stanley," I called.

He was too far away to hear and the crashing that was going on was terrific.

"Stanley!" I yelled.

Somewhere a door opened and a voice filtered through the darkness. "You can't have the axe. I'm using it."

The door slammed again and the crashing went on once more. I got up and walked down the hall, feeling my way. Stanley was in the laundry all right. I groped my way through the kitchen and out to where a candle flickered. Stanley, with his shirt off, was chopping up the kitchen cupboard. He was just getting in the last swipe as I entered.

"Stanley," I said, sorrowfully waving my hand at the

debris on the floor, "what is this?"

He hung his head.

"I did it, father, with my little hatchet," he murmured.

"Did you do this with the hope of becoming president of America at some future date?" I asked, when I had got a grip on myself again.

"Well—no," he said, "I hadn't thought of it. Is there a vacancy? I'd take it on, you know. I might get a motor-bike and side-car out of it."

I lowered myself to the floor and sat down.

"Stanley," I said, "I'm a sick man. Sorrow and domestic worries have left their mark on me. Don't toy with me. Why did you chop the cupboard up?"

"Going to make a cup of tea," he replied, idly chipping a piece out of the wash-tubs.

"What!"

"You see, before they left they turned the gas off at the main, and I blew the main fuse off the switch-board when I put the electric iron in the saucepan to boil some water——"

"Before who left?"

"Ma and Aunt Gertrude. I don't know where the gas tap is——"

I reached out and took the axe from him. "Listen, Stanley," I said, as he backed away, "explain from the start, speaking slowly and distinctly. What happened?"

He picked up a piece of the cupboard; a thick piece, with a nail in one end, eyed it thoughtfully, and then leaned back on the wash-tubs.

"After you went out," he said slowly, "they came upstairs to me and started questioning me."

"And you told them everything, you human cicada!"

"Well," he replied hotly, "isn't it better to tell

everything straight away and get the credit for being honest, than to have it dragged out of you and be regarded as a mug?"

There are times when I am proud of Stanley.

"Go on," I said, waving the axe.

"Well, Aunt Gertrude said that it was the last straw. She told ma that no woman would put up with it. She said you were a selfish, loafing, drunken——"

"Never mind about that."

"But she said you were a dipsomaniac and that when you were drunk you weren't responsible for your actions. She said you were not safe to live with and——"

"That's enough."

"Well, anyhow, they packed up and went before lunch. Aunt Gertrude said it would teach you to behave like a human being if Ma left you to look after yourself for a while. I think they've gone to Granny's place at Chatswood."

"When will they be back?" I asked, getting to my feet.

Stanley grasped his piece of wood in both hands.

"Dunno," he replied gruffly.

The blood throbbed in my temples; a roaring sounded in my ears and I felt as if I would burst. I gazed, axe in hand, at Stanley, till I could contain myself no longer.

"*Horray!*" I shouted. "Stanley! Bone of my bone!"

With a supreme effort I controlled myself.

"Bring out your mother's dressing-table, we'll need more wood than this," I said, removing my coat.

"I knew you'd be broken up when I told you," said Stanley, moving off. "Cheer up, dad."

"Bring something to boil the water in," I called after him, "and root around for something to eat."

A thought struck me. "Stanley," I called, as he groped

his way through the kitchen. "Why didn't they take you with them?"

"They wanted to," came the answer, "but I said I'd better stay and take care of you, and Aunt Gertrude said it would be a good idea to have someone to keep an eye on you, and I was to write regularly about everything you did."

"I can see you writing far into the night," I replied. "Hurry up with the dressing-table."

I heard him barging his way to the bedroom, and sat down.

Here was I, a lone man, left to look after the house and Stanley, my wife selfishly gone off to her mother's, leaving me to manage as best I could, with only memories for companionship. Deserted. Bereft. Alone...Hooray!

I rose as Stanley backed into the laundry dragging the dressing-table.

"Don't chop the mirror," he puffed. "It's seven years' bad luck. Besides, it won't burn."

"I don't see the use of keeping it", I replied, seizing the axe. "We have no use for the thing now. I look on a mirror as worse than useless."

"That's how I'd look on it if I were in your place," said Stanley.

I let it pass.

"Well, if you don't want it smashed," I said, rolling up my sleeves, "take it away and put it somewhere. Put it in the gas-stove where it will be out of the way. We must keep things tidy. Everything in its place. System, Stanley! That's what a house needs and a woman never has. I'll introduce some system into this place. You won't know it in a week or two."

"No doubt about that," he agreed, ducking as I turned

the first sod on the dressing-table.

When he was younger, Stanley was a Boy Scout. He was so enthusiastic about the training, especially the "one good deed a day" part of it, that the neighbours got up a petition and he had to resign. Before he left, however, he had accumulated such a rash of badges for path-finding, water-boiling, toast-turning, etc., that his uniform resembled an Oriental rug made by an epileptic Arab who had learnt to Charleston. Accordingly I allowed him to make the fire, boil the water, make the tea and fix things up generally, while I watched him. We sat down at last, beside the fire, with all the windows open to let out the smoke. There, reclining on our elbows on either side of the fire, we drank our tea and ate our burnt bacon and toast like North-west Mounted Police. The axe gleamed dully in the glow, and as the candle guttered out, the noise of crickets chirping came floating in on the night air. The smoke curled lazily off into the darkness and a shower of sparks shot up as I threw some wood on the glowing embers. A long-drawn-out wail came startlingly from out of the blackness of the night.

"Wolves!" gasped Stanley.

"Cats," I said. "That reminds me. I wonder if your mother and Gertrude really did go to Chatswood?"

"What does it matter," yawned Stanley. "I'll go and get a couple of blankets."

Taking a piece of flaring wood to light his way, he stumbled off, and presently was back with the blankets, and, as a concession to civilization, two pillows. I removed my vest, and rolling up in the blanket, got out my pipe and filled it. Stanley gazed across the fire at me; wistfully I thought.

"Worried, Stanley?" I asked as I lit up.

"Aw-n-no," he said hesitatingly, "just sort of unsettled."

I lay back on my pillow and puffed contentedly.

"Don't you think pipe smoking is bad for you, dad?" he asked after a while.

"Not a bit of it. You don't want to take any notice of that fool, Gertrude. Smoking is good for me. Those women don't realize that it's better for me to burn holes in the carpet and be contented than to take to knitting and go mad."

"Er, have you got plenty of tobacco?" he asked after a long pause.

I looked up. He was fumbling with a huge meerschaum, which, judging from its blackness, must have come from one of the old Egyptian tombs. He mumbled as I stared at it.

"Your mother and your aunt forbid it," I said harshly.

He mumbled again. I threw my pouch across to him: he made a queer, glugging noise in his throat, and fell on it. Dense clouds of smoke fouled the air before he spoke again.

"You're all right, Jack," he said, and spat into the fire.

I settled my pillow and fell to musing.

How on earth is it that women cannot make us men comfortable? Take Agatha for instance. For years I had been complaining about her cooking. Not that she couldn't cook, but she didn't seem to know what to cook. I'll admit she tried, after a fashion, but it is impossible to please a man once he gets particular about his meals. Why the devil hadn't she thought of lighting a fire in the laundry and giving me burnt bacon and toast? No imagination. Women are slaves to domestic routine and precedent. They are all alike, so far as I can see. Complaining when a man comes home a bit merry: like the time, for instance, when I pulled the front fence down and reared it against the wall so that I could get on to the balcony. What else was there to do? I couldn't find the keyhole. Then there is the perpetual asking for money, and worrying about the rent. Doesn't matter if a man goes short! Oh, no!

I knocked my pipe out on the floor and absent-mindedly reached for the switch to turn the fire out before I went to sleep. I was beginning to doze, when a belated thought tiptoed into my mind.

"Stanley," I said softly.

"Yairz."

"We might see Steak and Eggs again, and in that case——"

"Azzal right," he replied sleepily. "I had Eggs's telephone number so I rang her up this afternoon and they'll be here t'morrow night. Goo' night."

"Elephant's fins!" I gasped.

"Elefunz," mumbled Stanley dreamily.

He was asleep. The floor was concrete; not the best of beds; but the fact that I slept as soundly as a lift-driver speaks well for the clarity of my conscience and the adaptability of my hip-bones.

Chapter 6

It was somewhere about midday when I awoke, creaking in every joint. The sunlight streamed through the laundry window and a cat that had been eyeing me speculatively from the sill, leapt out of sight as I sat up. Outside in the street a dealer pleaded plaintively for empty bottles, rags, bags and old iron. Stanley was audibly asleep. I tossed a billet of wood gently on to his face, and he sat up clawing the air and gazing around wildly.

"Go and get my bath ready," I ordered.

"Go and get it yourself," he replied sulkily and fell back into his blanket.

"Stanley," I said, "is this obedience? Is this friendly co-operation? Is this looking after me? Did they teach you nothing when you were a Boy Scout?"

"Didn't have anything about baths in the Scouts," he mumbled.

I reached for another slab of wood.

"Aw, don't be silly, dad," he protested, raising his head from the pillow. "You're all right. You don't want a bath —you're clean."

"Stanley," I said, reasoning with him, "wouldn't it be easier and nicer for you to get my bath ready than to have to explain to Eggs how you got your face busted open through a piece of wood accidentally falling on it?"

He sat up, making savage, noiseless motions with his mouth.

"That's a good boy," I murmured, lying back on the floor, "and when you've done that, get the breakfast ready—and if what you are saying is what I think you're saying—don't say it."

He staggered to his feet and lurched out the door. In some respects Stanley is like his mother, bad-tempered when getting up or when asked to do any little thing. I had not dozed off exactly, but was in that blissful state when one is neither awake nor asleep, when I heard a bumping noise coming from upstairs in the vicinity of the bath-room and a wild, panicky yell from Stanley.

"Father! Father!"

I leapt to my feet, trod on an upturned nail that protruded from a fragment of the dressing-table, and rushed for the stairs.

"Father! Father!" came a despairing wail.

"Coming, boy!"

Taking too many steps at a time, I fell, crashed against the banister and rebounded on to my shin on the stairs. Clenching my teeth, I limped rapidly to the landing.

"Father!—Oh, there you are."

"Quick, boy! What is it?"

He surveyed me curiously as I stood panting on one leg, holding my shin.

"Your bath is now ready," he said coldly.

Mouth open I stared at him as he brushed past me and calmly descended the stairs. As though stunned, I watched him till the top of his head disappeared from view and then hobbled dazedly into the bath-room and sat on the edge of the bath. There are occasions when the English language, noble though it is, is inadequate to express one's feelings. Often I have yearned for the ability to speak Sanskrit, but strange though it may seem, I have never since uttered a word to Stanley about this so-called joke of his. It was beyond even physical expression, and I remained for months with this inhibition gnawing at my bosom until I saw a specimen of post-impressionist art entitled, "Picture of Workman Falling off Scaffolding". Gazing at it, I felt a load drop off my mind. I had been expressed.

Perhaps a psychologist could have relieved me at the time. I believe that once they get you hypnotized they relieve you of everything you've got, but as it was, even the warm bath failed to soothe my stricken faculties and, having bathed, I doddered downstairs like an old man. And yet fools who never had a son burble of the blessings of fatherhood!

Stanley was blithely humming the collection of sounds usually associated with the fox-trotting bouts. He stopped as I came in.

"What's for breakfast?" I asked dully.

Reassured, he made a more or less tuneful assertion that he wanted to go back to Dixie to see his mammie in the cotton-fields and then added that he had burnt bacon and toast to look forward to.

"Am I then condemned to finish my allotted span on a diet of burnt bacon and toast? Isn't there any other damn thing beside that?" I inquired.

"The trouble with some people," said Stanley, stamping on a piece of blazing charcoal that had once been bread, "is that they're too well fed. There's an onion behind the gas-stove if you're feeling fastidious."

I turned wearily to the wash-tubs where I had left my coat and hat the previous night. They were gone. I turned and raised my eyebrow at Stanley: "My coat and hat?"

"Oh, yes. They got burnt last night," he explained, "the fire was going out and I couldn't reach the wood without getting up, and I just accidentally knocked your coat down—and it sort of fell on the fire and—er—caught alight."

"And the hat?"

"Well, a hat is not much good without a coat, is it?"

Supporting myself with one hand on the wall, I made my way out of the room in silence. Even if I'd had a gun I could not have shot him. Hard to understand, I know, but living with Stanley has made me like that. When he strikes, he strikes me powerless.

"Where are you going?" he called out.

"To Flannery's," I gulped in a choked sort of voice, and closed the door behind me. Beer is a food as well as a drink, so I went to Flannery's for breakfast. The girl, Sadie, was behind the bar.

"Morning, Mr Gudgeon, beautiful morning this morning, nearly lunch-time too and I'm getting hungry. Hear you've been having some trouble, what is it, whisky?"

I nodded weakly. Sadie is a nice girl, but there are occasions when a man's sick, when a little silent sympathy, a little loving kindness, a little understanding pat on the cheek, goes farther than mere cheerfulness. I gulped my drink and drew a deep breath. Spirit called to Spirit.

"Sadie," I said, "flex the fingers, massage the little biceps and stand by the beer pump. If that bracelet is going to get in the way, take it off. I want action."

A foaming pint-pot thumped wetly on the bar as I

spoke and I clasped it by its big friendly handle, raised it, and the stuff swooped down my throat bearing a message of hope to my dejected internals. I replaced the pot, empty, on the bar and sighed—one of those deep, satisfactory sighs that seem to start from one's boots, gather all the little cares and troubles on the way, and from the mouth dissipate them in the air.

Back came my replenished pot.

"You look worried, Mr Gudgeon," said Sadie kindly. "You're so pale."

"If paleness is a sign of worry, Sadie, I ought to be transparent. I'm sick."

She clucked sympathetically.

"Poor boy. Why doesn't your wife look after you? 'S'shame!"

I put my empty pot down.

"Mr Flannery is sick, too," she said, whisking it away.

"Worry?" I said.

"No. Whisky," she replied, slapping her offering down before me. "Mugs of it! Drinking with some old fool as silly as himself."

I shook my head in a manner which I hope conveyed disgust.

"Madness," I said.

"You described it. Another? I'll have to be off to lunch presently—but I'll miss your company," she said, trailing off softly.

I am not dense.

"I'd like to be able to take you somewhere for lunch," I said in a tone of yearning, "but I'm not dressed for it and by the time I got home and changed, your lunch hour would be nearly over."

"What a pity," she sighed, straightening her shingle.

Strange, the lure I have for women. Sex appeal, I suppose.

"Oh, by the way!" I cried. "I'd almost forgotten it. We're expecting company to-night. Want some liquor. Say, four of lager, one small gin——"

"Is this in addition to Stanley's order?" she cut in.

"Stanley's order?"

"M'm. He was up here late yesterday afternoon." She was turning the pages of a book as she spoke.

"Here it is. Two dozen lager, six best gin—large, two claret, two sherry, two——"

"That'll do!" I cried, clutching at the counter. "I don't want to hear any more."

"It's going to be some party," she said, closing the book and gazing brightly at me. "Only a few people too. Just nice."

"Would you like to come?" I asked, mastering my emotions.

"Too right I'm coming!" she responded with a happy gurgle. "Stanley said he'd be real disappointed if I didn't come and bring a few friends."

She leaned over the counter and tapped me caressingly on the nose with one finger. "P'raps I'll get better acquainted with my little fat sheik," she whispered. She whisked away, pausing at the cash register, and turning, waved one lily-white hand. "Toodleoodle!" she cried, and was gone.

I closed my eyes and groaned. How much—Oh, how much was two dozen lager, six best gin large, and two of everything else, like Noah's ark! I clutched my hat and turned toward the door.

"Goin', Mr Gudgeon?" called the barman.

"Yes," I muttered. "Going—going."

"Ar, well. See y' t'night at the party," he yelled, as I hobbled out on to the pavement.

Like a weeping mother going to the electric chair, I set my face toward home and Stanley. Stanley....If I'd known what that party was going to start I'd have gone the other way.

Chapter 7

I had a meal; a meal which Stanley described as an artist's breakfast, being a combination of breakfast, lunch and afternoon tea. It lacked nothing in quantity, but it left me with the impression that if the tin-opener ever got mislaid while Stanley ruled the kitchen, we would starve to death. It seemed a long time since I'd had chops.

I wandered listlessly about the house while Stanley cleared the table and carried the crockery up to the bath and turned the shower on it. I really should have been at work, but what with one thing and another, I couldn't face the idea of going back to the office. The Gudgeons are temperamental, and I, perhaps the most temperamental of them all, coming as I do from a long line of Gudgeons—I, the end of the line so to speak, am over-civilized. When I say that I am the end of the line, I do not disregard Stanley. Stanley, so far as the family is concerned, is a blank file.

Being over-civilized and highly strung, there are times when the mere thought of work turns me sick. Had I not met Agatha I might still be making a comfortable and easy living at the billiard-room. But the propagation of the species is the sole aim of Nature and I was torn from the pool-table, and my cue was put back in the rack by the inexorable hand of Fate that Stanley might infest the world. Truly, there are some things that are beyond the understanding of mortal man. Things of which it is no earthly use to think. Still, there are times when thought, long held back by the physical activities of our daily lives, bursts all restraint and floods our minds like the restricted water bursting through a crack in a clogged sewer-pipe. I wandered aimlessly as a telegraph messenger from room to room and finally flung myself on the bed and surrendered myself to meditation and indigestion.

Lying there I seemed to see the difficulties of life line up, number off, and form fours. I have read in books that the events of a drowning man's whole life flash through his mind before he finally utters the word "Mother" and sinks.

I have not shared with the authors of these books the pleasure of being drowned, and so can offer no corroborative evidence, but I underwent a dreadful enough experience on the bed. Doubt descended on me and the confidence I have always felt in my ability to carry on the affairs of daily life drained from me. There were so many things to prey upon my mind. Agatha was gone. Gertrude was gone. My home was broken up. My bootlace was broken and I had not a clean collar to call my own. The tradesmen had to be paid, and the landlord—and Flannery.

Where was the money to come from? Agatha, with that careless disregard of responsibility common to all women, had calmly left me without making any provision whatever for my future. It would never occur to her that I needed money. That she would think gratefully of the pounds and pounds I had given her to fritter away on groceries; and that she would endeavour to repay me was a thought to be dismissed with a bitter laugh.

Apart from these problems of domestic economy, there was Stanley. That he was still out of jail was due solely to my unremitting efforts to keep him on the straight and narrow path, and in this endeavour I was unassisted and even opposed by Agatha and Gertrude. It was left to me to orient his moral compass and embark him on an occupation that would carry him safely through the stormy seas of life, with myself as adviser and supercargo. His sole ambition seemed to be to own a motor-cycle and side-car, his wavering inclinations were at present in the direction of bull-fighting, his only study was racing-form, his chief occupation seemed to consist in falling in and out of love with cat-like frequency. He had a positive flair for getting into trouble and everything he touched was automatically wrecked.

Could I have made him an alderman of the City Council he might have had some scope for the exercise of his peculiar genius. Given work where he would be in the position to assist in the resumption and demolition of whole blocks of buildings, in the tearing up of roads and putting them back, in the reviling of his colleagues, and the playing of practical jokes on the rate-payers—then he might have been happy. Contractors would have showered wealth on him from motives purely tender and his name would have appeared in the papers in company with society leaders, wife-beaters, archbishops, eminent murderers, modest hospital-cot endowers, and racehorse owners. But it was not to be, and failing the aldermanic life, I could only hope for the next best thing and make him a useful at Flannery's.

My melancholy train of thought was shunted into a side-station as Stanley burst into the room and commenced to roll up the rugs on the floor. The sight of him annoyed me.

"Stanley!" I snapped. "How often have I told you to knock before entering a room? The private detective manner does not become you. Next time you omit the necessary ceremony I'll lift you such a swipe in the teeth that your unborn grandchildren will stagger with the shock. Remember—knock or be knocked. Get out! Come here! What are you doing with those mats?"

He paused in the doorway and stood with his eyes cast down like a cab-horse in the rain.

"Well! Speak up! What are you standing there like a damn fool for?"

"I am abashed and confused, father!" he said softly.

"Bashed and contused!" I shouted wildly, rolling off the bed.

He leapt outside the door and, closing it, bellowed through the keyhole.

"I want the mats because I'm getting the place ready for the party."

The key clicked in the lock as I reached the door.

"You don't mind me locking you in?" he cried pleadingly.

Locked me in! His father! I looked around wildly for a moment, then wrenching the end off the bed, battered the door down. I do not wish to give the impression that I had lost my temper. Far from it. It was with the utmost calmness that I walked over the splintered door, carelessly swinging the end of the bed in both hands. My bedroom is on the ground floor. I proceeded rapidly along the hallway and tripped over a mat that Stanley had dropped. Smiling, I rose to my feet and called affectionately to Stanley. He did not answer, but I could hear him scurrying about, upstairs. The boy seemed to be avoiding me. I hurried up the stairs, and arriving breathless at the top, searched each room. Stanley was nowhere to be seen. There was only one place. The roof.

Throwing down the bed-end I hurried downstairs and secured the meat-chopper and then returned to the upper floor. By standing on the outer window-ledge of Stanley's room it was easy to reach the guttering of the roof and so haul myself up with the chopper gripped in my teeth. Kneeling on the sloping roof, I espied Stanley clinging to the chimney and staring at me in a most unfriendly manner with his mouth wide open.

"Vanvly," I called, "vor varver wavs you."

The chopper made it difficult for me to speak, but I kept it in my mouth and started the ascent of the roof. Stanley, after a savage attempt to tear a brick loose from the chimney, slid down the farther side. Reaching the ridge, I slid down after him. He was balancing on the balcony roof gazing desperately about him. Our house is separated from the next in the terrace by a narrow passage-way, four feet wide, and the roofs of both balconies are just that distance apart. I anticipated Stanley's intention and was almost on him with the chopper when he leapt. In his haste, he missed his footing, caught the guttering of the next-door roof, yelped as the guttering came away, and gasped quietly as the end of it held and he remained suspended in the air, swinging gently from about eight feet of galvanized iron. I had him. I had only to step across the intervening four feet and chop him loose to spend the remainder of my life in peace and quietude. Taking the chopper in my right hand, I placed one foot in our balcony gutter and stepped easily across. It was then that my rear foot became stuck. Straddled between the two houses, I vainly strove to dislodge it. Struggling, my other foot became wedged in the guttering opposite, and I was done.

Had I been younger I might have extricated myself fairly easily. Not that I lack either strength or agility; young flapnoodles can show me no points when it comes to strength and vigour, but a man of forty-eight accumulates a certain amount of dignity which breeds a distaste for violent physical effort. A rapidly increasing and very interested crowd was gathering in the street while my fiend son hung limply in the air and laughed himself black in the face. I missed him with the chopper, and it whirled past him and clattered into the passageway below. Nice position for a grown man of forty-eight to be in! Had it not been for Stanley's ridiculous desire to avoid me I should never have been exposed on the rooftops as an object of ridicule. It was always Stanley. Who, but Stanley, would have thought of cooking meals in the laundry at two o'clock in the morning?

My position was intolerable. I waved my arms to the mob in the street.

"Send for the fire brigade!" I shouted.

They cheered.

"Send for the——fire brigade!"

They cheered again.

I gazed sadly at Stanley. He was clinging with one hand and pointing excitedly at the crowd with the other.

I turned and gazed down at that sea of chattering nincompoops as a voice floated up to me.

"Ooo-hoo! Ja-ack!"

Two white handkerchiefs fluttered below.

"Cooee!" screamed Stanley. "It's Eggs! And Steak! Coo-*ee*!"

"Send—for—the—fire—brigade!" I bellowed.

"You must be pretty friendly with the fire brigade, dad," said Stanley, shifting his grip.

'"Oo-hoo! Ja-ack! Has the party started?"

"Send for——"

"For the love of Mike, father! We haven't enough lager for the fire brigade. I've invited all the people we want."

As the last word left his mouth the guttering gave a rasping screech and ripped away another eight feet, leaving him with an easy drop to the ground. Whether it was the sudden shock or the hand of fate that threw me back at the same time on to my own roof, I do not know, but as I lay back, perspiring, against the slope, a hoarse murmur of anger went up from the crowd and I looked to see numbers of them walking away with the attitude of people who wanted their money back. I had disappointed them. It was clear to me that they regarded me as a fraud; a person who gathered a good crowd and then didn't fall down and break his neck. They were dispersing sullenly, mumbling to one another, and at last all were gone except a few optimists and local residents who watched me, hoping against hope, until I disappeared from view. Climbing through the window into Stanley's room I surprised him furiously brushing his hair.

"Why don't you knock?" he demanded sourly.

"Sorry, son, I didn't think you'd be here."

"Thasall right, dad," he said, laying down the brush and turning to me. "Come and help me welcome the guests."

Stanley is given to sudden fiendish fits of bad temper, a deplorable trait which he inherits from his mother, but a relenting Providence has made him somewhat like me, in that he bears no malice after his fit has passed off. That is to say, not much. We descended the stairs together and proceeding arm in arm along the hall, opened the door and admitted Steak and Eggs.

"Come in, my dee-ars," crooned Stanley.

"You men are the limit!" said Eggs, wagging a roguish finger at Stanley.

"You silly boy!" exclaimed Steak, patting me on the cheek. "You might have been killed! Whatever were you doing up there?"

"Stanley got into difficulties and I went to his rescue," I explained with simple modesty.

"Oh, you big, brave man!" gurgled Eggs. "But what was my toreador doing up there?" she asked, snuggling her hand into Stanley's and looking up into his eyes.

Stanley paused and then spoke in a low voice.

"A poor little motherless kitten, blind and homeless, had collapsed on the roof and was mewing so plaintively that it wrenched my heart. I listened until I could bear it no longer. Then I hurled myself, careless of consequences, on to the roof."

"I'll say that was something like a hurl," said Steak admiringly.

"Later, the guttering gave way as you saw——"

I interrupted, thinking Stanley had been in long enough.

"I rushed to his assistance——"

"But what about the poor little blind kitten?" gushed Eggs.

"I—I gave it a drink of water," said Stanley, "which seemed to revive it, and it gazed gratefully at me for a moment and then spread its little wings and flew away."

"The kitten!"

"Ah, yes. I was thinking of the canary I rescued

yesterday. It just licked my hand and toddled off."

"You dear thing!" cooed Eggs, squeezing his hand.

I thought Stanley had gone far enough.

"Well, come on, girls," I exclaimed jovially. "Make yourself at home. Take your hats off, or your coats, or whatever it is you want to take off. Don't mind us; we're all friends together."

I herded them into the drawing-room.

"Stanley's been getting things ready. I suppose everything's fixed, Stan?"

"Well—no. Not quite," he replied. "I didn't expect anyone yet. You girls are a bit early," he added, smiling at them.

"We've been to enough parties," said Steak, "to know that the first-comers know where the beer's hidden."

"Where is it?" asked Eggs.

"It's in the stove, most of it, Maureen," confessed Stanley. "Care for a gargle."

"We wouldn't take much holding down if you wanted to force it on us," drawled Steak. "Trot it out."

I had seated myself and was admiring the shape of Daisy's ear, when what seemed like a herd of buffaloes struck the front door and a raucous howl came from the front of the house. For a moment I thought it might be the fire brigade. Stanley rushed into the room with a bottle in each hand and a delighted smile on his face.

"What's that?" I gasped.

"It's the Boys!" cried Stanley, and rushed to let them in.

Chapter 8

By eight o'clock, our quiet little party had, thanks to my son's efforts, swelled to the proportions of the crowd that gathers around the spot where the body was found.

There were the Boys: a crowd of immature dance-hall thugs who ran mainly to legs and reactionary suits. There was Sadie and a boy friend, and a girl friend and her boy friend, and the barman and the chief chucker-out at Flannery's. The milkman was there with an alleged female of the ultra-modern type, who could not be definitely placed as a boy or a girl and was best classified as a Boil. People I did not know kept coming in, in bunches. I tried to count them but they moved about too much. I don't suppose there were more people on the *Mayflower.*

Everyone, it seemed, had brought their music-books—for what reason I do not know, seeing that they had only ukuleles to play. The giggling and guffawing made the house sound like a large aviary being ravaged by bloodhounds. And the singing!

There was one girl who had been accused of being able to sing in the early stages of the orgy. Arraigned before a jury of panting ukulele players, she blushingly admitted that some people said she had a good voice but she was not so wonderful, really. After the usual assumption of bashfulness, and the orthodox statements as to not having brought her music, and having a bad cold, she consented to sing. The "Boys", who had urged her to sing, then left in a body headed for Flannery's side door, with three suitcases.

The girl sang "The Last Rose of Summer".

By some extraordinary fluke of an outraged glottis, she caught a high note on a neap tide, and held it. Like a draught-horse stalled with a heavy load on a hill, she held it. I shut my eyes and thought of knocking-off time at the steel-works and foggy nights on the harbour. Growing mottled in the face as Nature asserted herself, she was at last compelled to relinquish the note with a gasp and, amid a storm of applause, she finished off in a hoarse baritone.

"By cripes!" cried the milkman, slapping me on the back, "you wouldn't hear better than that at the Gaiety!"

Which was quite true. I've been to the Gaiety.

That priceless boon, "the life of the party", was a particularly virulent specimen. The Boil told me in a confidential whisper that he was *such* a character. The things he said! And the too-perfectly-funny-for-words things he did!

"Gee! I remember once," she said, ashing her cigarette on my coat-sleeve, "he blew up a balloon and sat on it. You should have seen the look on his face. Laugh! I thought I'd die!"

For once, I felt old.

I looked around for Stanley and failed to find him; neither could I see Maureen. I rose to my feet as the noble strains of "Pipe Ma Baby's Goo-goos" rose in the quivering air, and after a search secured a bottle of gin, two glasses and some ginger-beer, and lifting the eyebrow to Steak, headed for the front door.

"My gawd!" she said, following me out and seating herself on the gas-box beside me. "Does this happen every night?"

"Don't talk to me, Daisy, not for a while, anyhow."

"I understand, honey," she said.

"Take ginger-beer with it?" I asked.

"I hate ginger-beer."

I threw the ginger-beer away.

"I regard gin purely as a medicine," I said, filling the glasses.

"Absolutely," she replied, tersely.

We sipped quietly.

"You know—I like you, Jack. You're restful," she sighed, and leaned her head against my shoulder.

I felt rested, too. Some women affect men like that. They have the mother instinct without being mawkish; I felt that if I had laid my troubled head on Daisy's lap and said, "What a — — — of a world this is," Daisy would have said, "Absolutely."

Once a man reaches the forties he needs feminine company. Some men, indeed most men, like something young and fluffy, but I am not like that. I like a sensible woman. Not one of these hard, practical women, but a woman who doesn't *giggle*. A woman of the world who has had a couple of black eyes in her time is the best company for a man in his forties.

I liked Steak.

I filled the glasses and put them down on the floor.

"Daisy," I said, "I'm a married man. My wife has left me; Stanley is my son and I'm going on for forty."

I had made a clean breast of things—practically.

She patted my hand. "I guessed most of that but I thought you were a widower. Divorced, are you, Jack?"

I nodded glumly.

"Don't worry over things that happened long ago, honey," she said, smoothing my hair. "Did you like her very much?"

"I always respected her," I answered gently, "until——"

"Don't tell me if it hurts you, Jack."

"She ran away with a commercial traveller. Lord knows where they went. I tried to find her. I heard that he ill-treated her——Ah, well!"

I picked up our glasses.

"Some women don't know when they're well off," she exclaimed. "A fine man like you——! Thanks, Jack. Here's luck. Don't forget that there are more fish in the sea and quite a few pebbles left on the beach."

We quaffed.

"My word!" said Steak, after a pause, "what a row those galoots are making inside!"

"Bedlam!" I exclaimed.

"Absolutely."

I put my arm around her and we snuggled up. There was nothing wrong in it. Everything was all right. My wife had left me. Certainly, she had given me the impression that she would be back shortly, but the fact remained that she wasn't with me. And here was a woman, a friend, who understood me. Was I to insult her by spurning her affection? I think I am too much of a gentleman for that.

The noise of the party was increasing, a thing that I had not considered possible. They were stamping their feet, and singing "We're here because we're here because we're here because we're here." A very ancient and easily remembered song of some fifty-three verses, if I remember rightly. Extremely popular at smoke concerts and lodge meetings. I had got used to the monotony of the bellowing, much the same, I suppose, as factory workers get used to the noise of the machinery, and was feeling comfortable and almost drowsy when Temple, who lives next door, came to the gate.

"Gudgeon!" he barked, "what's all this damned uproar! Do you know it's nearly midnight?"

"It's Stanley's party," I answered in the soft voice that turneth away wrath. "It's his coming-out party."

"Coming out! Well, the sooner he emerges the better. It's a damned riot! Is he coming out in a tank?"

"Be nice, Temple. Be nice. You were a boy yourself once."

"I'll admit it," he shouted. "But there was no insanity in my family. I hope," he added, glaring at the doorway, "that when he comes out, he comes out on his ear!"

"Miserable old cow!" said Steak, as he bounced off.

"You can't take any notice of a man like that," I explained. "He's a fool. He said I looked old."

"Rot!" she exclaimed contemptuously. "He's mad."

That was a sympathetic, yet sensible observation.

I could see that Daisy was a smart, sensible woman. When I had told Agatha about Temple's ridiculous remark, instead of laughing heartily, she had said, "Quite right, too. Of course, you're getting old. You can't stay young for ever. You, with your hair parted in the middle and your tight-waisted coats and dynamite ties!"

It set me thinking.

It just shows the difference in women.

But then, every woman is different from every other woman; like finger-prints; and just as the dissimilarity in finger-prints leads to many a man's downfall, so with women. Some men think that because they have produced certain effects with some women by some particular method, they can do it at any time with any other woman, like the application of mathematical and chemical formulae. It is not so. It is decidedly not so. You may live comfortably with Jekyll for a long time, but sooner or later you are confronted with Hyde. No man can understand women for the quite ordinary reason that they don't understand themselves. In this they are similar to a lot of other animals. There is no mystery and no secret. If there had been, it would have been blabbed long ago. Solomon had more than his share of wives but he had to give it up at last and admit that a good woman was above rubies. And I think I have biblical backing when I say that Solomon knew his way about. It is not my wish to be considered a cynic. I like women. But the man who runs the circular saw cannot be called a cynic just because he realizes that it is a saw. Similarly, the man who puts a guard-rail around his machinery does not distrust the machinery, he only realizes his own fallibility.

My train of thought was interrupted by a smothered snort from Daisy. She shifted her head on my shoulder and mumbled something.

"Eh?" I said.

She was asleep. Never before or since have I met a woman so divinely conversationless. It is a sad fact that very few of them will refrain from speech when they see that a man wants to think; they imagine that he is either neglecting them, or thinking of some other woman, or merely sulking. I must have dozed, myself, shortly after that because the next thing I remembered was Flannery's barman carrying out the Boys and stacking them on the pavement. The girls had evidently gone home earlier. Sadie's boy friend came through the door on all fours, asserting that he was a cat, and mewing and enjoying himself immensely. The milkman emerged swaggering ponderously as though the best qualities of countless milkmen had been merged in him. He flung the gate open with a sublime gesture of dignity, marched out on to the pavement in massed formation, and fell into the gutter.

"Are they all out?" yelled the barman.

Artie, Flannery's chucker-out, loomed on the doorstep.

"Z'all out. Posilivly norar one lef'!"

"Lock up, then."

"Hold on!" I cried. "I want to get in."

"Can't geddin. Ish after hours."

"But I live here!" I protested.

"Zame ole tale."

I caught him by the sleeve. "Look here, Artie. I must get in, and I can't if you snap that lock."

He eyed me suspiciously.

"Well," he said after a pause, "I'll lesher go in this time but be kefful comin' out. Doan led anyborry see yer carryin' it."

"Come on, Artie," called the barman.

"Comin'," he answered, and rolled toward the gate.

"Now you be kefful!" he added, turning to me.

The barman caught him by the arm.

"I'm comin'!" he said testily. "Godder tellim—kefful."

They weaved their tortuous way up the street, Artie pausing now and then and exhorting the surrounding air to be very careful.

I grasped Steak by the shoulder and shook her.

"All right," she mumbled, "just half a glass."

She awoke at last and I left her to search for Eggs while I procured a taxi. Eggs had taken a fancy to some vases and pictures, and the wrapping of them delayed their departure, but after promising to phone me in the morning they rode away.

The chilly air heralded the approach of a new morning before I rolled into my disordered and broken bed and slept. If some of us were granted a glimpse of the future, most of us would remain asleep indefinitely, but no matter how battered, we must stand up to every round; so when the gong went in the morning I was on my feet and shaping up to another day.

Chapter 9

The postman was very late that morning, which surprised me as he was usually as regular in his movements as a government road-mender. Temple set his clock by him. When he did appear, it was plain that he had been a guest at our party the previous night. He flung a letter at me as he passed and moaned in answer to my cheery greeting. I called him back.

"Only the one letter?"

"There was one from the Gas Company, but I threw it down the drain like you told me to," he answered huffily.

"That's right," I said. "If you get one that looks as if it came from the Income Tax Department, put it down the same drain."

He grunted and moved off. I understood how he felt.

The envelope was addressed to Stanley, so I opened it. It contained a five-pound note which I pocketed for Stanley's own good. It might have got him into trouble and I had to look after the boy. The letter was written in Agatha's unique spiral back-hand and the gist of it was that she was sorry she had left him in the same house as myself, but that he was to keep pure and good nevertheless, and avoid me as much as possible. Followed sundry items of great interest about Stanley's grandmother and Stanley's grandmother's parrot. A postscript mentioned the enclosure of the five-pound note and added that Gertrude would write shortly and send another. Lastly, he was to appeal to Temple if he needed assistance or protection, or if someone was required to stand bail for me. Mr Temple, it seemed, was a very good man. As there was nothing of real interest to Stanley in the letter, I tore it up. The five was a crisp, new one, quite a rarity, and I thought I would like to take it up to Flannery and show it to him, calling in at the tobacconist's on the way back. It was my intention to buy Stanley some tobacco. I am afraid I spoil the boy.

It was a couple of hours later when I returned. Not until I was inside the house did I realize that I had forgotten the tobacco and I was annoyed at my own absent-mindedness. But perhaps Stanley was better without it. Tobacco is an insidious drug: although it has no harmful effect on a mature man it is bad for a youth. There are not many fathers who consider the welfare of their sons as I consider Stanley's. It is a weakness in me, this paternal assiduity, but I think a pardonable, even a commendable weakness. Passing through the house in search of Stanley, I came to the laundry and was surprised to hear voices in the back-yard. I listened.

I could hear Stanley's voice. "Now gimme a fair go," he was saying. "Don't crowd in on me. How can I get a good spin if you crowd in on me?"

"Come on," growled a voice that sounded vaguely familiar, "let some light under 'em."

There was silence, and then a faint tinkle.

"Two heads! You liddle beauties!" cried Stanley.

I peered cautiously through the window. The postman, the milkman, a time-payment collector and someone else whom I did not recognize, were standing in what was meant to be a circle around Stanley. He had a small piece of flat wood in his hand, on which were balanced two pennies.

The national game was in progress.

The boy was flushed with the glow of victory.

"I spin for the lot," he called. "Seven and eightpence. Set the centre! Set the centre!"

"Two bob you tail 'em," said the milkman, casting a florin on the ground. "That's all I've got."

"I'll set you for the eightpence," said the time-payment collector, casting his mite down beside the florin.

The postman looked worried.

"This is the fourth time you've headed 'em," he exclaimed. "If I'd known there was a game on I'd have brought some money."

"So would I," murmured the milkman.

The postman was rummaging in his bag.

"Look here," he cried, with sudden cheerfulness, "I got a registered letter here, it might be worth quids. If you'll take it on the off-chance, I'll chuck it in and call it five shillings."

"You're on," said Stanley, "stand away."

Up went the pennies.

"Oh, you liddle King Georges," chanted Stanley, "show those skulls. Nedkelly, Nedkelly, Ned——"

Clink!

"Two heads!" shouted Stanley. "Horray!"

The postman gave a grunt of disgust and made silently for the gate, closely followed by the milkman, the time-payment collector and the stranger.

"Come in again some time," called Stanley. There was no answer.

I left the window and hastened into the kitchen as he

turned to re-enter the house. He strolled in clinking the coins he had been tossing.

"How much did you win?" I asked.

"Fourteen shillings, counting a registered letter."

He spun a penny in the air and as he failed to catch it, it bounced to the floor and rolled toward my feet.

"My lucky penny!" he cried. "It's always been lucky. Hand it over!" he shouted as I put my foot on it.

I picked it up and twirled it between my fingers.

It was double-headed. Whichever way I looked at it, His Majesty's royal features confronted me.

"You snake!" I hissed. "You cheat! A son of mine—little better than a common thief!"

He mumbled and looked away. I laughed bitterly.

"A Gudgeon," I said, "with a double-headed penny! Have you no sense of decency? Is the honourable name of your ancestors nothing to you?"

I took a stride toward him.

"Father!" he cried weakly.

"Silence!" I roared. "Hand over half the winnings."

"Don't be silly!"

I turned and ran toward the front door.

"Milkman!" I shouted. "Milkman!"

"Come here!" shouted Stanley, bounding after me, "here's five shillings."

"That's not half. *Milkman!*"

A musical and peculiarly milkman-like gurgle answered me and the milkman came into view swinging his pint-measure.

"Here, damn you," hissed Stanley "seven shillings."

"'Ullo?" said the milkman, leaning against the gate.

"Leave an extra pint in the morning for the future, please, old chap," I answered.

He nodded and moved off to his labours and I shut the door.

I could see by Stanley's face that there would be trouble about this affair. He clicked his fingers in an exasperated manner and looked at me as a muzzled cat would look at a mouse-hole.

I didn't want to antagonize the boy. We had to live together as happily as possible, so I tried to win him over.

"Well," I said soothingly, "what have you got that face on you for?"

"Huh!" he grunted, and casting a glance at my left boot, he turned and strode back to the kitchen. It is hard to know how to treat a boy like Stanley. No matter how much I try I cannot please him. I remembered that he had not even thanked me for the tobacco I had intended to buy him. Second thoughts reminded me that I had not informed him of my intentions and I followed him, with the idea of bringing him to a proper state of gratitude for the tobacco and remorse for his resentment.

He was sprawled out in a chair near the table, with his hands in his pockets and the expression of an under-paid bailiff with an abscess.

"Stanley," I said, pulling a chair up to the table. "When I was going out a little while ago, I thought I would buy you some tobacco."

"*Tobacco!*"

I never knew until then, the possibilities of a word like tobacco. I have since decided that should a foreigner ever say "Tobacco!" at me with sufficient vehemence I shall give him in charge.

"What would I do with seven shillings' worth of tobacco?" he spluttered, after a long pause.

"Stanley," I said quietly. "Do not try to imagine

yourself as a member of the League of Nations and that you have been despoiled and are entitled to full reparations and then some."

"Haven't I been despoiled?" he demanded.

"You have not," I replied. "We will carry the League of Nations idea a little farther, so that I may explain to you. You, as a nation, have robbed other nations—that is, the milkman, etcetera—robbed them by means of the power given you by your armaments and superior equipment—the double-headed penny. I, another nation, cannot allow you to get away with fourteen shillings from your victim without stepping in——"

"For your cut."

"Don't be so vulgarly direct, Stanley. Remember you are at Geneva now. As I was saying, I must step in. Now I am a majority."

"Ho, are you!" he bawled.

"Yes, I am. I could lay you out in one hit if necessary, therefore I am a majority. I must step in and adjudicate and seeing that the milkman and other nations are unable to protect their own property, I will take over half the loot and guard it for them. You, I think, are treated very well in being allowed to keep the other half."

"I see," said Stanley. "If I had to give my half back it would amount to an admission that I had grabbed it, and then you'd have to give your half back."

"We won't go into those complications, if you please."

"And where do the milkman and postman nations come in? Do they stay robbed?"

"Not necessarily. You have to bear the opprobrium as the aggressor and all you get out of it is two shillings——" I held up my hand as his mouth opened. "Two shillings,"

I continued, "and a concession which will very likely prove valueless."

"You mean the registered letter?"

I nodded and rose to my feet.

"Supposing that it is not valueless," he cried gloatingly, "supposing that it is very valuable?"

"In that case," I replied, "there will be some more adjudicating."

I left the room. I had a feeling that the registered letter would contain a disappointment and I did not wish to be present at the opening ceremony. I was just entering Gertrude's bedroom, which I preferred to my own as its door was still intact, when he bounded after me waving the letter.

"Look here!" he shrieked. "Look at it!"

He held the letter before my eyes. The trembling of his hands made it difficult to read but as near as I can remember it ran:

> MY OWNEST,
>
> Why have you not written to me? Is anything wrong? This is the sixth letter I have written and no answer from my ickle one——

—and a lot more of that sort of rot, but no money.

"See it!" he shouted. "I get two shillings and you get seven!"

"Be a sportsman, my boy," I said. "You took a chance and you lost. There is nothing worse than a bad loser. Be a sportsman."

"Sportsman!" he shouted. "Why, if you were half a sportsman you'd share that seven shillings with me."

I smiled derisively and walked into the bedroom.

"I'll toss you for it," he cried, following me. "You're

such a sportsman!"

"I am a sportsman," I said gently, "and since you desire it, we will toss to see whether I halve the seven shillings with you or you pass over your two shillings to me."

"Right."

"I will toss," I said, "and call."

"You can't toss and call too!" he expostulated.

"Well then, we will place the coin on the top of the door so that the coin falls on the other side. Is that fair? I wish to be strictly fair with you, Stanley, and treat you in a sportsmanlike way."

"That's fair enough," he agreed.

I placed the coin on the top of the door, we stepped out into the hall and I heaved sharply on the door-knob and called heads.

"You said heads?" questioned Stanley. "That means that if it is a tail, I collect three and six from you."

"And if it is a head, you give me two shillings," I added.

We opened the door slowly. The penny lay on the floor, serene, fateful, decisive.

"It's a head," I said. "Give me two shillings."

He sighed and handed it to me. He gazed mournfully at me for a while and then shambled away. I put his double-headed penny in my pocket again as a coin of this sort is a valuable acquisition to a sporting man. I then shut the door.

Chapter 10

Sitting on the bed, I clasped my hands and stared at the clock on the little table near me. I don't know how long I sat there. I was not thinking. I was just looking at the clock. Not that there was anything particularly remarkable about it. I did not regard it so much as a clock, as something to look at. I am not a man who goes about seeing sermons in stones or lectures in bricks, or the descent of man in a piece of bone. I can see material for a debate in a heap of road-metal but I am not the type that can gaze on a Seville orange and weep for the glory that was Spain. Had I been like that I would have gazed past that clock to its old home-town in Switzerland. I would have visioned the Swiss clock-makers perched on the Alps and yodelling happily over their work. I would have seen the Swiss maidens condensing the milk and throwing the nuts into the chocolates. The cows browsing in the streets. The cheeses by the lake. The lakes clogged with tourists.

But I was just looking at the clock. It was as if my mind had said, "Now you look at that clock till I come back" and had then departed leaving me a mere body, a shell whose whole outlook in life was clock. Utterly blank-minded. Governmentally employed, so to speak. It is hard to describe my state of mind—or my lack of any state of mind; but it is necessary to describe it. I believe that when one is in this state one gets messages from Beyond. The line is clear, there are no statics, and one has premonitions, vague prophetic feelings loom on one; the great Darkness is lit for a while by a feeble blue flame before one is hurried back to earth and the darkness again.

I had a feeling of impending trouble. As the browsing lamb sees the shadow of the hawk on the grass, so I saw trouble. Gradually the clock forced itself on me. It ticked at me. Its little hand went around. Every tick was a second nearer the grave; my life was ebbing away, ebbing away—second by second.

I was in a very bad state.

There was a loud knock on the door, and Stanley appeared. A real Stanley, plain human meat, of the earth earthy. At sight of him my fit of abstraction vanished and my mind resumed business at the same old stand.

"Well?" I queried.

"Steak just phoned and said she's going to the races with Eggs and she wants us to come and meet her out there. You'll have to hurry. I'm almost ready. Don't bother about a shave. Come on, hurry up."

"Races? What races?"

"Randwick races. Get a collar on and a coat. Just as well you have another coat besides the one that got burnt. I'll have to get you a hat somewhere. Look lively or we'll be late."

He scurried out of the room, and the bedroom door, the front door and the gate slammed almost simultaneously behind him. I rose to my feet. I didn't want to go to the races. I just wanted to sit down and think. Besides, I had only about eight pounds including Agatha's contribution and I wasn't going to be financially butchered to make a holiday for the gimme-girls. I sat down again. A loud crashing of doors and gates resounded through the house and Stanley suddenly appeared in the room like a stage demon.

"Not dressed yet!" he squeaked breathlessly.

"I'm not——"

"Here's a hat of Temple's I've borrowed for you," he gasped, and threw it to me.

"I'm not——"

"Come on. Get your coat. I've phoned for a taxi; it will be here any moment."

"I'm not going!" I shouted.

"Don't be silly, dad. This collar looks clean enough. I found it in the hall. Got your studs?"

"Listen to me, Stanley. I am not going. Don't try these tornado tactics on me; I'm not going."

"Aw, be yourself, dad! You're not working. There's no money coming in. Steak knows an absolute cert for today. Opportunity only knocks once. Come on!"

The door-bell rang.

"That's the taxi-man!" he exclaimed. "Here, put your coat on."

I clambered into my coat as he rushed out of the room. He was back in something under a second with my tie and studs.

"You can put these on in the car," he gasped, slamming a hat on my head. He grasped me by the arm, swung me out of the room, out of the front door, out the gate and into the taxi.

"Randwick!" he cried. "Drive like hell!" and the car leapt forward.

"Keep close to that car in front," I added, "and if it

stops, shoot to kill."

I struggled out of the hat, which was much too small and jammed down on my ears.

"What are you talking about?" said Stanley. "What car in front?"

"There's always a car in front," I replied testily. "A black closed-in car, and it winds in and out streets until it pulls up at a deserted house and they all get out and carry the unconscious girl into the cellar and we surround the house and capture the Master Mind who turns out to be the butler."

He stared at me.

"You're mad!" he said.

"Have it your own way," I replied, and proceeded to adjust my collar.

I made no complaint to Stanley for literally dragging me out of the house and throwing me into a taxi. I had been practically abducted—shanghaied; but the thing was done. It was no use objecting. It was all of a piece with my presentiments and I sensed the presence of the finger of fate. I am a fatalist and believe that what will be, will be; what is, is; and what was, was; and so on through the verbs. I am not alone in my belief, the modern trend of thought is more and more in that direction and I sometimes suspect that even the Railway Commissioners operate their passenger services on the same principle. Stanley must have been thinking on similar lines. He had been gazing at the taximeter, a thing I never do in a taxi as it takes half the pleasure out of the ride. He seemed to be fascinated by the cold-blooded inexorableness of the thing.

"You know, father," he said, "all life is a gamble."

"A highly original remark, my boy," I replied, "I suppose then that Randwick race-meeting is the quintessence of life and a royal routine flush would be the peak of existence?"

"It would be the end of your existence if you were playing at the camp with the boys. Wouldn't it be funny if we won a thousand pounds today?"

"Funny! The braw laddies of the Highland Society would laugh their sporrans off. May I inquire the basis of these hopes for fun? How are we to participate in this huge joke?"

"Don't try to be sarcastic, father. It lessens my respect for you."

"Your respect for your poor old father is already a minus quantity. It only appears on pay-days. You haven't answered my question."

He leaned over and clutched my ear.

"Steak has a stone moral," he whispered.

"A stone moral."

"Ssh!"

"What's a stone moral?"

"Don't talk so loud. It's a certainty. It can't be beaten. There's only one horse in it."

"Oh, well, in that case," I said, leaning back in my corner, "it certainly must win."

"Of course it'll win; you can put your undies on it."

"Seems rather strange, though," I ruminated, "having only one horse in the race. Any fool ought to see that it must win."

"Arrgh!"

I relapsed into my corner again.

The taximeter, foaming at the mouth, demolished another shilling and gnashed its teeth in anticipation of the next. The tick menace is not confined to our country districts.

"Who is going to pay this lightning calculator?" I asked, pointing to it.

"That's all right. I'll see to that," replied Stanley with a contemptuous flirt of his hand that must have greatly disheartened the meter. "It's only twelve shillings," he added.

"Where did you get it?" I exclaimed.

"Temple. Good feller. Stung him for a couple."

"Great!" I cried. "Serves him damn well right!" I had begun to dislike Temple and to hear of his lending money to Stanley was sweet music to mine ears. Anything lent to Stanley can be lined up with the Pyramids, the Sphinx, the national debt and such-like time-defying monuments.

"Leger reserve, sir?"

The driver spoke through the back of his neck after the manner of his kind. The car pulled up and we decanted ourselves on to the pavement. Stanley paid the driver and we walked toward the entrance.

"Synagogue rules," he said. "Take yourself in and pay for yourself."

We clattered through the turnstiles.

A horde of race-book sellers detonated in our faces. "Book! Book! Book! Bookertherazes! Book, sir?"

I bought two and handed one to Stanley.

"That squares us," I said. "You paid for the taxi and I've paid for the programmes."

"If there's a harder man than you," he said, taking the book, "I'll bet he stands on a pedestal in Hyde Park, wrought in solid bronze."

"Where have we to meet Steak?" I said coldly.

"Over by the first stand—there she is!"

I looked as he pointed, and saw Steak and Eggs with

two men, one of whom seemed to be drunk.

"Who are those men?" I asked, waving my hand at the same time to Steak.

"Dunno," he answered in a puzzled voice.

As we drew nearer to them a strange feeling of apprehension stole over me. Their faces left me perturbed. I felt that the only way these men could attain popularity in a civilized community would be for them to become radio announcers. Unseen Uncle Georges gravely announcing a glut of onions in the market. Later, when I heard their voices, I was forced to deny them even this faint hope. We doffed our hats and greeted the ladies.

"So glad you came," said Eggs in an enthusiastic voice. "I don't think you've met our friends. Mister Simpson; Mister Gudgeon. Mister Stanley Gudgeon—Mister Slatter—Gudgeons. Mix!"

As we shook hands I made a mental note of Stanley's perfidy in divulging my name. Smith is good enough for me.

"Gonna back all the winners?" asked Mr Slatter pleasantly. Or as pleasantly as he could. He was not the type of man I usually associate with. He was tall and very broad about the shoulders, attired in a silvery-grey suit and a hard hat. His features reminded me of the cliffs at South Head, and his nose, which had evidently been broken at some time, had a disposition to lounge about his face. I pictured him shaving with a hammer and a cold chisel.

"I hope so, Mr Slatter," I replied.

"Call me Woggo," he said, spitting over my shoulder. "All the boys call me that. Where's Dogsbody?" he added, gazing around.

I concluded that "Dogsbody" was the inebriated Mr

Simpson's trade name and turned to see him a little distance away, leaning on Stanley and breathing very confidentially into his face.

"Come on, Dosb'dy," bawled Woggo. "We're going inter the ring."

I took Steak's arm and moved off toward the betting-ring.

"Your friend has evidently been looking on the wine when it was red," I remarked to her.

"He'd look on it if it was purple and had frogs in it." She squeezed my arm. "Glad you came, honey," she said.

"Have you known Mr Slatter long?" I asked.

"Woggo? He's all right. We get the dinkum oil off him. He knows all the jockeys and trainers and everything. He was born in a horse-trough and carried round in a nose-bag when he was a child. You don't want to worry about him."

"What does he know for this race?"

She stopped and put her mouth close to my ear. "King Rabbit," she whispered. "He's an outsider and he'll be any old price. Put a couple of pounds on for me."

She kissed me on the ear.

She was a gimme, but twenty years of life fell from me, and I kicked them out of the way as I walked on. The frantic clamour of the bookmakers roared around us as we entered the ring. Men and women surged about the stands hurling money away with both hands. Punters pleaded to be allowed to lay odds on the favourite and elbowed each other out of the way in their earnest desire to be robbed. Tip-slingers, urgers and whisperers slunk like jackals through the crowd, and grave and massive policemen placed their furtive bets. I shrunk from the ordeal, but how can man die better than by facing fearful odds? The rest of the gang came up and with a parting glance at Steak, I plunged into the riot.

Pausing at a stand, I addressed the open mouth of a bawling bookmaker.

"What price King Rabbit?"

" 'Oo? King Rabbit? Never 'eard of it. King Rabbit?— Ar, yes, four to one, King Rabbit."

I turned away.

"Well, eight to one," he bawled. "Tens!"

I continued on my way.

"Fifteens!" he yelled. "Twenties! Well, go to blazes!"

I emerged at long last with my head throbbing under Temple's hat and the dust of conflict clinging to my boots.

Steak was waiting for me, with Eggs. I handed her a ticket.

"Sixty-eight pounds!" she shrieked. "He must have been thirty-three to one!"

"You went to a good school," I said.

"Gimme half if it wins," pleaded Eggs.

Steak impaled her with a glance.

"This is my ticket," she said coldly. "Stanley will get yours."

"But he's only putting ten shillings on for me," wailed Eggs.

"Faulty work," said Steak succinctly. "Come and we'll watch the race, honey," she added, taking my arm.

Never, never shall I forget that race. When I am old and peevish, sans teeth, sans hair, and shod with elastic-sided boots, I shall be content merely with the memory of that race. When St Peter asks me my greatest display of charity and fortitude on earth, my answer will be that I refrained from choking Steak when King Rabbit won the Grantham Stakes.

When the barrier went up, the jockey seemed quite oblivious to the fact that I had four pounds on his mount. He appeared to go to sleep on the horse's neck. They wallowed round the bend behind everything else that had legs. The jockey seemed to be about as useful as a wart on the hip and I groaned aloud.

To this day, I believe the horse heard me. He laid his ears back, opened his mouth and accelerated. He threw his legs about in wild abandon. His hoofs touched the turf merely here and there. He flung himself along like a thing gone mad. His tail stood out. Like a chestnut bullet he sped past the field, past the favourite, past the winning-post, and twice around the course before he could be pulled up. Doped, of course.

The great, beautiful, brave beast, may he live for a hundred years and die in a lucerne paddock surrounded by his progeny.

Hoarse with shouting, my hands sore from beating the railing, I assisted the almost unconscious Steak out of the crowd. The stricken punters were very, very quiet and the happy laughter of the bookmakers plunged the iron into their souls.

Thirty-three to one! Even now my hand trembles as I write.

One hundred and thirty-six pounds I collected, and sixty-eight for Steak. If horses have halos when they die, King Rabbit should look like a zebra. We were joined by the rest of the party. I wanted to go home. I was padded with notes. Steak was crying on my shoulder; Eggs was in charge of the matron in the ladies' waiting-room; Stanley and the drunken Simpson were dancing like bears in the midst of an interested crowd. Woggo Slatter stood aloof and not a pore of his skin opened or shut. Not a smile disturbed his granite face. A cigarette hung from the corner of his mouth, and when I sighted him he was buying a packet of chewing-gum. Chewing-gum! Fancy being able to chew!

I parked Daisy in the grandstand and went to him.

"Thanks for the tip, old man," I said, grasping him by the hand. "Thanks very much."

" 'Sall right," he drawled. "We has our lucky days. I might want ter put the fangs inter you for twenty or so one er these days. What are you goin' to do now?"

"I'm going home."

He shifted his cigarette to the other side of his mouth.

"Don't go yet," he said. "Got another one. Be a short price, but it's good."

He tipped his hat over one eye and walked away.

Stanley touched my arm.

"Hello!" I said. "Corroboree finished?"

"The police stopped it," he whispered.

"What are you whispering for? Are they after you?"

"No," he said in an almost inaudible voice, "it's my throat. I couldn't talk at all a while ago. I don't care if I'm never able to yell again. Wasn't it wonderful?"

"Oh, fair performance, I suppose. What are you going to do now?"

"I'm going home if I can get away from Eggs," he whispered.

I studied the nail on my little finger for a moment. "Don't go yet," I said. "Got another one. Short price, but good," and tilting my hat over my forehead I strolled away and left him gaping.

Returning to the stand, I found Maureen and Daisy sitting with their heads close together. Their talk ceased suddenly as I came up to them. I know women. I buttoned my coat and sat down warily.

"Oh, gee!" sighed Maureen, "wasn't it just too lovely! Whatever are you going to buy me with all that money?"

"If you'll excuse me, Maureen," said Steak in a chilly voice, "Jack is *my* friend. Go and find Stanley."

"I like Stan," murmured Eggs, "but I don't value his friendship half as much as Jack's. Besides, he's only a boy, really, isn't he?"

I felt that I was being haggled over. Stanley had evidently been weighed in the balance and found to be under the limit.

"What about Woggo?" I suggested.

"Woggo!" they echoed. "Ha! Ha!"

That let Woggo out. He was either a member of the syndicate or an abandoned mine.

"Do you know what this next winner is going to be?" I asked, to change the subject.

"Dunno," answered Steak. "Woggo will tell you when the time comes. Here he is now."

Woggo strolled into view and halted before us. Fixing his gaze on the horizon, he slowly stroked his left ear with three fingers, spat aimlessly in the general direction of the betting-ring and moved on. Maureen and Daisy hurriedly turned the pages of their race-books.

"Useless Annie!" they gasped in unison.

"What about her?" I queried, looking around.

"That's it," gabbled Eggs. "That's the pea. Where's Stanley?"

She jumped to her feet and scurried away.

"What do I do now?" I asked, turning to Steak.

"All you've got to do now is to empty the roll out on Useless Annie—and make it snappy. Off you go! I'll wait here."

"The whole lot!" I gasped.

"Absolutely," she said, giving me a push. "Put a pony on for me."

I hurried away and burrowed into the betting-ring. A striving elbow bored into my ear as I squirmed through the crowd. It was Stanley. I might have known that with practically the whole population of Sydney collected in one place, Stanley would single me out for injury.

I stamped heavily on his foot.

"Sorry, Stan," I said, patting him on the shoulder, "it's the crowd you know. What's a pony?"

"Thassall right, dad," he replied, "that wasn't my foot. A pony is a little horse."

He was swept away on a wave of punters before I could land him one. Useless Annie, as Woggo foretold, was a short price. One Hennessy, on the outer edge of the ring, who may possibly have been one of the lost tribe, offered to lay me fifty pounds to forty and I passed up the money. He made a quivering stab with his pencil at the betting-ticket and passed the result down to me.

"What's this?" I asked, staring at the Morse code on the ticket.

"Useless," he snapped, glaring at me. "Fifty pounds to forty. That's vat you vant, ain't it?"

"Useless Annie?" I inquired meekly.

"Ah, Gor!" he moaned. "Can't you read?"

"All right, all right," I muttered, and wandered away to the bar.

A flying barman, handling glasses like a nervous octopus, extracted the order from between my teeth before I could utter it, and sped away.

"Snappy, eh?" commented Stanley. He was at my elbow. Ubiquitous.

"Stanley," I said, producing the ticket, "what do you make of this?"

"Useless Annie," he said, glancing at it. "Who put you on to that zoo fodder?"

"Slatter."

"The urger with the ironstone complexion."

I nodded uneasily.

"Born every day," he muttered, shaking his head at his glass. "One a minute."

"What's wrong with it?" I demanded.

He leaned towards me. "Useless Annie's in the bag," he whispered. "I've backed Bonser Baby. Get on while you've got time."

"But——" I faltered, waving my ticket.

"Well, of course, if you don't want to—don't," he said, shrugging his shoulders.

"Do you think I ought to?"

He glanced at me pityingly. "Anyone picked your pocket yet?"

"No."

"Hmm, funny," he said. Then fiercely he added, "Go and get your money on. Leave your drink; I'll look after that."

I gulped my drink and hurried away with my mind in a whirl.

The bookmakers were howling that they were prepared to lay five to one against Bonser Baby and I took a hundred and fifty pounds to thirty pounds in three bets. I stood to win one hundred and fifty, or flay my thirty pounds' worth out of Stanley. Something seemed to tell me that I would win. I felt confident. I decided to avoid Steak for the nonce, and took up a position near the track to watch the race.

It wasn't a race. Some dissatisfied gentleman close to me remarked that it was a mere sanguinary, lightning-struck, blasted, confounded and unmentionable procession. Useless Annie might have been sired by a rocking-horse, and as regards its dam, it was damned by all present. The jockey made a ferocious display with his whip and then realistically fell off and left his horse to browse on the track. Bonser Baby was in front, with another horse gaining on it rapidly and for a moment it looked as if the jockey of that horse would have to fall off too. Fortunately Bonser Baby, with the fear of the bone-yard in him, speeded up his lollop and staggered past the post amidst a chorus of congratulatory groans. The race had not the thrill of the previous one, and although I was pleased to collect my winnings, I was not excited. My presentiments were returning.

I sought Steak and handed her the ticket for Useless Annie. "I put fifty on for you," I said with a wry smile, "the remainder I put on for myself."

I sat down heavily beside her.

"Oh, what a pity!" cried Steak. "You poor thing! Are your absolutely broke?"

"Penniless," I muttered.

"And you put fifty on for me! That was sporty of you, Jack. Here, you'd better take this fiver."

I waved it aside.

"Don't be foolish," she said, pressing it into my hand.

I took it and thanked her. "Hard luck," I groaned.

"Absolutely."

The stand was half full, but she put her arm round my neck, and drawing my head close to her mouth kissed me on the chin.

"There's possibilities in you, honey," she whispered.

" 'Ullo! Wot's this?" grated a harsh voice.

I looked up and quickly declutched. Slatter was glaring at me and chewing his lip. He looked, to put it mildly, discontented. I felt an empty feeling in my stomach as I rose to my feet. It looked like an even chance of my becoming a co-respondent or a corpse.

"It's all right," cried Steak, rising.

Keeping my eyes on Slatter, I edged, crabwise, away from him.

"Well—so long," I called, waving my arm.

"'Ere!" growled Woggo.

I hurried on.

"Come 'ere. I want yer!" he bawled savagely.

I broke into a trot.

"'Ell!" he bellowed, and started after me.

It was then that the benefits of living a more or less clean life came to my aid. There, on that day, without thought of honour or reward, I put up a performance that would have given any Olympic games aspirant a lesson. I flashed past Stanley who was strolling towards the gates with Eggs clinging to his arm like some parasitic growth.

"Father!" he yelled.

"Pace me, boy," I gasped.

"Hey!" called a policeman, dashing toward me.

I slowed down as Stanley came up beside me.

"Whatever you've pinched," he panted, "hand it over to me. They're bound to search you."

"What's all this?" boomed the constable.

"It—it's his wife," gasped Stanley. "She's dying. We must get a taxi."

I caught a glimpse of Woggo temporarily off the scent in the crowd.

"Dying?" queried the constable.

"'Yes," I gulped.

"While the Spring Meeting's on!" he gasped incredulously.

I nodded vigorously. Woggo had sighted us.

"My gore!" said the policeman. "You can't beat women."

"Come on, Stanley!" I cried, and bounded toward the gate.

"'Ere!" shouted Woggo.

"Stop!" bawled a policeman.

"Taxi, sir," queried an angel in uniform, as we dashed out the gate.

I hurled Stanley in and threw myself on top of him. "Woollahra!" I yelled. "Drive like hell!"

Stanley sat down and straightened his tie as the car bounded away. "Referring to the car in front," he said, "do we shoot to kill, in the event of its stopping?"

"If you're trying to be funny, Stanley," I said, scrambling to my knees, "you have selected an inopportune time and run a grave risk of disfigurement for life."

"Well, what's it all about?"

"Woggo was going to assault me," I hissed, seating myself.

"Was he? And yet when I first saw him I didn't like him. Funny how you can be mistaken about a feller." He shook his head. "And I helped you to get away," he muttered.

"What do you mean?"

Ignoring me, he leaned forward and spoke to the driver.

"Go to Castlereagh Street first," he directed.

"What for?" I asked. "What's on at Castlereagh Street?"

"I want to buy a motor-bike and side-car," he replied, producing a cigar.

"Now!"

"Of course!" he exclaimed, staring at me.

"But it's a holiday. The shops are not open."

"Aw, gee! No," he moaned. "I'll have to wait till tomorrow."

"What part of Woollahra?" inquired the driver.

"You're not going home, are you?" protested Stanley.

"Why not?"

"What is the symbol of achievement, the delight——"

"Steak and eggs!" I exclaimed. "King Street, driver."

"Can we get steak and eggs at the Ambassadors?" inquired Stanley, handing me a cigar.

"We could, I suppose, but it would be called *viande* of the bull *avec oeufs* and you'd get it on four plates and have to eat it as if you didn't want to."

"It must be terrible to be in Society. You've been in Society, haven't you, dad?"

I nodded. I've been in everything in my time, from the harbour to the Salvation Army.

"What do you do when you've got your mouth full and someone asks you a question?"

"Well," I said, "you can pretend you didn't hear, or you can swallow the lot, or appear to be thinking over the question and chew like mad, or you can shake your head and give it up—the question, I mean."

"Sounds pretty rotten. I don't think I'd like it," he decided. "And what about finger-bowls? Do the caterers supply the towel and soap?"

"Well, my boy, nowadays people dance between courses so if you really needed a wash, I can see no reason why you should not have a warm bath after the asparagus," I replied.

"We'll go to Guisippi's," decided Stanley. "Pull up at Guisippi's, driver."

The car slowed to a stop and we alighted. Stanley handed the driver a note and waved him off with a lordly air. "Keep the change, my man, and don't get drunk," he drawled, and strolled into the restaurant like a retired pawnbroker. I wadded my notes well down into my pockets and followed him. Seating myself on the opposite side of the table, I twirled my thumbs while he perused the menu.

"H'm!" he mused. "Devilled lambs' kidneys. Hmm. Murray cod. Hm."

The waiter fluttered his pinions fretfully and handed me a menu card.

"Mm!" continued Stanley, stroking his chin, "asparagus on toast. Any bath here?" he asked, glancing at the waiter.

"Nossir."

"Hmm! Fricassee of tripe. Blah! Broiled whiting. Mm!"

I flung my menu card down disgustedly.

"Steak and blasted eggs!" I said.

"Steak and blasted eggs. Yessir. Steak and blasted eggs, one."

"Er—mm. Yes. Steak and eggs," said Stanley. "Extra special eggs, waiter, and porterhouse steak."

"Stand the confounded eggs on their edges for him," I added.

"Yessir. Edge on their eggses—er—eggses on their——"

"Never mind," I said kindly, "waft away with the order."

He wrinkled his forehead and padded off.

"Excellent cuisine?" muttered Stanley. "Never tasted

it. What's it like?"

I snatched the menu from him and tore it up. My nerves were worn to a fine edge with the afternoon's events and I couldn't bear it. "Another word out of you and I'll brain you with the sauce bottle," I growled.

He scratched his ear slowly with a ten-pound note and eyed me speculatively.

"What's crawling on you?" he drawled. "You're practically swathed in money; you've had a wonderful afternoon, and here you are, acting like an Arab who wants to steal away and can't get his tent to fold up."

The boy was right, to a certain extent. Despite the fact that I was nearly two hundred and fifty pounds to the good, I was not contented. My presentiment still gnawed at me. Then there was Slatter. I groaned quietly and commenced the assault on the steak. Stanley must have read my mind.

"What was Woggo chasing you for, dad?" he asked, resting both hands on his fork and staring curiously at me.

"He wasn't chasing me."

"Well, what were you running away from him for?"

"I wasn't. Do you think I'd run away from that ignorant slob!" I demanded, mopping the gravy off my vest.

"Yes."

Stanley can be disconcerting at times.

"I avoided him," I said, "because I was afraid that I might lose my temper and hit him. I have killed men, Stanley, with a blow."

"Fancy having a breath like that!" he gasped.

"At the very least," I continued, "I would have disfigured him."

"You couldn't disfigure a face like that. Almost any

alteration would be an improvement," he commented. "All the same, I wish you'd had a go. The boys will have the laugh on me, now. Anyhow, how do you know he won't follow you?"

"If he follows me, he does so at his own risk," I retorted.

Had I not felt so depressed I would have been amused by Stanley's questions. The only way I ever discovered what fear meant, was by looking it up in the dictionary, when I found it to be "a painful emotion excited by impending danger", and that is all the knowledge I have of fear. I have been called a brave man. Modesty permits no discussion of the matter, but I have lived with Agatha and Gertrude, I have seen the hotel door shut in my face on a Saturday night, and I have pinned an Orangeman's badge on a drunken Irishman. The Irishman was colour-blind, of course, but I took the risk with his instinct. I was not afraid of Slatter; he was something tangible that could be dealt with. It was the dreadful feeling of impending trouble that perturbed me.

I had finished my meal and was scooping the last vestiges from my plate. Stanley tapped me on the arm and I paused with the knife half-way into my mouth.

"Have they any bigger cups than those they gave us last time?" he inquired.

"Stanley," I remonstrated, "surely you must know that it is a very rude and vulgar thing to interrupt people when they are eating? I might have cut my mouth off."

"Sorry, dad," he faltered. "Is it vulgar to drink champagne out of tea-cups? Or do we have to use coffee-cups?"

"The bigger and oftener the cups, the less necessity for the observance of trivial conventions. Ask for jugs."

The waiter coasted down to our table and pulled up

with the silence of a Rolls-Royce hearse.

"Yessir?"

"A bottle of champagne, waiter," ordered Stanley.

"Two bottles," I put in.

The waiter's eyes glistened.

"Three bottles!" declared Stanley.

"Four no-trumps!" cried the waiter.

We stared at him.

"Sorry, sir," he stammered. "Pardon—forgot myself. Three bottles. Yessir."

Stanley tapped his forehead as the man hurried away.

"Bridged," he muttered pityingly; "probably from birth."

I nodded. I had seen too much of that sort of thing to pity the man. In the early days of my married life Agatha had threatened to divorce me for failing to lead the ten of diamonds. By some outrageous whim of a malicious fate we subsequently won the rubber and she stayed with me. I have never played the game since.

The champagne enlivened me. It thrilled and uplifted me like the fangs of a bull-ant. Champagne is another symbol of achievement. It puts a laurel wreath back among the rest of the shrubs. If headaches were created for any practical purpose, it was to show the glory of champagne. To emphasize the beauty of the rose by the magnitude of its thorns. And we had five bottles, altogether.

It was with great difficulty that the waiter and I managed to carry Stanley out to a taxi, some time later. It would have been easy, only the fool waiter, muddling round with his end of Stanley, made me lose my balance and fall to the floor several times before reaching the footpath. The man was obliging enough and I gave him a handful of pound notes as some slight recompense for his trouble, urging him at the same time to bank some. He offered to go in the taxi with us and wanted to brush me down. I couldn't stand for the brushing down. Positively couldn't stand for it.

We left the restaurant, with the waiter standing in the doorway gazing sadly after us, as though he had missed an opportunity to relieve his fellow-men.

Chapter 11

I forget how we got home, and how it came about that we both decided to sleep on the door-mat instead of in bed. Probably it was a hot night. I do not indulge in the stupidity of cluttering up my mind with the memory of insignificant details and I am unable to remember anything about it. The milkman disturbed me in the morning and I had hardly snuggled back on to the mat when the man who delivers the morning papers struck me in the ear with a deliberately aimed *Herald*. By the time the postman arrived Stanley was awake and I sent him to the gate for the letters. There were three of them and as a number of female broadcasters in the terrace opposite were hanging out of their windows like dogs' tongues, we retired into the house before opening the letters.

Stanley flung them on the kitchen-table and we sat down. Only one was addressed to me and that was from the Easy Payment Company. Easy payment; the savage irony of the term!

It was a final notice to the effect that they would remove the gramophone if payment was not made within seven days. I filed it away among the other final notices, wondering why the postman had bothered to deliver the thing. Perhaps the drain was full. I resolved to speak to him about it. The other two letters were to Stanley, from

Agatha and Gertrude. I read Gertrude's letter while Stanley was reading Agatha's. Gertrude's letter I read once then, and several times afterwards. It burnt itself into my brain. It hoisted my gorge. I can quote it almost word for word. It ran:

DEAR STANLEY,

I have prayed for you every day since your mother and I left the house. I feel like a murderer, leaving you there with your father. Although he *is* your *father* I feel it is my *duty* to warn you to be wary of him. Not only is he a lazy, drunken, vulgar, hypocritical old blackguard, but he is a *dangerous man*. Your mother has done well to leave him, if only for a time. Your grandmother thinks so, too. It is a blessing that you take after your mother's side of the family.

I had wondered why you did not write each day giving particulars of J.G.'s conduct, but remembered that you would be busy studying for the Public Service examination that you told me about. We are having some *very* hot weather here, and Granny's parrot is looking very poorly. I hope you are studying hard to fit yourself for a position in the world and have not forgotten to wear your flannels. Keep an eye on J.G. and be *constantly* vigilant, because (I hate to say this, Stanley) I think your father is a *philanderer*.

Love and best wishes from Aunt Gertrude.

P.S.: I am trying to persuade your mother to sue for a divorce, so don't be alarmed if you see any *men* lurking around the house, as they will only be private detectives.

The mere memory of that letter makes me grind my teeth. What a poisonous woman! The tolerance of civilized communities is overdone when such women are allowed to reach maturity. The people of Australia are too easygoing. In any other country she would have been dealt with. America would have had an Anti-Gertrude League and prohibited her. On the Continent, the whole commonwealth of peace-loving nations would have outlawed her like poison-gas and submarines. But here in this land of too much freedom she is allowed to take her place with human beings and go about without even being muzzled! I felt bad enough as it was, without having insult flung at me through the post. I chewed my finger-nails and looked across at Stanley.

He was looking at me and holding his forehead on with both hands. I could see that he was in a vile temper.

"About that fiver!" he grunted.

"About what fiver?"

"The five-pound note ma sent me. Where is it?"

"I don't know what you're talking about. How long have I been treasurer?"

"Ever since you've been secretary and correspondence clerk."

"Stanley," I said, pushing my chair back, "if you have so far forgotten yourself as to accuse your own father of having robbed you; if you are so despicable as to think that I would open your letters; if you are so niggardly as to haggle over a filthy fiver—take it."

I sorted out a fiver and flung it at him.

"Keep it," he growled, and threw it back at me.

"It's worth five pounds to retain the grudge, isn't it?" I replied sarcastically. He made a strange rasping noise conveying contempt.

"Here," I said, throwing the note back to him, "go and get five pounds' worth of aspirin tablets for yourself."

His mouth flickered in a feeble smile.

"Aw, gee! Yes. Aspirin tablets." He pulled himself to his feet and plodded to the door.

"Aspirins!" he gasped, fumbling with the handle. "Motor-bike."

The telephone bell rang with a piercing tingle that set my brains beating against my forehead.

Stanley groaned, and staggering to the phone lifted the receiver off. "Oh, go on," he moaned in a stricken voice. "Say what you've got to say. It's me speaking, hullo, damn you."

A moment of silence.

"Oh—Daisy! Oh, I'm splendid, thanks. Dad? Yes. He's in the kitchen. I'll call him."

"I'm not in!" I shouted.

"Hello. He's not in. Yes, he was in the kitchen a while ago. Up on the roof, I think. Eh? Yes. Another kitten. Don't know when he'll be down—got to take part of the roof off. Yes. Call him a bit later. Good-bye."

He dropped the receiver on the floor and dragged his feet toward the front door.

"Going out, Stanley?" I called.

"I think so," he replied weakly. "I'm flickering."

The door slammed behind him and I pressed my forehead against the gas-stove. The touch of the cold metal was like the hand of a faith-healer. It was uncomfortable kneeling on the floor with my head to the stove, so I lifted the door off it and carried it into Gertrude's room and laid down on it.

And misery swooped on me like a plague of locusts.

Woggo and Daisy, Stanley and Maureen, Gertrude and Agatha, divorce, private detectives, and Woggo and Woggo and Woggo. My brain pounded along on three cylinders and my thoughts plodded round and round like divers with lead boots on. I thought of Slatter. Slatter would stop at nothing. A man with a face like that would be capable of anything from assault and battery down to selling mining shares. Steak was his accomplice; she was the vampire who had clutched me in her coils and would seek to drain me in the depths of her web. Eggs would help her. Gertrude was a scorpion bent on surrounding me with private detectives. My every movement would be watched. Agatha was straining every nerve to drag my name through the divorce court. I pictured myself playing an accordion in the streets to raise the alimony.

Stanley! The blight of my life. The waster who would not go to work. Studying hard for the Public Service examination! Who was going to support me? What did Stanley care? Even now, I thought, he may be careering round on a motor-cycle with a side-car full of aspirins, while his poor father lies sick and worried at home with only the door of the gas-stove for company. My forebodings had eventuated. My presentiments had unfolded into reality. True, I had money. The taxi-driver had either missed his opportunity or had not been in the business long for I still had over two hundred pounds. But what is wealth? Dross. A man spends half his life chasing it, and if he catches it he spends the other half of his life trying to hold it down. Can wealth get one into heaven? If it can, what is to stop Henry Ford from getting there? Ridiculous. Imagine a heaven smeared with lubricating oil, with all the angels in overalls, standardized harps and halos with inner-tubes! In the great moments of life, wealth is as nothing. What are riches to the man who has just been stung by a bull-ant? No. My money was only my fare through the vale of tears. That is the injustice of this world. You pay your fare and walk. What interest had I in life? Leaving out the door of the gas-stove—nothing. Where was I being led? Whither was I going? I was being carried hither and thither, willy-nilly, in endless circles, like the stranger who has hired a cab to go two blocks.

There is a limit to one's mental endurance; at least,

there is to mine. My mind works fast and finishes early. Overtime is a double draft on my physical resources, and as I had practically exhausted myself the previous evening, I fell asleep.

I slept till well into the afternoon and was awakened by Stanley bringing a motor-cycle into the room. I did not wake completely until he started it up and accelerated it. The plaster commenced to fall from the ceiling in flakes. I sat up with my hair on end.

"What do you think of her?" asked Stanley proudly after he had switched it off.

I told him.

"Well," he said after I had finished, "there's no need to go on like that. You ought to be pleased. I am."

Having relieved myself to a certain extent, I regarded him more calmly.

"Where's the side-car?" I asked.

"Outside," he replied, jerking his thumb in the direction of the street. "It got knocked off as I was coming around Flannery's corner. I don't know why the devil they want to put telegraph poles near corners—it's madness. Just as well it came off though; I couldn't have got the bike through the doorway with the side-car on it. That is, I don't think so. It'll be easy to put on again. Of course, it's dented a bit——"

"Did you bring anything to eat or drink?" I put in impatiently.

"No," he replied, "but I'll go straight up to Strathfield now, and get something."

"Strathfield!" I yelled. "Strathfield is twenty miles away!"

He patted the cycle.

"She'll do eighty, all out," he bragged. "Lemme see—

twenty miles there and twenty miles back. Forty. I'll be back in half an hour."

I got off the bed and stood up.

"You'll go to the grocer's and call at Flannery's and be back in five minutes," I snapped.

"Oh, all right then," he muttered peevishly.

"Leave that thing here!" I shouted as he made to mount the cycle.

"But, father, I could be so much quicker on the bike. I'd be so quick——"

"You'd meet yourself coming back and catch your own dust, I suppose. Never mind about that; get out and get something to eat."

He murmured and moved away reluctantly.

"Go on!" I shouted.

"Just wait a minute," he mumbled, and snatching a sheet off the bed, he draped it over the cycle and tucked it in. He patted it affectionately on the handle-bar.

"Be back shortly," he said, and tore himself away.

"If you're not back in five minutes, I'll smash it," I shouted after him.

I was irritable. The room was filled with exhaust gas. The floor was speckled with white flakes from the ceiling, the stove-door lay in the middle of Gertrude's disordered bed, the dressing-table lay on its back and an easy chair, upside down, mutely appealed with its upstretched legs. The whole room was horribly suggestive of the final act of *Hamlet*. I left the room, shuddering. My own room was just as bad, which was Stanley's fault for locking me in. The splintered door leaned tiredly against the wardrobe. One end of the bed stood on its own legs, the other end, having no legs to stand on, rested on the floor. Sheets, blankets, pillows and mattresses lay about in gorgeous profusion, giving the room an air of an abandoned seraglio. Wandering from room to room I was appalled at the disorder. The laundry was merely a receptacle for a mass of debris covered with grey ashes. The kitchen was indescribable. Stanley's room was an impression on a small scale of the Tokyo earthquake. The bath-room had sunk with all hands. The floor was faintly visible beneath a sheet of greasy water and the bath itself was filled to the brim. In its depth rested the remains of the household crockery. The trail from the kitchen to the bath-room was littered with knives and forks, and the whole house was cloaked in dust and death-like calm which somehow reminded me of the excavations of Pompeii. Had I been a vindictive man I would have sent for Agatha and Gertrude, and shown them around. It would have been a simple method of killing them both. Stanley, of course, would never think of trying to straighten things up a little, and as for myself, I do not regard it as a man's sphere to be pottering about tidying things. Man makes the mess; it is the woman's privilege to clean it up. I thought of hiring a woman for an hour or so to give the place a thorough cleaning out. On second thoughts it seemed to be a job for the City Council. I dismissed the problem and wandered out to the front gate.

Stanley was not yet in sight, and I felt hungry and miserable and unsettled. I had too much responsibility, too many things to think of, too many worries. I yearned for sympathy. I needed encouragement. So I went up to Flannery's.

Some men, when they are worried, find relief in violent exercise, some put their faith in a cold shower, others go to their beds early and relate their troubles all night to their wives; but Flannery's will do me. Flannery's is a home, and better than a home. You can knock your pipe out on anything and spit anywhere you like at Flannery's. Always a welcome there, a kind smile and a cheery word. And if they don't like you, they throw you out. A virile place. A place where he-men with red blood may fill their open spaces—where they fetch Grandad his old Martini and mend a broken heart with a gin sling; where every man can give his order and be obeyed; where everyone gets shot and no one dies. Such is Flannery's.

Chapter 12

At three o'clock, after I'd had a drink, I felt that there was still hope left in life; at three-thirty, my troubles seemed to dwindle; at five o'clock, I felt quite confident that if any difficulties really did present themselves I could overcome them.

At six o'clock I determined to look for Slatter, and having purchased a baked rabbit and a tin of sweet corn, I returned to the house to get the axe. What a wonderful difference decent surroundings make to a man!

Dusk had stretched its tired arm across the sky and a little breeze, forerunner of the night, frolicked with scraps of paper on the road. I seated myself on the gas-box and filled my lungs with the cool, sweet air. I am a child of nature and susceptible to her moods, and watching the little clouds hurrying home before it got too dark, and seeing the blush on the horizon's cheek where the dying sun had kissed it, all thoughts of seeking Woggo vanished from my mind. The twilight gave way to the night, the moon strolled out, fat-cheeked and fatherly, among the stars, and I lingered on the gas-box and munched my rabbit. I like rabbit.

I rose after a while and went inside to get the tin-opener. Glancing into Gertrude's bedroom as I passed, I noticed that Stanley's motor-cycle was gone. I was not surprised. It was only natural that the boy should want to ride it all over the globe. He would ride it and ride it and wear the thing down until it was the size of a scooter and then throw it away. I returned to the front of the house and sat on the mat and opened my tin of sweet corn. I like sweet corn. I was pretty messy when I'd finished, but I wiped my hands on the mat and lit my old pipe. If I had to choose between my family and my pipe, I'd keep my pipe. Of course, I'll admit that if I had to choose between a boil on the neck and my family, I'd prefer the boil, but what I mean to say is that a man can get a family anywhere, but a good pipe is irreplaceable. I was at peace with the world.

Lying on the veranda with my head on the doorstep, I watched the glow in my pipe darken and brighten as I puffed. It beat like a human heart.

I love my pipe.

A cricket chirped in the little strip of grass that our landlord calls a lawn. A pianola tinkled somewhere far enough away to make it sound like music, and for once there was no one gaping out the window of the house opposite.

Quietness and peace. Peace and quietness. It seemed too good to be true. It seemed as if it couldn't last. It didn't.

Stanley vaulted over the fence, and I thought of poor Adam looking back on the angel with the flaming sword.

"How many times have I warned you about jumping over the fence and trampling the grass?" I remonstrated.

"Oh, hullo, dad! Didn't notice you there. I was too tired to open the gate. I've had a hard day."

"Vaulting a fence because you are too tired to open the gate is a variety of perverted laziness I cannot hope to understand."

I rolled over on my side and knocked the ashes out of my pipe. "You're incurably lazy," I said.

"I suppose so, father," he agreed.

For the first time I noticed that he was clad in a short leather coat, leggings, gauntlets, riding-breeches and goggles.

"Where's your crash helmet and parachute?" I asked.

"All good riders dress like this," he answered huffily.

I stood up and looked up and down the street.

"Where's your motor-cycle?" I inquired.

"In a garage," he answered glumly. "It wasn't insured either."

"What's wrong with it?"

"Come inside and I'll tell you about it," he said.

I followed him into the house, wondering.

"We'll sit in the hallway, dad; it's too dirty in the kitchen."

I spread myself out on the floor, refilled my pipe, and prepared for the worst.

"You remember when I left here this afternoon to get something to eat?"

I nodded.

"Well, I met Maureen up the street——"

"Eggs!"

"Yes. She was coming down to see you—wanted to tell you something. Don't interrupt me. I'll tell you everything if you give me a fair go. I asked her if she'd care for a ride and she said she would, so I came back here and got the bike and fixed the side-car on—you were out somewhere—and she got in, and away we went. Gimme a match."

I handed him a box and waited while he lit a cigar the size of a carrot.

"Well," he continued, "we got down town and Maureen saw some silk stockings she wanted for a sick friend, so I bought them and a few things more, and then some more things for herself——"

"You poor, abysmal, protoplasmic mug!"

"If you're going to interrupt——"

"Go on. After that, I'm speechless."

"We were waiting for the traffic cop's arm to get tired, just there near the Post Office, when—whom do you think I saw?"

"Dunno," I said.

"Have a guess," he entreated.

I wrinkled my brows in thought.

"You'll never guess it," he piped gleefully.

"Well, what the hell's the use of me guessing!" I snapped.

"I'll tell you. It was Oscar Winthrop with Estelle!"

"Who's Oscar Winthrop?"

"You don't know Oscar Winthrop! He's the prawn who took Estelle away from me, with his rotten motor-bike!"

"Oh! Go on."

"Of course, as soon as I saw him, I just said, 'All right, you——' "

"Now! Now!"

"Well, the traffic cop forgot, and scratched his ear and about two hundred of us got across before he knew it. Then I told Maureen to hang on to her parcels, and went after Winthrop. I caught them in Macquarie Street. Oscar's got a broken leg and concussion. Estelle is not hurt much, it's just shock. Eggs was treated for abrasions and allowed to go home. It happened right outside the hospital. Wasn't that lucky for them!"

"My word, it was!" I gasped. "What did Maureen say?"

"She couldn't talk much. I don't think she said anything."

"Were there any police about?"

"Droves of them."

"Take your name and address?"

"Yes, but of course I didn't tell them everything quite exactly."

"That's all right, you fool, but what about the number on your cycle! They'll find out everything from that, and then where will you be?"

"Oh, I fixed that," he said, waving his cigar, "I just stood next to what was left of Oscar's bike and told the police that I'd take care of Oscar's bike for him and leave mine in the gutter because it was a total wreck. Of course, they took the number of Oscar's bike, thinking it was mine, and I took my own bike away—and—I dunno——"

He scratched his head and looked puzzled.

"I know I tricked someone."

"Didn't they take the number of both bikes?"

"Yes—no. Oh, I dunno! I took the number-plate off my bike when I got it to the garage, but I think someone saw me throw it away."

I tapped him on the knee.

"The best thing you can do is to grow a beard and smuggle away to South America and get shot in a revolution," I said gravely.

He rose to his feet and flung his cigar into the gramophone.

"Ah, well. I busted him, anyhow," he said, cheerfully.

The telephone bell rang as I was scrambling to my feet.

"The telephone!" we gasped.

"You answer it," I said.

"You answer it."

"Answer that telephone!" I ordered sternly.

"Aw, dad. You answer it. Go on. You can disguise your voice, or something. Go on, dad!"

"Why boy, I believe you're frightened!" I scoffed.

"I'm not. I answered it for you this morning. Listen to it ringing!"

I walked to the phone and took the receiver off.

"Yeth," I said, "vat ith it?"

"I'd like to speak to Stanley Gudgeon, please," answered a voice.

It was Maureen. I put my hand over the transmitter and beckoned to Stanley.

"It's Eggs," I said.

"I'm not in," he whispered hoarsely.

"'Ullo? Misther Thtanley Gudgeon ith out. Ith there any methage?"

"Is Mister Jack Gudgeon there?" inquired the voice.

"Oh, no. My vord, no. He'th gone for good. To Meckthico."

"Do you know where Stanley is?"

"Vell, I'm not thure, but I think he'th up on the roof; that'th vere I last theen 'im."

"Is someone spraying your—roof with—kittens?"

Her voice nearly scorched my ear off.

"Madame!" I replied, in a dignified voice, "I refuthe to 'old any further converthation vith you."

I put the receiver back with a click.

"What did she say?" gasped Stanley.

I patted him on the shoulder reassuringly.

"Never mind, boy, your father will protect you," I said

affectionately, and walked thoughtfully into the kitchen.

"What is she going to do?" he asked, following me. "What did she say?"

I shook my head gravely and sat down. "One-hit Mulligan, eh?"

"The champion heavyweight? What's he got to do with it?"

"He's her brother," I murmured in a voice full of sympathy.

"Of course," I mused, "it might all blow over but——" I paused and shook my head. "Thousand pounds damages!" I continued. "It seems a lot of money to claim for a little thing like that. I suppose you haven't got a thousand pounds, Stanley?"

"I've got a thousand uses for a pound."

"It means jail!" I moaned.

"What for?" demanded Stanley.

"Criminal assault with intent to murder, wilfully damaging property, false pretences, robbery, arson, barratry—anything. And then there's her brother. You're in a terrible fix."

Stanley sat down and stared at me grimly.

"Of course, you're not," he scoffed. "Do you know what Maureen told me? Do you want to know what she wanted to see you for?"

I shook my head and he pointed his finger at me menacingly, like the man in the correspondence college advertisements.

"She told me that Woggo Slatter was Daisy's husband. He's looking for you and—stop me if you've heard this—he killed two men in Melbourne last year for sending Christmas cards to Daisy. The police are scared of him. He's after you!"

He dropped his voice to a harsh whisper and leaned across the table. "And he gets his man!" he whispered.

"Does he carry a gun?" I inquired hoarsely.

"No."

I smiled.

"He doesn't need one. He garrottes them!" whispered Stanley. His eyes were bulging with excitement.

I wiped the perspiration from my face.

"You can't frighten me," I told him.

"And you can't frighten me," he declared emphatically.

"I don't know what fear is," I insisted.

"It's never too late to learn," he quoted, rising from the table.

I was rummaging in my mind for a devastating retort to put an end to this bickering when something happened which did more to Stanley than anything I could have thought of. Someone knocked at the front door. My hand, on its way toward an itchy ear, paused half-way and remained motionless. Stanley, with his back toward me, stiffened like a pointer. Slowly he turned his head and looked at me.

"The door!" he whispered. "A knock."

"Well!" I said, "answer it."

"You answer it," he pleaded.

I rose, and pulling the ice-chest away from the wall, crouched behind it. The door-bell rang like a summons to the operating-theatre.

"Go to that confounded door," I whispered. "I'm not in."

"Neither am I," he replied, and bounded softly into the darkness of the laundry. I drew myself up to my full height behind the ice-chest.

"Come out of that, you coward!" I called softly.

The door-bell rang again.

"Go on, dad," urged Stanley. "You're not frightened, are you?"

"Did you ever see your father frightened?" I demanded.

"Never, dad."

"Did I not tell you that I don't know what fear is?"

"You did, father. It makes me proud to think that I am your son—of the same blood."

I stepped out from behind the ice-chest.

"Hand me the axe," I ordered sternly.

The handle of the axe poked out from the darkness and I grasped it.

The blood of the Gudgeons surged within me.

"Stay there, you banana-spined dingo. I shall return presently."

"I hope so, father. I hope so," whispered Stanley.

I crept out of the kitchen and up the hallway. Groping my way into my own room which is in the very front of the house, I peered out the window. A girl of about seventeen was in the act of pressing the bell-button. I felt my way out of the room and strode back to the kitchen.

"Stanley," I said, hurling the axe into the laundry, "you may have this."

"Have you killed him, father?" gasped Stanley, peering around the doorway.

"No, not yet. When I do kill him, I shall kill him with my naked hands. I am a Gudgeon."

I turned and strode up the hall.

"Oh—er—hullo!" said the girl, as I flung the door open.

"What do you want here, One-hit Mulligan?" I

demanded, loudly.

"I—I'm not Mulligan," gasped the girl, "I'm Estelle Jones."

"Estelle?—Estelle?"

She nodded brightly.

For a moment I was puzzled, and then I understood. This was Oyster-mouth. Stanley's erstwhile love.

"Stanley!" I shouted. "Your bicycle accident is here."

"I'm not in," came a smothered voice.

"It's me, Stan! Estelle," yelled the girl.

"You'd better come in," I said gently.

I closed the door behind her and guided her up the hall.

Stanley was in the kitchen, standing with arms outstretched.

"My de-ar!" he cried.

"Oh, Stan!" she murmured, and fluttered into his arms.

I smirked contemptuously at Stanley as he motioned me to get out.

"Well?" I drawled.

Stanley came out of his clinch as the girl looked around.

"This," he said, with what seemed to me an unnecessary emphasis on the "this". "This is my father."

He flopped a careless hand in my direction. The girl smiled at me, and turned to Stanley.

"I see where you get your good looks from," she simpered, and taking both of his hands in hers, stood back and gazed at him.

"Oh, Stanley," she cried, "you beautiful, ruthless brute!"

She kissed him.

I walked out.

Fathers don't count these days. It's hard. Things were different when I was a boy. I remember the time when my father was the head of the house. My mother used to ask him what he'd like for dinner! What he said was *it*. No argument. I obeyed him and went to him for advice. Those were the days when fathers were fathers. Nowadays, a father is nothing more than a family pay-cart. When he does break out and seek to make himself heard, the family merely shrugs its shoulders and murmurs, "What's bitten the old geezer?" If the son of the house brings a girl friend home, father is sent off to bed. He goes to the barber's shop to find himself done out of his turn by his daughter. The only place where the head of the house can air his opinions is in the bar-room. Even there the prohibitionists frown on him. There ought to be a Discarded Fathers' Union.

I went to bed, and they turned the light out in the kitchen.

Chapter 13

Stanley came to me in the morning with the news that there was a breakfast loose in the house. He was in a remarkably good mood and informed me that the bath was cleaned out so that I could have a real bath instead of a series of ablutionary contortions in the wash-tubs. He went away whistling and he was still at it when I came down from my bath to the kitchen.

"Stop that blasted whistling!" I exclaimed.

I never feel much good before breakfast.

"Righto, dad," he said cheerfully, and stopped it.

Eyeing him suspiciously, I sat down to the table, which was laid out as though for human beings.

"What's for breakfast?" I asked. "If there's any more of those damned sardines and baked beans, I don't want to see them."

For days I had been handed a tin of beans, a tin of sardines, and a can-opener for breakfast.

"Chops, fried tomatoes and chipped potatoes," said Stanley. "Will you have porridge?"

"Don't joke, boy. I can't stand it. Bring out the b—— beans."

He set a plate of porridge down before me and I stared at him.

"Is it true!" I exclaimed. "All this chop and tomato stuff—is it fair dinkum?"

"It is," he replied. "Splash round with that porridge or the rest will go cold."

He sat and watched me, beaming. I finished the porridge in a daze and he whisked the plate away and replaced it with another. On it, two noble chops, done to a turn, supported an assembly of little slices of fried potato. Fried tomatoes furnished the background. No poet has ever written a sonnet to fried tomatoes. And yet they are supposed to be able to discern beauty and capture visions. I eyed Stanley mutely.

"Estelle," he chuckled proudly. "She done it."

"Did it," I amended dreamily and took up my knife and fork. The full realization of the thing struck me as I tasted the chop.

"Estelle!" I exclaimed. "She done it?"

"Did it," he replied gently. "Came in this morning and did it. She cleaned the bath out. She's coming back afterwards to wash the dishes and tidy things up a bit."

"What a girl!" I whispered. "She knows her tomatoes."

"Well, I'll leave you to it," he said, strolling to the door, "I want to talk to you when you've finished, dad."

I wondered vaguely what he wanted to talk about, but my mind and soul went on with the breakfast and my mental vision was obscured by chops. When at last I had finished the meal and was breathing regularly once more, I put my feet up on the table, lit a cigar and, with chair tilted back, surveyed the ceiling with a kindly eye. Sticklers for etiquette might view this after-breakfast attitude with disfavour, but if a man can't put his own feet up on his own table in his own house, where can he do it? Agatha once read to me a newspaper article which told of an explorer who shaved regularly and dressed for dinner in the heart of the jungle. I picture this convention-haunted empire-builder doffing his sun-helmet to female baboons, shooting wart-hogs in their order of social precedence, and drinking his own health in a glass of quinine. True, politeness costs nothing, but then, taking into account the laws of supply and demand, anything so plentiful as to be given away without cost must naturally be common; or to use another word, vulgar. I abhor vulgarity.

These are my own opinions, of course, the conclusions of a mature mind, but I have brought Stanley up in strict accordance with all the rules of good society. It is not so very long ago since I chastised him at the table for flipping pieces of butter at my guests from the end of his knife. It was a sheer waste of butter and he was a rotten shot, anyhow. Having brought Stanley up on strict lines, as I have said, I was not surprised when he entered the kitchen and kicked my feet off the table as a sign of his disapproval. I sat up and he seated himself opposite me.

"Well," he commenced, "what do you think of Estelle's cooking?"

I had to admit that I could not have done better myself.

"She'll be doing most of the cooking now," he said. "She'll do anything for me."

"After what you did to her!" I exclaimed.

"Yes," he said smugly. "I've a way with women. I know how to treat 'em. That's all she wanted—a good belt in the back with a motor-bike. Pity I never thought of it before."

"Do you mean to say——" I began.

"Exactly," he interrupted. "She's eating out of my hand. She can see now that I am hard and determined and strong and ruthless. What I want, I take."

"That's all right in the desert," I said, "but we work things differently in this city. And besides, taking what you want is easy compared with getting rid of what you don't want. Any fool can collect a harem, but it takes something more than a sheik to disband it and stay physically and financially whole."

He smiled complacently.

"She is going to square things with Oscar Winthrop, so there will be no trouble from him," he continued. "She begged me to allow her to come here and make the place comfortable for me, and after thinking it over, I decided to allow her."

I shook my head sadly. "What a pity you never had a motor-cycle when your mother was here," I murmured.

"Oh, yes," he drawled, "but I don't think the bike would stand it; and then of course, you've got to understand women. You've got to know how to——"

The whirr of the door-bell interrupted him.

"That's Estelle!" he cried, and leapt from his chair. He had taken two strides when he stopped and returned to his seat. "I'll let her wait for a while," he said.

I rose to my feet and made for the door.

"Sit down!" he hissed. "I'm handling this case."

I returned to my chair and waited. We are never too old to learn.

The door-bell had rung three times before he strolled to the door and let the girl in.

"Hello, little one," he drawled. "How are you this morning?"

"Oh, Stanley——"

"Hush! I am not in a listening mood this morning. Go through into the kitchen."

She entered the kitchen and greeted me. She was

rather a nice-looking kid. About seventeen, perhaps, with auburn hair and a few freckles, which doubtless kept her awake at night and anguished all day. She was evidently at that romantic age when she could invent a blighted life for the milkman and a tragic past for the grocer's assistant, but nevertheless I gave Stanley two days in which to change his programme or lose his licence as a cave-man.

I talked with her in a kind, fatherly way for a while, but it was obviously a strain for her to talk without dancing, and she gave a little sigh of relief when Stanley entered the room with a heavy masterful tread.

"The telephone's ringing," he announced.

"Answer it, then," I said.

"You know, father, I have taken a vow never to use a phone again," he declaimed, folding his arms.

I turned to Estelle.

"Will you answer the phone, my dear?" I asked.

She rose obligingly and we followed and crowded round her as she put the receiver to her ear.

"Hello," she yodelled, and listened.

Stanley took the receiver from her hand.

"Who is it?" he hissed.

"It sounds like a woman," she said, staring at him.

"Eggs!" gasped Stanley.

"Steak!" I whispered.

Stanley handed the receiver back to the girl.

"Tell her," he instructed hurriedly, "tell her it's Mrs Gudgeon speaking."

He smiled at me and I smiled back and winked.

"Hello," said Estelle, "Mrs Gudgeon speaking. Yes; Mrs Gudgeon. G-U-D-G-E-O-N. All right. Just a moment."

She turned to Stanley and offered him the receiver.

"Stanley," she said. "Your mother wants to speak to you."

"Holy Moses!" I gasped, and staggered to a chair.

"Hullo!" cried Stanley shakily. "Hullo! Hullo! Hullo!"

"Cut off," he whispered, and taking Estelle's hand, he gazed at me fearfully and then rushed for the door as I leapt to my feet.

"Come here, you blighter," I shouted.

The door slammed and I was left alone.

Chapter 14

Oh, what a tangled web we weave when first we practise to deceive! The seed had been sown and two private detectives would now grow where only one grew before. I would be dogged, and my lightest word would be taken down in writing and used in evidence against me. And heaven knew what they might dig up. I had led a blameless life, never having been found out yet—that is to say, in anything serious—but with a horde of paid jackalls burrowing into my past——! Thinking of what they might discover made me shudder. Already I saw the headlines: "Gallivanting Gudgeon Goes Gay"—and the alimony! Surely it is a strange law that, not content with depriving a man of his reputation and his honour, must needs go farther and make demands on his pocket.

Stanley had done it again, this time in collaboration with Oyster-mouth.

I wandered wearily toward the door, checked myself in the act of opening it and peered through the window-blind. A pale thin man stood on the opposite side of the road, gazing across at the house. He had the face of a Judas who had only received twenty-eight pieces of silver, and the expression of a defiant rabbit. A born slinker. I made my way through the house to the back gate. As I opened it, a low soft whistle came from the corner of the street and another bloodsucker slunk out of sight. Evidently Agatha was sparing no expense. I cursed gently to myself and scrambled over the fence into the yard of the adjoining house and crept stealthily up the side passage. Peering around the corner of the wall I saw that Rabbit-face had gone and I let myself out the gate and hurried up the street to Flannery's. I had not been there five minutes when Flannery, to whom I had unbosomed myself, nudged me slyly with his fist and nodded toward the other end of the bar. The money-changers had got into the temple. It was Rabbit-face. I looked away quickly but it was too late and I signed to Flannery to pass me a heavy bottle as the fellow came toward me.

"Mr Gudgeon, I believe?" he inquired with lifted eyebrows.

"At your service," I answered, taking the bottle from Flannery.

"Representing the Easy Payment and Household Benefit Co.," he said, taking a sheaf of papers from his pocket. "You bought a gramophone from us, Mr Gudgeon, in—let me see—1927. We have been trying to get in touch with you in regard to——"

"How much is it?" I asked, putting back the bottle.

"Seven pounds, fifteen shillings, Mr Gudgeon. You understand——"

"Here," I said, holding out a handful of notes, "sort it out of that. Why didn't you ask me before? Have a drink?"

His mouth worked and he mumbled considerably before he could speak. "Good gracious, Mr Gudgeon!" he cried. "I don't drink as a rule, but really——Yes, I will have a drink."

"Think he's all right?" whispered Flannery from the corner of his mouth.

I nodded as the man handed me the receipt.

For one who did not usually drink, his technique was good. He was in a hurry to go at first but after a while seemed to settle down and when Sadie came into the bar I introduced him and left him to his fate. Although Flannery was still distrustful of the man, I felt almost certain that I had make a mistake, and though keeping a sharp look-out for detectives on my way back home, I felt less inclined to suspect casual loiterers. Although I was quite right in suspecting casual loiterers. A man who loiters is justly suspected by any civilized community. He is up to no good. Policemen move him on, motorists run over him, pavement salesmen mark him down as a victim and matrons with daughters stare coldly at him. In the eyes of the perambulating populace his grade is low, but I am a broad-minded man and can admire and respect one who has the hardihood to stand still in the street and thereby risk his life, his pocket-money, his social status and the attention of some ambitious probationary constable.

I entered the house with a light heart and a bottle of rum beneath my vest and ascended the stairs to Stanley's room. As I expected, the bed was made and the room swept and tidied. Estelle had seen to the comfort of Abdul Stanley and I laid myself down with a sigh of contentment.

To the habit of lying down whenever the opportunity offers I attribute the preservation of my youthful appearance, and it is my belief that if more men lay down and rested in their spare time, there would be fewer arrests, divorces, bankruptcies, suicides and marriages. The rum was not a restful rum. It was Australian rum. The sort of rum that stormed the heights of Gallipoli, and makes Australia a nation of singers. It was therefore with something like satisfaction that I heard the scraping of boots on the roof immediately above the room and perceived a leg hanging from the guttering above the window. With the alertness of mind which is characteristic of the Gudgeons, I slipped beneath the bed and awaited the intruder. A loud creaking of springs announced that he had scrambled through the window and stepped on the bed with both feet. I watched his rubber-soled shoes slink silently from the room and make toward the bath-room. Cautiously I crept from beneath the bed and followed him on my hands and knees. Arriving at the bath-room, I peered through a chink in the doorway and saw him crouched beside the wash-basin staring intently at the wall, as though listening. Slowly and gently I rose to my feet. He heard me, glanced around nervously, and whipping a spanner from his pocket, commenced to unscrew the water-pipe. It was no time for hesitation. I flung the door open and leapt on to his back. He gave a startled grunt and spread out on the floor. I grasped the spanner he had dropped and rapped him sharply behind the ear.

"'Ere!" he exclaimed feebly.

"Move an inch and I'll loosen your nut with this spanner," I muttered harshly.

It has always been my opinion that if a thing is worth doing, it's worth doing with trimmings.

"Jes' wait till I get up," he spluttered threateningly, and I passed him a blow behind the other ear.

"You bungling home-wrecker!" I exclaimed savagely.

He ceased struggling and rolled one eye at me. I was holding the other against the floor.

"That's what they all say," he said bitterly. "Bunglers!

Home-wreckers! It's enough to make a man give up the game. Lore knows it's a dirty, thankless job."

I seated myself more firmly on his back.

"Any man born of woman, who so far forgets his heritage as a vertebrate animal as to become a divorce detective, deserves to be herded with rattle-snakes," I growled.

He twisted his head around till both eyes stared at me.

"I'm not a detective!" he yelled. "I'm the plumber!"

I laughed bitterly and dealt him another one with the spanner.

"A plumber!" I jeered, "and you came straight into the bathroom and started work immediately. Do you think I don't know anything about plumbers?"

"But I can prove it!" he cried, "I've got all my tools with me."

The man sickened me.

"Don't make it worse," I said contemptuously. "Who ever heard of a plumber with all his tools with him? Do you think I'm a fool?"

"I tell you, I am a plumber!" he shouted. "I've just been mending the roof."

"Oh, and who told you to come into my bath-room?"

"Nobody. I just thought I'd make sure that everything was in good order——"

"That's enough," I cut in. "A conscientious plumber! Ha! Ha!"

Still chuckling, I removed his belt and bound his wrists behind his back, gave him a parting blow with the spanner and stepped quickly out the door and locked it.

"Hey! You——"

I did not wait to hear what he had to say. Whatever he said, it left a brown, burnt-looking stain on the ceiling of the bath-room which has never been removed since. I descended the stairs to my own room, well pleased with myself. I had no plan as yet for disposing of the body in the bath-room but felt that there was no immediate hurry as he was securely locked in, and provided the door withstood his poundings, could be kept locked in till hunger weakened him.

I pottered idly about the room, humming a tune and wondering where Stanley was. Possibly he had pitched his tent on another part of the desert and did not intend to return. The prospect of his absence did not perturb me. I glanced casually out the window—casually for a moment, and then stared in amazement.

Woggo Slatter was strolling slowly down the street, gazing at the house numbers. There sprang to my mind the words of Stanley: "He garrottes 'em", and I sprang open the wardrobe door, scrambled in, and pulled the door to.

I was not afraid. I simply did not wish to see Slatter. He was not the sort of man I like to entertain and I hold it as a British subject's birthright that I should be allowed to choose my acquaintances and regulate my own visiting list. To put it in the social jargon, I was merely not at home to Slatter.

A loud and prolonged ringing of the door-bell proclaimed that he had found the right number. I breathed gently. Upstairs, the bath-room shuddered with blows and shouts. Slatter was impatient. He kicked the door with his feet, pressed the bell-button, knocked with his fist and shouted, "Hoi, Gudgeon!"

The air was thick in the wardrobe and redolent of moth-balls and lavender, but I plugged the keyhole with the corner of my handkerchief. I hate noise.

"Hoi!" bellowed Slatter.

"Open this door!" shrieked the bath-room occupant.

I leave out the various trade technicalities with which he embellished his demand. The telephone bell was ringing loudly and insistently, the window-sashes rattled, and vaguely and disconnectedly I thought of the trump of Gabriel and the sea giving up its dead. As though by some prearranged signal, the noise suddenly ceased. So still was it in the wardrobe that I could hear the moths rolling the moth-balls out of the way to get at the clothes. Then the window-pane rattled as someone tapped it.

"Arryone in?" cried a voice that sounded familiar yet strange.

" 'Sno good, Simp," came Slatter's voice, " 'e must be out. We'll get 'im later. Commorn."

It seemed that Slatter had the drunken Simpson with him. I listened as the gate clacked shut, and opened the door gently to hear their departing footsteps. Gingerly I scrambled out of the wardrobe and stretched myself. The prisoner upstairs had become silent. The house, after all the recent noise, seemed as quiet as some wooded grove, and after a preliminary peep through the window-blinds, I opened the front door slightly and peered out. Women in all stages of house-cleaning *déshabillé* craned from every window in the opposite terrace. Carelessly they risked their lives leaning over balconies to gaze up the street after the disappearing forms of Slatter and Simpson. I shut the door quietly and went into my bedroom and lay down. The shower in the bath-room was running and the plumber was quiet. Possibly he was making the best of things and having a bath. I had begun to suspect that the man really was a plumber.

For some hours I dozed and it was late in the afternoon when I suddenly started to my feet with a sound of crashing and yelling ringing in my ears. It was the plumber, very earnestly trying to get out of his cell, and I rose and went to see if the bath-room was still intact. I knocked at the door.

"Are you there?" I asked gently.

"Where the blazes do you think I'd be?" shrieked the hoarse voice. The man seemed to be irritable.

"All right. All right," I said. "I only wanted to know. Your manners are rotten."

"What are you going to do now?" he demanded querulously.

"Oh, I'll think of something presently," I assured him. "Just plumb around for a while and amuse yourself."

He started to stamp his feet and chant loudly, so I left him. He had asked me what I intended to do with him, and thinking it over I had to confess to myself that I had no idea what to do with him. I have made it a rule never to worry about trifling matters so I forgot him for the time being. The telephone was ringing as I came down the stairs and as I failed to see how it could cause any more trouble than it had already done, I answered it.

"Woollahra, 4381," I answered in a snappy, business-like manner.

"Is that you, Stanley?" answered Agatha's voice.

I lifted my voice an octave.

"Yes, ma."

I held the receiver tightly with both hands and leaned against the wall as the diaphragm quivered to the blast. The poet who wanted to see himself as others saw him, never had a wild woman talk to him on the telephone. She weakened at last.

"Are you still there?" she demanded.

I nodded and then, remembering where I was, answered, "Yes."

"Well then, don't you forget," she snapped. "Your aunt and I will be around at eleven o'clock tonight. Leave the door unlocked. We will have witnesses with us and I'll make it my business to find out what that—what your father is doing with hussies in the house. Don't forget. Leave the door unlocked. Do you hear me?"

I replaced the receiver. I had heard enough.

Wearily I turned from the phone, to see Stanley's head poked around the half-opened front door. He ducked back quickly as I looked.

"It's all right," I called, "come in."

He entered warily.

"How was I to know——" he commenced.

I silenced him with a motion of my hand.

"It's all right. Where's Estelle?"

"Didn't she come back here?" he asked in a surprised tone.

My brain worked rapidly.

"Perhaps she did and perhaps she didn't," I replied smiling.

"Come on now, dad; where is she?" he asked playfully.

"I didn't say she was here, did I?"

"No, but I know you're hiding her somewhere. Out with it, dad."

I beckoned him to come closer and he came very slowly and cautiously. It was evident that he was not too sure how he stood with me. I caught him by the arm and whispered in his ear.

"There might be a surprise for you in the bath-room, but I don't think you should go up there, my boy."

He winked and made for the stairs, chuckling.

"Mind you," I called after him, "I only said there might be. Just peep in."

He bounded up the stairs and I crawled under the table and rapidly pulled the chairs in close. I heard him fumbling with the lock. "Did oo finkums could hide from me?" he cooed.

Whatever else he was going to say was drowned in a wild shout of rage and triumph as the plumber leapt on him. For a few minutes the house shuddered. Stanley screamed like a frightened horse, and the air quivered with the battle-cry of the Amalgamated Plumbers' Union. I tried to resemble the pattern of the linoleum as much as possible as the noise subsided. The plumber clumped heavily down the stairs, paused in the hallway sniffing like a prowling puma and then trudged out of the house. Several ornaments fell off the mantelpiece as he slammed the door. Crawling from beneath the table, I tiptoed to the foot of the stairs, and called softly:

"Are you there, Stanley?"

A moan answered me.

Alarmed, I dashed up the stairs. He was lying on the floor, mumbling to himself; saying the same words over and over again. He repeated them loudly as I bent over him. The modern youth has no respect at all for his father. Stanley's injuries were slight but well distributed. Time and bandages would easily stale their infinite variety.

"Well," I said sadly, "you've been getting yourself into trouble again."

The breath whistled through his nostrils as he looked up at me. I stepped back a pace and grasped the stair-rail.

"Why you should assault a harmless plumber who was merely doing his duty, goodness only knows," I continued. "You certainly resemble your mother's side of the family in your sheer wilful malice. Your outrageous temper will get you into serious trouble one of these days."

More in sorrow than in anger I descended the stairs while he lurched to his feet and tottered into his room. At the foot of the stairs, I sat on the bottom step and thought.

Things were getting mixed.

Chapter 15

The slings and arrows of outrageous fortune were descending on me in matted clumps. I was hemmed in with things happening and things about to happen, and peace of mind was as far off as a reduction in the Naval Estimates. I am a strong man and have borne many sorrows and suffered under dreary burdens, but I must admit that now and then, I feel as if I'd like to lie down and be bedridden. Just to look out a window at nothing, to be turned over and washed, to have my temperature taken from me and my meals brought to me. To be like the three wise monkeys of the East; to see nothing, hear nothing, know nothing, and damn everything. But the indomitable spirit of the Gudgeons raises its battered head and I carry on, bloody but unbowed.

With my chin cupped in my hands, I disciplined my mind and laid out my troubles for inspection. It is essential to get a proper grasp of a problem before it can be dealt with.

Woggo Slatter was on my trail. Eggs was after Stanley. Agatha and Gertrude would arrive with a gang of witnesses at eleven o'clock that night. I had lost my job; this did not worry me much but I put it in with the rest, as a difficulty. Perhaps there was nothing much to worry about, but I had had only two decent meals since Agatha's departure and that in itself was an excuse for morbidity. I was practically marooned in the house with Stanley as my man Friday and he was at that moment moaning on a bed of pain through his own foolhardiness. There was trouble between us. Now, when co-operation was needed more than ever before, there was a rift in the lute and the even tenor of our companionship had sunk to a rumbling basso. The only thing to be done was to go to Stanley, put the case before him and enlist him as an ally.

It is characteristic of me that when I come to a decision, I immediately carry it out. Otherwise I'd forget it. I trudged up the stairs once more and entered Stanley's room. He was standing before the mirror examining his eye and he turned with a low bestial growl and glared at me as I shut the door.

"Stanley," I said soothingly.

"Blah!" he exclaimed and flung himself down on the bed.

I sat down beside him and patted him on the shoulder.

"I know you're having hard luck, my boy," I said. "What with the motor-cycle accident and now these black eyes and things, it's hard on you. Cheer up, my son, I've got some bad news to tell you."

He grunted and looked curiously at me with the less swollen eye.

"I've been talking to someone on the phone," I continued.

"Maureen," he exclaimed. "Or was it only the police?"

I shook my head gravely.

"Eggs it was. She—I don't like to tell you this, son."

"Go on," he urged weakly.

"She wanted me to leave the front door open."

"What for?" he asked in amazement.

"They're coming!" I whispered. "Droves of them. The

two women, Maureen's brother—One-hit Mulligan, that is, and two or three more men in case you put up a fight."

"When?" he gasped, sitting up on the bed.

"Eleven o'clock."

"I'll go now!" he cried. "I'll leave before they come."

I caught him by the arm as he jumped to his feet.

"Don't you think they have foreseen such a probability?" I pointed out gently. "Don't you understand that they will be watching for you?"

He slumped back on the bed and stared bleakly at me.

"You see the position you are in?"

He nodded dumbly.

"Well then," I cried, slapping him on the back, "trust to your old father to get you out of it."

"Hmph!" he grunted.

Silence fell between us.

"To think," he broke out at last, "after all I've done for her! Took her for a ride in the side-car, gave her money at the races, bought her silk stockings and a fur coat, paid for——"

"Hold!" I interjected. "What's this about a fur coat? Motor-cycle—fur coat! How much did you win at the races?"

"Seven hundred and something," he answered carelessly. "I forget exactly how much. And now," he went on, "she hires a gang to besiege me in my home!"

"Split infinitives!" I gasped. An oath which I use only when absolutely astonished. A journalistic friend who subsequently and, of course, inevitably died of starvation and alcoholic poisoning, taught me it and I use it rarely. I was more than astonished, I was dumbfounded. That the boy should be so secretive about his winnings amazed and pained me. I resolved to teach him poker at the earliest opportunity.

"What are you looking at me like that for?" he demanded irritably.

I bent over him.

"You and I must be friends, Stanley," I said in a conciliatory voice, "we must combine to rebuff your enemies."

"What about your enemies?" he sniffed suspiciously.

"I can handle them," I assured him. "Now," I said, standing up, "the first thing to be done is to get something to eat. An army fights on its stomach."

"I don't want to fight on my stomach," he moaned.

"I speak figuratively," I explained. "Where is your inamorata?"

"I think it's all right," he replied weakly. "Seems to be bruised," he added.

"Where is Estelle?" I snapped impatiently.

The door-bell rang.

"That'll be her," he exclaimed.

I left the room and went down to let her in.

"Is Stanley all right?"she inquired fearfully, as I held the door open.

"No," I said gravely. "He is very badly injured and needs nourishing food sufficient for two. I'm glad you came. Go up to him."

She skittered past me and up the stairs and I followed slowly. I paused at the door as the murmur of Stanley's voice came to my ears:

"And then four more of them rushed me," he was saying. "I clutched one by the neck and held him up for a shield while I battered the other three down with my free hand. Then all of a sudden——"

I coughed and walked in.

"Estelle," I said, "would you do something to help Stanley?"

"Oh, I'd do anything!" she trilled, regarding him with shining eyes.

"Well, then, go and get about six pounds of steak and potatoes and stuff, and cook it for him. If there is any left over when he has finished, I'll have a bite myself."

She glanced again at Stanley.

"Please," he pleaded with a wan smile.

"You're lucky to have such a kind, thoughtful father."

Stanley writhed, coughed violently, and started to mutter.

"I'll go now," she said anxiously. "I won't be long."

"Better take the key and let yourself in," I said. "I'll have to stay with poor Stanley."

She took it and hurried out of the room.

Stanley rolled off the bed and stood up, wincing.

"Eleven of them," he said meaningly. "Attacked me, they did. Eleven hoodlums; and I beat them off."

He gazed at me defiantly.

"All right, son," I agreed. "I won't let you down."

"You better stay in your room till Estelle has gone," I added. "We'll have plenty of time to barricade the place afterwards."

I left him and went downstairs to the kitchen and switched on the light and sat down. Things were going well.

A plan was forming itself in my mind. Of course, I could have risked the possibility of detectives watching the house and simply left the place. But I did not want to see Slatter. I had an idea he was hanging about the house, waiting to spring.

I felt more comfortable in the house.

Chapter 16

It was a quarter to eleven. Estelle had come in, cooked, cleared up and cleared out. I had dined well and Stanley had been supplied with steak both inside and out, and was lying on his bed with nearly two pounds of perfectly good, cookable meat on his face.

At first, I had thought of barricading the place, but a better idea had suggested itself to me, devilishly effective and childishly simple. I merely knocked the back out of the wardrobe in the front room and left the front door ajar. Nothing more.

With Stanley as an additional witness, I intended to secret myself in the wardrobe and when Agatha and Gertrude entered with their private detectives and came, in the course of their search, to the bedroom, I would confront them and demand to know what they were doing sneaking into the house with men companions. There was no escape for them; I simply would refuse to believe their explanations and their mouths would be sealed for ever.

Stanley, with the fear of the mythical One-hit Mulligan in his soul, was inclined to doubt the wisdom of my arrangements. He could see no good reason for allowing Maureen and her gang into the house, and I had to explain that they would batter their way in, anyway. I at last smoothed his objections by agreeing to rush out of the wardrobe at the right moment, lock the front door, and burn the house down.

It wanted eight minutes to eleven when I called Stanley to take up his position in the wardrobe. With the back removed, there was plenty of air, and although the odour of moth-balls still hung about and Stanley insisted on taking his eye-steak with him, we were as comfortable as we could expect to be.

The seconds doddered along and the minutes crawled after them. Stanley kept hissing questions into my ear, playing round with his piece of steak, shifting his feet and sniffing, until the mere proximity of his body irritated me almost to the point of choking him.

Eleven o'clock boomed out from somewhere far away.

We held our breaths. The house seemed full of things that creaked. The silence got up and walked about.

Stanley chewed the end of his steak nervously.

"Will they never come?" he mumbled.

"Courage, my boy," I whispered.

"What does One-hit Mulligan want to bring his gang for?" he whimpered.

I handed him a moth-ball with the vague idea that it might console him, and he became silent.

The front door creaked and the murmur of hushed voices filtered through the darkness. I could hear Stanley crunching the moth-balls. He trembled as the soft sound of wary footsteps came muffled from the hall.

"It's very dark," came a voice, 'I don't think there's anyone here."

"It's ma!" gasped Stanley.

I clutched his throat and held it.

"Not so loud!" whispered Gertrude's voice. "He's here all right. Stanley would see to that."

As they paused in the hall, I released Stanley's throat and glared at him.

"Not a word out of you," I whispered savagely.

I opened the wardrobe door the merest fraction and peered out. The two women had come into the room and were just discernible in the darkness. Someone stumbled in the hallway, cursing softly in a man's voice, and I shut the door hurriedly.

Stanley looked at me with a strange expression on his face. "I'm going to sneeze," he whispered.

"Don't!" I implored hoarsely.

"What's it worth?" he whispered gloatingly.

I manoeuvred my hand into my trousers pocket and passed him a note. Rage possessed me as he handed me a moth-ball.

Gently, I pushed the door.

"What carryings-on!" Gertrude was murmuring. "Look at that bed. Broken to pieces."

"Hs—hs—hs—hs!" hissed Agatha, tapping her foot on the floor. I had heard that noise before from Agatha and it sent a chill through me.

Stanley tapped me on the shoulder.

"It's coming on again," he whispered, covering his nose and mouth with his hand.

I poked another note at him with quivering fingers. He made a queer sizzling noise with his mouth and continued to hold out his hand. Hurriedly I gave him two more and he grunted softly and relaxed.

"Here, this way!" hissed a voice from outside the wardrobe.

A confusion of soft footsteps sounded in the hallway; Stanley clutched my arm and pointed frantically to his open mouth. I slipped the remainder of the notes into his talons and stroked him gently on the neck so that he trembled. The footsteps died away.

I turned my face toward Stanley and smiled like a sick tiger.

"All's f-fair in love and w-war," he faltered.

He caught the hand I stretched toward him.

"Listen!"

Someone was very gently pushing the window up.

"Now be careful! Get in gently or you'll break something. One at a time."

"Maureen!" quavered Stanley, squeezing my hand in a frenzied grip.

"And gang," I added. "I feel queer, Stanley."

"Aw, dad!"

"I'm afraid I'm going to sneeze, Stanley."

He scrabbled frantically in the narrow space and pushed a bundle of notes into my hands.

"Dad!" he implored in an agonized whisper.

"Is that all?" I replied.

He handed me a few more notes and some silver. The voices of two men, as well as Maureen's were mumbling in the room.

"P'raps they're in the side-car," said one.

"Side-car me foot!" scoffed Maureen. "Stanley's the chap we want to find."

"Might come across the old man," put in a harsh voice. Woggo's voice.

The silence of the tomb descended on the wardrobe and we put our arms about each other's necks for company's sake.

"Here they come!" said Maureen. "Now we'll get them."

"Don't see why you should go to all this trouble when

you could——"

"Shut up!"

There was a clatter of feet in the hallway.

"In here!" cried Gertrude.

The light flicked on and I peered through the wardrobe keyhole with Stanley trying to elbow me away. The scene was extraordinary.

Gertrude, Agatha and two men stood motionless in the doorway of the bedroom. Woggo Slatter and Simpson were facing them, and Maureen stood irresolute between the two groups with her mouth open. Daisy, obviously a late arrival, was half-way through the window. She had pink and blue garters on.

Woggo was the first to speak.

"Ho!" he said.

The spell was broken.

"And who might you be?" demanded Gertrude shrilly. "What are you doing in this house?"

Woggo stepped back and leaning with one hand against the window-sash, crossed his legs and pushed his hat over his eye.

"One might arst the same question," he drawled. "Oo might you be?"

Agatha pushed her way to the front.

"Who are these hussies?" she screamed, pointing to the girls.

Steak swung her other leg over the window-sill and advanced in battle formation. Woggo swept her back with his arm.

"Oo are you?" he shouted to the group in the doorway.

"My name is Agatha Gudgeon," answered Agatha crushingly. "I live here."

"Poor Jack," muttered Maureen.

"Ar, y'are, are yer?" mumbled Woggo.

"Now perhaps you will tell us what you mean by trespassing on our premises!" hissed Gertrude.

"We came here to find——" commenced Maureen.

"'Old!" cried Simpson dramatically. "Before another word is said—Oo are them two rat-faced coots 'angin' round in the background? Seems ter me I seen 'em before."

"These two gentlemen," replied Gertrude, with an air of Polar politeness, "these two *gentlemen*," she repeated, "are private detectives."

"Har! Har!" growled Simpson and threw his hat on the floor.

"*Ds!*" shouted Woggo. "Ho! Simp!"

"Har, I loves detectives," pealed Simpson, shedding his coat.

Shouting with savage joy they leapt for the two men in the doorway. Gertrude screamed, Maureen cheered, and Steak pulled off her hat and made for Agatha.

Stanley heaved at my arm in a vain attempt to get at the keyhole. "It's my turn," he muttered. "You've been looking all the time."

I fended him off with one hand.

"I'll sneeze!" he threatened.

"Sneeze, damn you!" I muttered gleefully.

Agatha had escaped and rushed out of the house and Daisy had taken on Aunt Gertrude, the next best thing. Simpson had finished his man, but Woggo toyed with his victim, knocking him down and picking him up for the sheer innocent joy of it. It was a glorious sight.

Presently the room quietened. Gertrude had followed Agatha into the open air, and Steak, surveying a torn dress, breathed heavily.

"Commorn," said Woggo, "we'll go."

His voice sounded elated and even boyish.

"Just a minute," said Maureen, busily scooping a brush, comb and scent-spray off the dressing-table.

"I like these and I know Jack would give them to me if I asked him. That reminds me—what about Stanley and his old man?"

"Aw, we'll find 'em later," growled Slatter. " 'Urry up out of this."

"Yes, but we came here to get 'em and we're going to get 'em."

"Why harp on it?" said Daisy.

"Harp on it! How would you like it?"

Still arguing, they trooped out the front door and slammed it shut.

We listened as their voices grew fainter and fainter in the distance and then flopped out of the wardrobe. The two detectives lay peacefully side by side in the hallway.

"Do you think they're dead?" asked Stanley, staring at them.

"I'm afraid not," I sighed. "Give me a hand to throw them over the front fence."

"It doesn't matter," said one of them, sitting up. "I'm all right."

"Well, take up your fellow buzzard and walk," I snapped. "Walk and walk and keep on walking."

"Go on!" snarled Stanley, brandishing his fist in the man's face.

"All right. All right," he mumbled weakly.

"Get!" shouted Stanley as the other detective opened his eyes. "Get out before I kill the pair of you!"

Cursing silently, they staggered to their feet and swayed out into the street.

"Humph!" grunted Stanley. "I'll show 'em."

He glared after their retreating forms.

"Quicker'n that!" he barked.

They glanced back piteously, and he slammed the door and swaggered up the hallway.

"That sort has to be dealt with firmly," he flung over his shoulder as I followed him.

"You're a tiger, all right," I replied admiringly.

He paused in the kitchen and turned to me with a puzzled look.

"What did she mean by 'harping on it'?"

I shook my head. I was wondering about that myself.

He sat down and wrinkled his forehead to give me the impression that he was thinking.

"Steak seemed to be on our side and Eggs said—what did Eggs say?"

"She said something about how would you like it—or something," I answered.

"H'm! Ah well. No use worrying about it. Suppose we'd better hit the kapok."

"Hit what?" I queried.

"Hit the kapok. Bungidoo—snatch a stretch of shut-eye, somnolosa, go to sleep—— Gee, you're dense!"

"I suppose I am," I muttered. "I'm tired."

"Ah, well. You'll soon be wrapped in the arms of Murphy's. I'm going to sleep out here. Good night."

I went off into Gertrude's room and sat down, thinking deeply.

Chapter 17

Queer, the incongruous thoughts one has occasionally. Especially in times of mental stress. The mind seems to set aside all major worries and considerations and fool about with something entirely remote from them. It is a common thing and happens to all of us. The parachutist leaping from his plane wonders if the canary has been fed. Derelicts about to suicide have misgivings about the spelling in their farewell notes. The explorer, bound for the Pole, wonders if he wound the clock and put the cat out before he left home, and the battered boxer, prone upon the mat, wonders what his mother will say. And I wondered how and where I could find a position for Stanley. Perhaps this care for Stanley's future had become a star boarder in my subconscious mind; perhaps my tired brain could not control my thoughts and they wandered where they listed. An easy job, with easy money and plenty of it. I mumbled them over, starting from the As.

Architect, alderman. Beauty specialist, building contractor. Car lifter, catarrh curer. Dope pedlar. Evangelist. Face-lifter.... Politician, pugilist.... Despairingly, I stumbled on.... Xylophonist. Yeast prescriber. Z—Z—Z——?

I got up and went to look for the dictionary.

Passing down the hall in the darkness, I bumped

Stanley coming from the kitchen.

"Where are you going?" I asked.

"Up to the garage to get the bike," he replied. "It ought to be repaired by now."

"At this time of night!" I exclaimed.

"Garages are always open," he explained. "Day and night; like the lock-up. Get in any time you like, but you're lighter when you come out."

A brain-wave surged over me.

"How'd you like to be a zodiaccer?" I asked him.

"Aw, I dunno. I'd have a crack at it. What is it? Anyhow," he added hastily, "I'm not broke yet, you know."

"A zodiaccer," I explained, "is a man who studies the stars and knows all about them and can tell——"

"I know!" he cried, "a film-actor! Or do you mean one of those he-chorus girls, or is it a blackmailer?" he added bitterly.

"It's the only one I can think of with a Z," I replied.

I could see it was no use talking to the boy.

"I'm going to be among the Bs," he declared.

I nodded in emphatic agreement.

"I'm going to be a bike-rider. A professional, trick bike-rider," he continued, walking toward the door.

"And you'll end up appearing on some speedway fence as a professional trick corpse," I called after him.

He sniffed loudly and walked out.

I strolled into the kitchen, thinking the matter over. If the boy was really sincere in his desire to become a professional motor-cyclist I could insure him and rest assured that whatever sacrifices he made to improve the breed of motor-cycles would not be made in vain. In such a profession he could not fail to provide for my old age by some means or other; and as a father, with a proper sense of my paternal responsibilities, this method of providing for our joint futures appealed to me...

Someone knocked at the door.

I switched the light out in the kitchen and kept still. Lately it had seemed that every time I opened the front door, something happened.

"Anybody in?" bawled a voice from the street.

The knocking was renewed.

It could not be the police. The police knock once and then bash the door in. Anyhow, what did it matter if it was the police? The sturdiest of us get fed up at times. I went to the door and opened it.

" 'Ullo," said the darkness.

I opened the door a little wider and peered out.

A man about seven feet high, with a travelling-rug over his arm and a suit-case in his hand greeted me.

"It's me," he announced.

"Well?"

"Is this where the Gudgeons live?"

"Yes," I answered after a momentary hesitation.

"Is your name Gudgeon?"

"Er—yes."

"Well, I'm your brother-in-law. Here, take these."

He threw his suit-case and rug at me, pushed the door back, and walked in.

I threw his bag and rug out on the mat.

"This isn't an hotel," I said. "Eight visitors have just left. We have no accommodation."

"I'm all right," he said peevishly. "Isn't Agatha here?"

"No," I snapped.

"Thank crikeys! I'll stay with you for a while."

"Agatha is at present visiting her——"

"Don't tell me," he shouted. "I promised to call on

her when I came to Sydney. If I don't know where she is it's not my fault, is it?"

He struck a match.

"Where's the lamp?"

"What lamp?" I asked.

"Ain't there any light in the place?"

I switched the light on.

"Ar!" he gasped. "Electricity."

I looked him over, starting from the base. There was nothing niggardly about his feet. He had on an enormous, one might say palatial pair of knobby-nosed boots of an ox-blood colour. His tight trousers showed two inches of thick woollen socks. A leather belt, like the surcingle of a horse, girded him, and two bony wrists, from which dangled a pair of outsize hands, stuck out from the short sleeves of his coat. His hat and collar were too small. His face was a reddish-brown and freckled largely, like a banana.

His face fell apart in a grin as I looked up at him.

"Decent sorta turn-out, eh?" he said smugly.

"You look swell," I agreed.

"Yes," he said, retrieving his rug and case, "I wasn't goin' to have these city blokes pickin' me for a bush-whacker so I filled in a coupon for a complete rig-out from Sydney. Five pounds. Everything. Suit, hat, boots—even a handkerchief and a watch and chain. Cheap, eh?"

I nodded. I was wondering what Stanley, the man about town, would say.

"What's your name?"

"Gudgeon," I replied.

"Ar, yes. Of course. But what's your other name?"

"Jack."

"Shake," he said, displaying his manual acreage. "My

name's George. George Weldon."

My hand disappeared in a forest of fingers and was clenched tight in a desert of calluses.

"Lead on," he said.

I walked into the kitchen, switched the light on and waved him to a seat. He put his case on the floor and, leaning over, unlocked it. "I've come a long way," he said, flinging the lid back, "but I'm travelling light. Got bushed trying to find your house or I'd have got here earlier."

"Where from?" I asked.

"Split Rock," he answered. "Have a drop of snake charmer?"

I waved aside the proffered bottle.

"Is that all your luggage?"

"Aw, I got a few things here. Goin' to do a bit of shopping while I'm in the city. Better have a drop of this. I brought it all the way from Split Rock."

I took a sip from the bottle pushed toward me, and my throat contracted. My tongue curled and flopped as, coughing, I put the bottle down.

"Better have a drink of water now, it stops the liquor from taking the enamel off your teeth. Good stuff, eh?"

I nodded as I made for the tap.

"Well now, let's hear all the news," he said as I seated myself once more.

I rather liked the man. There was something about him; an air of frankness, honesty, openness—something that I liked but could not define. A sort of innocence. I hoped he had some money. He was someone in whom I could confide, and I unbattened the hatches of my reserve and told him everything. I told him of the circumstances leading up to the departure of Agatha and

Gertrude, and of the subsequent happenings. Of Woggo and Steak and Eggs and Estelle and Stanley. Of the police, the divorce detectives, the motor-cycle and all the things that had happened or might happen. It did me good to see him nod his head and hear him grunt in sympathy. He patted me on the back as I finished.

"Never mind, Jack," he said. "You and me's going to be cobbers. If there's any fightin' to be done, leave it to me. As for that Slatter bloke—I'll fix him all right."

He commenced to unlace his boots.

"My crikeys!" he added. "That young Stanley must be a bit of a doer!"

"You said it," I agreed.

He jerked off his boot.

"Me feet ain't really as big as this," he remarked. "I got me roll in here. I heard about the sharps in Sydney and I'm taking no chances."

He commenced raking notes from his boots and shaking them on to the floor. "Got a cheque for three thousand in the other boot. Sold out me share in a little mine we had up at Split Rock."

He looked into my open mouth.

"You show me round the town and help me do some shoppin' and I'll stand the damages. That all right?"

"That's all right, all right!" I gasped.

"All right. That's all right, then."

A muffled roar sounded in the street, grew louder and louder as we listened, and terminated at the front door with a fearful crash that sent the crockery clattering from the shelves.

George pushed me back into my seat. "I'll go," he drawled, peeling his coat off.

I followed him along the hallway and stood behind

him as he opened the door. Stanley, astride his motor-cycle, blocked the view.

"Dented my mudguard!" he whined.

I looked past him at the splintered fence.

"Haven't you got any brakes?" I demanded.

"Ar—brakes!" he replied contemptuously. "Why didn't you leave the door open?"

I turned to George.

"This is it," I said. "Stanley, this is your Uncle George."

" 'Ullo, Stan," said George, grasping his hand.

" 'Lo, Uncle," replied Stanley, looking up at him. "Gee, you're big, aren't you?" he added admiringly. "I bet you're strong."

George simpered.

"I bet you can't push the motor-bike and side-car over the step and into the front bedroom."

"Har! 'S'easy!" replied George as Stanley dismounted.

I turned and walked back into the house with Stanley behind me, leaving George to handle the machine.

"He's going to be useful to have about the home," remarked Stanley, removing his gloves. "Is he staying long?"

"Depends," I replied.

"Straight from the Never-Never by the look of him. Is he cashed up?"

"You leave your Uncle George alone!" I warned him.

"Oh, all right. You saw him first, of course; but I'd just like to know."

"You must treat Uncle George with respect," I snapped.

"Oh," muttered Stanley. "I see. Well, I'll want a

commission on the takings, you know."

I made a swing at him as George entered.

"Ar, leave the boy alone," he drawled, "he didn't mean no harm."

"He's always hitting me," blubbered Stanley, screwing his face up.

"Never mind, Stan. You try and be a good boy. Here!"

He handed him a pound and patted him on the shoulder.

"Boys will be boys, Jack," he said, turning to me.

Stanley grimaced at me behind his uncle's back.

"That's all very well," I cried, "but where am I going to get ten pounds to have the front fence fixed up?"

"Don't worry about that, Jack. I'll see to that. Here, grab hold of this."

"I can't let you pay for it," I remonstrated, pushing the note away.

"Gorn, take it. I've got plenty."

"No, thanks, George, old chap."

"I'll tell you what, uncle——" put in Stanley.

I grabbed the note out of George's hand. Stanley shrugged his shoulders and sat down.

"Well, it must be getting late," yawned George. "Where do I sleep?"

"Go and have a look around," I replied. "If you see a bed you like, sleep in it. My home is yours. Use it."

"Righto," he said heartily, gathering his boots up. "Good night."

Stanley rose from his chair as his uncle lumbered off.

"Good night, daddykins," he said.

"What's the strength of this 'daddykins' talk?" I queried suspiciously.

"We're friends, aren't we, dad?"

"I suppose so," I replied, slightly mollified.

He held out his hand and I shook it.

"Well, nighty-night, dad."

"Good night, son. Sleep well."

He left the room and I was about to wind the clock, when he poked his head around the doorway.

"Dad," he said, "you go halves with me in Uncle George, won't you?"

He was gone before I could think of anything.

Chapter 18

Uncle George was up at the ridiculous hour of five o'clock the next morning and blew the front out of the stove trying to boil some water. Evidently they didn't have gas at Split Rock. He lumbered into my bedroom and gazed at me while I lay with both eyes shut tight, breathing deeply. Nobody gets me out of bed at five o'clock in the morning without using force. He tiptoed out of the room and five minutes later Stanley entered with his pre-breakfast face on. He sat on the edge of the bed and glared at my trembling eyelids.

"He's mad!" he ejaculated.

I never answered.

"He came to my room," he continued savagely, "and said that it was about time young fellers were out of bed. Said he'd overslept himself and it was five o'clock. You'd think it was five o'clock in the afternoon! He said they always had breakfast at half-past four at Split Rock. Wants me to show him how to light the gas! Damn Split Rock! What does he think I am?"

I snored.

"Oh, I know you're awake!" he snorted. "You can't fool me."

I snored again and turned over, muttering as though dreaming.

"Uncle George!" he yelled. "Father's awake now."

"You dirty dog in the manger," I mumbled, sitting up. "Out—before I choke you, you life-shortener."

I lay back suddenly as George entered the room, but it was too late.

"Ah, there you are, Jack. My crikeys, you've slept in this morning! Do you know what time it is?"

I shook my head.

"Quarter past five!" he declared impressively.

"My word, is it?" I gasped. "And here am I still in bed! Has Stanley cooked the breakfast yet?"

"He's just out of bed, the young rascal."

"Off you go, Stanley, and cook the breakfast—take him with you, George. I'll be along presently."

"But, gee, you don't expect a man——"

"Come on, Stan, you young rascal," said George, grabbing him by the arm.

Stanley ground his teeth at me and left the room and I lay back in bed for a few more minutes' rest.

If there is one thing I hate more than any other thing, it's getting up early. How on earth people can make a habit of it is beyond my power of understanding. I have always regarded an early-riser as one mentally afflicted, or hounded by circumstance. One has only to study history to know that the higher the civilization, the lower the percentage of alarm-clock slaves. In this respect, milkmen and their kind are but one remove from the ice-age. Their place is with the cows. However, I thought it best not to give George a wrong impression for the start and I dragged my body unwillingly from bed and hoped earnestly for his ultimate salvation. If all other methods failed, I could give him some knock-out drops with his supper before we went to bed.

Breakfast was a rough and ready sort of meal. The

kind you might expect on a submarine that had been submerged for a week during a battle.

I persuaded Stanley that his presence would serve no useful purposes on our shopping expedition and he roared off on his motor-cycle in low spirits and high gear and disappeared in a cloud of smoke. As for the actual shopping, little need be said of it. George was very disappointing. For a man with a cheque for three thousand pounds in his left boot he showed an extraordinary lack of enterprise. He was so determined that no one should rob him of a few shillings that his caution would not allow him to put a penny in a weighing-machine unless he could see where the coin went and got a receipt for it. Not that he was mean. He was just suspicious. Coming from remote regions where the kangaroos shook the earth with their boundings and the eagles darkened the sky, the city was to him a den of iniquity where security depended on perpetual vigilance.

It is a bushman's failing. They have heard so many tales about city sharps; so many of their friends have come back home on foot after an unsuccessful attempt to pick the ace; so many have returned with a lease of Hyde Park for agistment purposes; so many of them have been sold telephone booths, traffic signals, sun-dials, and public fountains that they have become suspicious and will prod the blind man in the eyeball to see if he is really blind. It was with the greatest difficulty that I managed to get George into a tailor's where I could get a little commission for introducing him. As the moth is attracted to the flame, so some evil instinct drew him to sell-out-and-move-on establishments that sold him the cheapest goods at the highest possible prices. The same instinct led him to hotels where simple, honest bushmen, similarly attracted, yearned silently over their beers, longing for gum-trees and suspecting their fellow yearners. We dined in a hash-house, his plea being that in any more pretentious place people would look at him. He was shy. I understood how he felt, and for business reasons forgave him; nevertheless, I suffered.

We attended a matinée at a theatre of his own choosing. The spotlight was half a lap behind the song and dance artist, the song and dance artist was a lap in front of the orchestra, and the orchestra was so far off the key that it should have been locked out for the night. The Instinct again. A basso-soprano with tonsillitis recited the words of a song while the orchestra backed her up with a little music; and a woman with two babies, sitting next to me, had brought a bundle of fried chip potatoes with her in order that her children might grease everyone within a certain radius. The popping of peanut shells was almost deafening. An infant prodigy played "Home Sweet Home" on the concertina with more feeling than restraint, and the delighted clapping of George's huge, horny hands left me with all the symptoms of shell-shock. The only thing I enjoyed in the whole performance was when the acrobat landed on the wrong part of his neck and had to be carried off the stage on a stretcher. George was greatly taken with one of the Vere de Vere Quartet. He communicated his opinions to me in a hoarse whisper that may not have been heard outside in the street. She had a red and white face, red trunks, yellow hair, and a sort of emergency, jury-rig chest-protector held up in a disappointingly secure manner by two ribbons. She was mature. If her physical development had been at the expense of her mental powers she could not help but be an idiot. George said she reminded him somehow of Split Rock. He asked me if I knew her. In my role as guide, philosopher and friend, and in order to preserve my prestige, I had to tell him that I knew them all. I was hardly prepared for his request for an introduction after the show. He was evidently gnawing his way out of the cocoon. Loath though I was to impede his development as a man about town, I was compelled to excuse myself as we made our way out of the place over a crackling bed of peanut shells.

I knew by bitter experience gained in my early days, what an afternoon in the Vere de Vere strata of the theatrical world would be. I have met and consorted with the denizens of these peanut infernos where every usher is an ex-pugilist. Memory takes me back to Lascivia Lotelli whose family name was Higgins. She was in the "legitimate" business, whatever that is—I was too tactful to inquire—and called herself, not an actress, but a "turn". She was more than a turn, she was a revolution. She had a kleptomaniacal complex and no inhibitions. She was surrounded with such an aura of eau-de-cologne that the flies couldn't get near her, and consequently there were none on her. Her parents were Protestants, but her tastes were catholic, although she never touched methylated spirits because she thought it unladylike. In many other ways she was refined, but I have since thought that she must have had a lot of lime in her bones because I have never since met a woman with such an extensive natural thirst. Her motto was, "Anything Once", and she had it stuck up over her bed at home. Whenever I see a clove I think of her and her memory is as green as ever, though I am not. I explained all this to George as we were walking up the street and he grunted glumly, and said I was hard but he supposed I was right.

"Are you a woman-hater, Jack?" he asked after an interval of heavy thinking.

I assured him that I was not and proceeded to expound. I like George, otherwise I would not have bothered.

"There is the man who thinks he is unsuccessful with women—only thinks it, George, he's never really tried—he's one sort. There's the man who is married on five pounds a week; there's the man with an ideal—poor devil; there's the sheik who has stolen into the harem and can't get out, and there's the invalid, but there are no woman-haters."

"What are you, then?"

"My eyelids are unstuck," I said quietly.

"Well, Agatha——" he began.

"Say no more, George. Look at these ties."

I reined him in at a shop window.

"My crikeys!" he exclaimed. "Ain't they humdingers. Look at that yellow one. 'Eau-de-banana'—what's that?"

"That's the colour."

"I think I'll get that," he said, struggling to free himself.

"An all-yellow tie! Have some taste, George. You'll antagonize all the policemen in town. If you must buy another tie, get that one marked 'Snappy', the red and green one."

"What'll I ask for?" he inquired, pausing at the door.

"Ask for 'Snappy'." I was getting a bit fed up. It is no joke shopping with a man who picks on butcher's apron material for a lounge suit. He reappeared at last with a large parcel under his arm.

"They said I'd have to buy the collar and shirt and handkerchiefs and pyjamas to go with the tie," he explained sheepishly. "A man's gotter look smart."

"All right," I sighed. "Go and give that parcel back and tell them to send it. When will you learn that no one ever carries anything?"

He gripped me by the shoulder and pointed across the road. "What place is that?"

"The Blue Garter," I said. "It's gone off a lot lately. Hasn't been raided for a fortnight. Why do you ask?"

"Stanley's motor-bike is outside, so I was just thinking that he might be inside."

"The young hound!" I exclaimed. "Wallowing in that den of iniquity, casting his body and soul into the melting-pot, tearing his moral fibre to rags and enjoying himself generally, while his father walks about the streets, shopping!"

"Aw, leave the boy alone, he ain't done no harm," pleaded George as I prepared to cross the street.

"All very well, you siding with the boy, but what about his soul and his fibre?"

"Aw, don't worry the boy about his soul and all that just when he's enjoying himself. Anyhow there won't be anything much doing in there till later, will there?"

"No, that's right," I mumbled. "But what's Stanley in there for if there's nothing doing?"

"P'raps that's why he's there."

"You don't know Stanley," I said sadly. "If there is nothing doing at the Blue Garter, Stanley will start something—and I want to be in it."

"Is he like that?" inquired George, edging me toward an hotel on the corner.

"You've no idea of the depths of degradation to which that boy will descend."

"Aw, well. We were all young once. Come and have one."

I went with him, just to please him.

Chapter 19

We idled about town for hours, filling in time.

We followed two pairs of lace stockings up George Street as far as the Central Railway and then they threatened to give us in charge so we caught a tram back. George bought a ready-made suit and put it on in the shop. The coat was so tight across the back that he had to breathe like an exhausted dog. We attended a picture-show for a few hours and altogether spent a miserable evening. Nevertheless it was after eleven o 'clock before we passed the Blue Garter again. Stanley's motor-bike was still parked at the kerb. Doubtless a hundred police note-books contained its number.

"I am going to save Stanley from the sinister influence of that place," I declared firmly.

"Me, too," said George, accompanying me across the road. "It's terrible to think how a young feller can be lured into them joints and come out with his soul all mushed up, ain't it?"

"It is, it is," I agreed passionately.

We ascended the stairs and, entering the crowded café, gazed about.

George plucked my sleeve.

"Do you see him?" I asked.

"That girl smiled at me," he simpered. "That one over there. I wonder how I could get an introduction?"

"You seem to be pretty strong on these introductions. We have done Stanley an injustice," I added. "He is not here. We were a bit hasty, accusing the poor boy as we did."

"She waggled a finger at me!" giggled George, screwing a piece out of my elbow. "How can I get introduced?" he pleaded.

"Go and buy her a drink and may the Lord have mercy on your soul. I'm going to speak to the manager."

I left him and accosted the head demon.

"I'm looking for a young man," I said, "tall, inclined to be fair, rather soopy expression. Probably dressed in motor gear. Have you noticed him about here?"

"No. I'm sure he never came in here," replied the manager. "We never allow undesirable characters in here. Sure you haven't made a mistake?"

"H'm!" I grunted, stroking my chin.

"Come now, sergeant, you know that I'd give you any assistance I possibly could. The man is not here. Come and have a cup of tea—or something, sergeant."

"I'm not a detective!" I exclaimed.

"You aren't!" gasped the manager. "Well what the blazes do you want to come in here looking like that for! Who are you, anyhow?"

"Now listen——" I began.

"Get out!" he commanded. "Coming in here," he spluttered, "frightening everyone—looking like that——"

"Look here——"

"Get out! And take that animated fire-escape with you!" he hissed, pointing a quivering finger at George.

George strode in between us.

"Listen to me!" he said in a deep voice that made the chandelier tinkle. "We're looking for a boy called Stanley

Gudgeon. Is he here or is he damn well isn't here?"

Three waiters drifted up to the manager's side and gazed calmly over our heads.

"What do you know about him?" he demanded fiercely. "Who are you, the pair of you?"

I peered around George's elbow.

"I am John Gudgeon," I replied haughtily.

"Stan's old man!" gasped the manager. "Is that a fact?"

I nodded.

"Well! Well!" he cried, extending both hands. "I *am* sorry, Mr Gudgeon. Why didn't you say so at first? I really must apologize to you—and to Mr—er——"

"Weldon," whispered George, dazedly. "Stanley's uncle."

"Mr Weldon. Yes. To be sure. Step this way, gentlemen. I really am sorry. I hope you won't mention this to young Mr Stanley, Mr Gudgeon. It is so easy to make a mistake—one can never be sure—of course I should have known at once—the resemblance. Dear me, I am sorry—tut-tut."

He pattered on, walking sideways and waving his hands and we followed him dumbly through four doors and down three flights of stairs.

"I do hope you will overlook our little misunderstanding, gentlemen," he said, pausing before a baize-covered door. "I'd like to retain young Mr Stanley's patronage—be very glad to welcome both of you too—any time—make it a sort of family affair, eh? Ha! Ha!"

I mumbled something as the door opened. A large thickly-carpeted room, blue with smoke and sprinkled with tables was visible through the open doorway. I counted seven doors in different parts of the room. The bar at the end of the room was deserted but the tables were crowded.

"This way, gentlemen; Mr Stanley will be in the two-up room, I think."

We followed on.

One of the seven mysterious doors opened to the manager's magic touch and we had one fleeting glimpse of a large room entirely covered with green baize. Tiers of seats lined the walls. A man stood in the centre of a square of eager faces with a flat piece of ivory in his hand. And then Stanley appeared at the doorway, backing out.

"Positively won't have it!" he was muttering. "Sort of thing has to stop. Nice state of affairs——"

He stopped as he caught sight of us, paused wide-eyed, and then shut the door with a gentle click.

"What the devil are you doing here?" he gasped.

The manager bowed, raised his eyebrows, and left us.

I was about to assert myself, when a shout went up from a vision of such sartorial magnificence that the sight of him struck me temporarily dumb. He eyed the pair of us peevishly. George shuffled his feet.

"Follow me," said Stanley curtly, and strode off without another glance at us, as though we were two out-of-work labourers. Several men nodded to him as we passed through the room and the blasé nonchalance with which he returned their courtesy was galling to see. We ascended the same stairs we had just come down, passed through the various doors and found ourselves once more in the café. It looked as if he was going to put us out. Speech returned to me and I gripped him by the coat.

"Look here!" I commenced.

"Now shut up or I'll have you thrown out!"

I drew a deep breath. Parental affection slunk back

into a crevice of my being and I felt myself getting red in the neck.

"Aw, leave the boy alone, he ain't done no harm," said George, grasping my arm.

I was about to assert myself, when a shout went up from a far corner of the room.

"Gudgeon!"

One glance was sufficient. Slatter, with Maureen, Daisy and Simpson, were on their feet and pushing back their chairs.

"The bike!" I cried, clutching Stanley in a frenzied grip. "Start it, boy, while we hold them back."

"Don't be silly," he replied loftily.

"What's the matter with him?" queried George, gazing at Slatter, who was approaching with his arms hanging gorilla-like at his sides and a smile of deep satisfaction on his face.

I hauled Stanley to the top of the stairs and pushed him in the back. He rolled most of the way.

"Slam him!" I shouted to George. "Hand him one and then run for it!"

George stared at me with astonishment oozing from every pore.

"Him!" I shrieked wildly, pointing to Woggo. "*Dong* him!"

I could wait no longer. My feet touched the stairs twice before I reached the bottom. Stanley was outside, stamping viciously on the kick-starter of his cycle.

"There was no need to go on like that," he gabbled nervously, fumbling with the gadgets on the handle-bar.

"Start the damned thing!" I yelled.

The engine roared into motion as I spoke.

Stanley leapt into the saddle.

"Pile in," he snapped. "Here comes Uncle George."

George dashed out on to the pavement and rushed toward us. "I think they're after me!" he gasped.

He flung himself on to the side-car and clutched me around the neck as the machine swung out from the kerb. A crowd of men belched out from the doorway as we gathered speed, Woggo among them.

"Taxi! Taxi!" they shouted, and then rushed for an unattended touring-car that stood at the kerb.

"My crikeys," gasped George. "They *are* after me!"

Shops, lights, streets, loomed in front of us and then flashed behind us.

"Flatten yourselves down," shouted Stanley. "Too much wind resistance. Lean out going round this corner."

"Flatten yourself, George," I said. "I'm flat."

"I'm too long!" whined George.

"Lie along the top, with your feet on the nose of the side-car," directed Stanley, shouting above the roar of the engine.

George wriggled on top of me with his face pressed on my ear, breathing hotly down my neck.

"You're not flat," he said reproachfully. "Your knees are bent."

"Do the best you can," I replied. "I'm stuck."

A roaring wind snatched my hat away and hurled it down the street. George's followed it.

He peered over the top of my head.

"They're still after us," said George.

"What are we crawling along like this for?" I shouted to Stanley.

"Doing fifty," he snapped. "None of these damned corners are banked."

Perhaps he had some justification for his snappishness. Although most of the late traffic had left the streets, we were far from having the road to ourselves. Three cars had run up on the footpath as we approached them. Courtesy of the road, I suppose.

"My crikeys, they're coming up now!" gasped George, as we bumped over a railway crossing. "There's another car coming behind them."

"That'll be the traffic-cops," said Stanley, peering over his shoulder. "No wonder they're gaining on us. Hang on!"

The roar of the engine increased in volume and the rushing air put its hand in my face and pushed. The houses thinned out as we swooped past the suburbs. A khaki-clad figure on a motor-cycle swung around a corner we had just passed.

"He's coming too," remarked George.

"That's another traffic-cop," I explained. "We're done now."

"Can't beat him with a load like this," said Stanley despairingly. "Seems to be a dark clump of bush or something about a mile farther up the road. We'll be there in a minute. One of you hop off as we pass it."

"Control yourself," said George contemptuously.

A sudden loud report sounded behind us and George clutched me by the neck with both hands.

"He's shooting!" he quavered.

"Let go," I gurgled, striving to free myself. "I think he's got me."

"Where?" gasped George, releasing me.

"Here," I moaned. "In the back."

Stanley gazed over his shoulder.

"Shot—me eye!" he jibed. "The cop on the bike has

had a blow-out."

"I'm sure I'm shot," I muttered.

Indeed I would have sworn to it. I felt a distinct twinge in the back immediately after the report. I explained it to George.

"Ar, you and your back!" he said. "How far have we gone, Stan?"

"About thirty miles, I think. I'll open her up presently."

George became silently thoughtful.

"Good-oh!" he yelled suddenly. "They've caught Slatter's mob. The cops have got 'em."

"A very good thing too," I remarked.

And it was a very good thing. Exceeding the speed limit as they were, they were a menace to traffic and a danger that threatened the life and limbs of every pedestrian on the road. I hoped that they would be punished severely.

"We can slow down now, can't we?" asked George, poking Stanley with his foot.

"I suppose so," he replied reluctantly.

"I think we'd better keep going," I said. "There are two more policemen coming after us on motor-cycles."

He crouched over the handle-bars and we roared on through the night.

"They don't seem to be trying to catch us," said George after a while. "They're just keeping behind us, waiting for us to break down or something. Have you got plenty of petrol, Stan?"

"Had a full tank to start with," answered Stanley.

I gazed over George's neck at the moonlit road. Bushes and trees swept up to us on either side, flitted past us and were swallowed up in murkiness. To the right, a range of hills sloped blackly against the starry sky. I could see no houses at all, and the only lights were the headlamps of the pursuing cycles. Stanley's cycle had none.

"George," I said, "you're a bushman—where are we?"

"Blowed if I know. Stanley, do you know where we are?"

"No, uncle," replied Stanley. "But I can guess where we'll finish."

"Where?"

"Clink," said Stanley succinctly.

George looked at me interrogatively.

"He means the cooler," I explained.

"Quod?"

"Yes."

"Well, why didn't you say so at first, instead of using all those silly slang terms?"

We relapsed again into silence and the miles rolled behind....

Coming to a cross-road, Stanley swept around the bend and a most annoying thing happened. George shot off the side-car into some bushes, taking my collar with him. Stanley, with his eyes fixed on a rutty road, did not seem to notice. George's going had been swift and strangely silent considering the circumstances. I was upset. I hate being seen in public without a collar. I don't think a man looks respectable without a collar. I was tempted to advise Stanley of George's departure, but my position in the side-car was so much more comfortable that I decided, although with considerable reluctance, to let the collar go.

It was but a few minutes later that the barking of dogs heralded our approach to a collection of houses grouped on either side of the road. The road widened out into a dusty, moonlit street, and an excited dog raced alongside us and leapt at Stanley. The machine swerved, we crashed through a little white fence and came to a dead stop against a low, wooden veranda.

Stanley picked a piece of splintered wood out of his hair and sighed deeply.

"This," he said, "is where we get pinched."

I pushed a picket off my chest and sat up.

"We must have lost the two traffic-cops," said Stanley, glancing down the road.

"Well, why should we get pinched?" I demanded. "What are we sitting here for?"

"No use running," he replied gently. "We'd get lost. The machine is busted."

"Yes, but——"

"Read that," he said tiredly.

I glanced to where he pointed. An enamelled iron sign glinted dully against the dark background of the cottage wall:

POLICE STATION

"Righto," came a calm voice from a window near the ground. "Wait till I get my boots on. Don't go."

Stanley gazed at me and spread out his hands, palms up, in the Hebrew manner.

"There you are, you see. I knew we'd get pinched."

He glanced back at the battered fence and then at the side-car.

"Where's Uncle George?"

"Fell out a couple of miles back," I explained, jerking my head in the direction where I thought George might be.

"Lucky cow!" grumbled Stanley.

I was telling him about George's selfishness in clinging to my collar when he left the side-car, but a harsh voice interrupted me.

"Get off that bike and come inside."

I dragged my cramped body out of the side-car and followed Stanley through the doorway of the cottage.

A kerosene lamp shed a mellow glow over a small room which was almost wholly taken up by a table and a roll-top desk. The constable, clad in trousers and boots and a pyjama coat, seated himself and commenced a search through the litter of papers on the table.

"Got a pencil?" he asked, looking up.

Stanley handed him one.

"Now then," he said, wetting the end of it, "name and address."

We told him. Morality and the new number-plate of the cycle urged us to truthfulness.

"Occupation?"

"Salesmen."

"Both of you?"

"Yes."

"Turn out your pockets."

We emptied out.

"What do you want to carry all this gear about with you for?" he queried disgustedly. "I've got to make a list of all that muck."

We stood in apologetic silence.

"Aw, put it back and I'll fix it up later," he growled, biting the end off a yawn.

"Three o'clock in the morning!" he exclaimed. "Don't you think a man wants any rest!"

We scooped up our belongings and replaced them in our pockets.

"Lemme see," he mumbled. "Wilful destruction Gov'ment prop'ty, exceeding speed limit, riotous behaviour, riding without licence——"

"I've got a licence!" protested Stanley.

"Don't interrupt!" roared the constable.

"Riding without a licence, resisting arrest," he glanced at a small patch in the knee of his trousers, "tearing uniform, no vis'ble means support—Ah, I'll write the damn thing out in the morning."

He pushed his chair back, and unhooked a bunch of keys from the wall.

"Follow me," he grunted, "but go in front."

He guided us along a narrow passage that led through the building, out to a large gravelled yard.

"Straight on," he directed, motioning toward a whitewashed, stone lock-up.

We stumbled across the yard and paused at the iron door while he opened it.

"We've only got one cell," said the constable, apologetically. "You'll find a stack of blankets in there and don't knock the sergeant's push-bike over. And mind the wheelbarrow," he cautioned as we stepped into the darkness.

The door clanged behind us.

The cover of the spy-hole swung back and the light from the policeman's torch shone through.

"And don't kick up a row, or I'll come out and quieten the pair of you. No singing. D'ye hear me!"

The light blinked out and we heard him trudging away.

Still listening, we heard him trudging back.

"And don't go scrawling your names all over the walls, or drawing on 'em, or you'll have to whitewash the whole blooming lot."

He strode away again and we were left in the darkness.

Vainly I strove to accustom my eyes to the gloom.

"Where are you, Stanley?" I whispered.

"Here," said Stanley.

Groping my way toward the sound, I collided with something solid and sat down with a bump on the hard floor.

"That'd be the wheelbarrow," said Stanley, "unless it's the blankets. It wouldn't be the blankets, would it?"

"Damn you!" I cursed.

"It's the wheelbarrow," muttered Stanley.

"Nice confounded mess you've got us into this time," I growled savagely.

"Ho!" exclaimed Stanley. "I like that! *I* got you into it! If it hadn't been for you and Uncle George following me around, this would never have happened!"

Silence ensued for what seemed like hours. I sat on the floor, and searched myself for matches one hundred times....

Footsteps sounded outside the cell.

"Listen!" hissed Stanley.

The door opened.

"The blankets are in the wheelbarrow," came the policeman's voice, "and if there's any more of you they can go to hell and sleep out on the road—and don't write on the walls."

The door closed again and the bolt shot into its socket.

"Who's there?" I called softly.

"Is that you, Jack?"

It was Uncle George.

A match flared up and his expression soured as he saw us.

"My crickeys, this is a nice blooming mess you've got me into!" he grumbled.

"Ho!" I exclaimed. "I like that!"

"Ah, shut up, dad, and pass me over some blankets," said Stanley wearily.

"Mind the sergeant's push-bike," said George hastily. "Wait till I strike a match."

"We know all about the sergeant's rotten push-bike," I replied. "We don't want to hear any more about the filthy thing. Catch these blasted blankets."

"Now don't get upset," said George, soothingly. "You just sit down there and I'll fix everything up, so's we'll be comfortable."

I sat down mumbling.

"There's two iron beds here," he said, "but they're piled up with boxes. We'll just shift these barrows and things and spread the blankets on the floor. That'll be nice and all right, won't it, Jack?...Eh, Jack?...Won't it, Jack?"

"Ah, shut up!" I growled.

"Don't take any notice of him, uncle," said Stanley. "I'm sorry he pushed you out of the side-car," he added.

"I fell out," confessed George.

"Oh, well, as long as you think so——" replied Stanley carelessly, and left the sentence unfinished.

"There you are," said George, presently. "Everything's set. Come over here, Jack."

I got to my feet and lounged over to the blankets. We seated ourselves, side by side, with George in the middle.

"Fine confounded mess——" I commenced.

"Light your pipe, dad," interrupted Stanley. "Don't start that all over again."

It was a good suggestion and I fumbled around for my

pipe and filled it. George held a match and the three of us lit up.

"Very unlucky for three to light off the same match," remarked Stanley after a brief interval of silence.

"My word, yes!" agreed George. "Never thought of that."

"Bah!" I exclaimed. "Old women! Do you think we could be any unluckier than we are now?"

"We could be lost in the bush," suggested Stanley.

"Or kicked to death by Slatter's gang," said George, brightly.

"Go on," I urged bitterly. "Cheer me up."

Stanley yawned.

"Uninteresting sort of cell," he murmured. "Is this the first time you've been in, uncle?"

"Yes," said George. "I ain't a hardened criminal. This is my début."

"Hang around with Stanley for a few weeks," I interposed. "You'll be lucky if you escape the noose."

"How did you manage to get pinched?" continued Stanley.

"Aw, I didn't manage, exactly," replied George. "No-writing-on-the-walls caught me. After I fell out of the side-car, I got up and ran along the road after you, but you didn't seem to notice that I'd gone, so I kept up a bit of a trot for the next mile and then I perceives the bike up against the veranda. When I sees the fence all smashed in, I says to myself, 'That's Stan's bike,' and I goes over to see what's happened. While I'm there, out comes No-writing-on-the-walls, and here I am."

He turned to me.

"How was it you didn't notice me fall out?"

"I told Stanley that you had been thrown out and

asked him to pull up, but he merely laughed and refused," I explained.

"Stone the crows!" exclaimed Stanley indignantly. "I——"

"Silence!" I hissed, "or I'll brain you!"

"Aw, leave the boy alone——" commenced George.

"Yes, yes," I snapped. "I know. 'He ain't done no harm.' That's it, isn't it? He has only got us into the lock-up. If we are let out, we are at the mercy of Slatter and his fellow garrotters. If we stay in, we'll stay for six months. That is what comes of being a conscientious parent. This is what comes of trying to save him from that Blue Garter den. He has had too much liberty and not enough discipline. Things will be different from now on."

"Aw, leave——" said George, and stopped.

I tucked the blanket around me and chewed the stem of my pipe.

"Stan," said George, "how comes it that you're such a big person at the Blue Garter?"

"What do you mean?"

"Well, you seem to be ace high with the manager, and you're terrible well in."

"Oh! Well, you see, uncle, I'm a good customer. And then of course, I brought 'em a lot of custom. All the boys go there now. And then there's the two-up room. That was my idea, and another thing, the proprietor had been losing pretty heavily with the wheel one night and the bank went broke. Of course, the game was stuck. He took a risk and slipped, and then he had to pay out. I backed him up with a cheque for a thousand—"

"Eh?" I gasped.

"Of course," he continued, "the cheque was no good, but he wasn't to know that. The luck turned and I got my cheque back the same night, so you can see that I'm entitled to a little respect and preferential treatment."

He yawned again.

"I'm very tired," he continued. "I'm afraid I've been overworking myself lately. What with one thing and another——"

His voice petered out wearily and he curled up in his blanket and lay still.

For a long time George never spoke. His pipe had ceased to glow. At length he tapped me on the arm.

"Why do you want to bother yourself about getting that boy a job?" he queried in a husky voice. "Why don't you turn him loose on the community?"

"Too insecure," I sighed. "The time would come when he would have to leave the country, and then where would I be? Besides, you may think him shrewd, but I know him. He's young, he's had no experience, baited traps gape for him, and he's dying to fall in."

"What sort of traps?"

"Women."

"Ar, there you go again!" said George disgustedly. "Why don't you get a divorce?"

"Just what I'm trying to avoid," I objected. "Remember, too, that Agatha is your sister, George."

"I ain't forgetting it. That's why you've got my sympathy. What's wrong with getting a divorce?"

"The alimony, George. The alimony!" I exclaimed. "And the publicity. Supposing the court awarded her three pounds a week—Stanley won't pay it! And think of the name of the Gudgeons being connected with sordid divorce proceedings, in the press."

"H'm. And think of your photo on the front page of the Sunday *Truth*."

"Yes, yes," I murmured. "There's something in that; I take rather a good photo. I've got one at home, George, that I must show you. I've got my lodge regalia on and I'm standing with one hand on my hip and the other like this."

I showed him as best I could in the dark.

"It's a full-length picture," I concluded.

"If we ever get out of this, you can show it to me," said George. "I'd like to have a full-length photograph taken of myself."

"Not with your height," I corrected gently. "You'd have to be taken as a group, unless you lay down and let them make a panorama of you."

"They ain't going to make no paramour out of me——!"

"Panorama, George."

"Well, they needn't think just because I come from the country that they can make me a piano-rammer!" he declared hotly.

"Now, now, George! Don't be hasty tempered and raise your voice. You'll wake Stanley."

He subsided, grumbling.

I filled my pipe again.

"Tobacco, George?" I inquired, offering him my pouch.

"No," he said sulkily. "I'm going to sleep."

"Give me a match before you go," I requested.

The grey fingers of a cold dawn were clawing their way through the barred windows. Cocks crowed in near and distant barnyards. Crowed and listened. And from over the hills and far away came the answer. The mournful hour before the sunrise stretched its clammy length over the country. The wheelbarrow was faintly visible, and the sergeant's precious push-bike. Two blanket-enveloped forms lay motionless beside me, and the earth sighed and shut its eyes for just a little longer. Never have I felt more alone nor more despondent. Truly, man that is born of woman hath but a short time to live and is full of sorrow. He cometh up as a flower and has his head knocked off by an idle switch from the careless cane of Fate. He cometh up as a flower and is trodden on. He cometh up as a flower and is cut, bunched and sent off to the hospital to wilt in an atmosphere of iodoform and misery.

Ah, the little worries of life! The little ones! The little ones! Stanley needed a mother's guiding hand. He had become unmanageable since the home had been broken up. What had the future in store for him? And what for me? Would I, in future years, gaze from the window of the Old Men's Home and wonder, "Where is my wild colonial boy tonight?"

Somewhere out in the world the first sunbeam of the day was rippling along the tops of the wheat. Birds twittered. Quite close, a chain rattled as a dog emerged from his kennel and shuddered off his lethargy. A tree that grew outside the window of the cell shook out its dewy leaves to dry in the breeze. A horse clopped by in clinking harness. A bucket clattered. Someone was singing....

I fell asleep.

Chapter 20

Something was nudging me in the ribs and I pushed it away.

It came back and butted me. It was the policeman's boot.

"Now come on out of that!" he bellowed. "Up with you! It's nine o'clock and the sergeant will be here any minute."

"Fold up your blankets," he added, and walked away, leaving the cell door open and the sunlight streaming through.

"Stanley," I moaned, staggering to my feet, "fold up my blankets."

Without a murmur of objection, he caught hold of them and commenced.

That was some indication of how he felt.

George swayed out into the yard, rubbing his eyes.

"Water in the tank," bawled the constable from the cottage, "bucket in the corner, wash yourself, look smart, breakfast here, cost you a shilling each."

"Breakfast a shilling each?" echoed George in a puzzled voice.

I filled the bucket with clear, chilly water from the tank and ducked my head into it. Blowing rainbow-coloured spray, I emerged in time to hear the constable's "Hurry up before the sergeant comes."

"He seems to be afraid of this sergeant," I remarked.

"Come away from that bucket," said George sourly.

I dried myself on my handkerchief and the lining of George's coat and watched the constable arranging a number of thick slices of bread and golden syrup on top of an upturned barrel.

"Three shillings," he demanded, turning to me.

I paid him.

"Want some milk?" he inquired in a pleasanter tone.

"Yes, please."

"A shilling."

He brought out about half a gallon of milk from the cottage and the three of us stood around the barrel and breakfasted in the sunshine. The bread was thick but fresh, the milk was cold but pure. I have tasted worse breakfasts. We were squatting against the fence, smoking, when the constable emerged, fully dressed and shaved.

"Come on," he commanded, waving us toward the cottage.

"Speak civil to the sergeant," he whispered as we filed through the doorway, "otherwise he'll make it bad for you and the J.P. will give you six months each."

"Words of comfort," muttered Stanley.

We lined up before the table in the little office. The sergeant was poring over some papers and the top of his massive head was grey.

"Six charges," he muttered.

He looked up. A smile dawned on his fat, red face.

"God prisarve us!" he exclaimed. "If ut ain't little George!"

George grinned, blushed, and extended his hand.

"Didn't know you were in these parts, Mr O'Toole," he stammered.

"Well! Well! Well!" said the sergeant, leaning back in his chair. "Yer gettin' more like yer ould father ivery day!"

He folded his hands on his stomach and beamed delightedly at George. George grinned back and Stanley kicked me on the ankle.

"Phwat are the charges aginst the gintleman?"

"Breaking and entering, loitering...."

"Soilence man!" roared the sergeant. "A foin mimber of the foorce ye are! Can't ye see this gintleman is a gintleman!"

The constable shrugged his shoulders.

"Be off with ye and nail up the fince!" growled the sergeant disgustedly. He turned again to George.

"Y'know, George; they sint that feller up to me from Sydney and not an ounce av since has he got. He's been nothin' but an eyesore to me since he came here. The first day he arrives, phwat must he do but go and knock me push-bike over!"

I brought up a gasp of horror.

"Indade, he did!" exclaimed the sergeant, swinging in his chair toward me. I shook my head sorrowfully.

"A beautiful bike like that! Pushed it in the dirt, eh?"

"Pushed it in the dhirt, he did! You're a frind of George's, I suppose?" he added kindly.

"I'm his brother-in-law," I explained. "This young chap is Stanley, his nephew."

"Well, well, well," he muttered softly. "George's father and me came out in the same boat whin we was bhoys togither."

He stared at George as though trying to see his father in him.

"Ah, well," he sighed. "Ye'd better come over with me

and have wan, gintlemen. I'll never be seein' yer father inny more, George."

"You stay here, sonny," he added as Stanley prepared to follow us. "The houtel is no place for little bhoys. Fix up yer motor-cycle."

We filed out of the room behind him, leaving Stanley to think over the insult. The town was a mere blister on the main road over which we had travelled the previous night. It had an ice-works, a garage, a blacksmith's shop, two general stores and four hotels. I should say that the population would allow five persons to each hotel. One of those calm, quiet, sunny places where people stop and say good day to each other and only hurry when there's a dog fight on. Sergeant O'Toole informed us that the town had once been flourishing and had shown signs of becoming a second New York but the railway had diverted the traffic from the road and now the place was a mere backward village where progress and the community spirit were so dead that nobody ever got arrested.

The sergeant was inclined to be a little morbid about George's father. I gathered that the elder Weldon had migrated from Ireland in company with the sergeant and had landed in Sydney full of hope and ship's biscuits and pregnant with possibilities. Together at first, they drifted apart after a few years and Weldon got married to the woman who was now George's mother and my mother-in-law. Fate had relented some years later and released him from his bondage and Sergeant O'Toole had gone to his funeral. It was all very sad. George offered to pay for the fence and Sergeant O'Toole, refusing with deep emotion, declared that the son of Patrick Weldon could knock the police-station down and he would regard it as an honour.

We returned to the police-station infected by the sergeant's mournfulness. Stanley promised to have the motor-cycle repaired in a few hours with the assistance of the garage man, and we lunched with O'Toole.

We departed regretfully at two o'clock in the afternoon, and the sergeant in a husky voice told George that any time he liked to drop in and bring his friends the police-station fence would always be up, waiting for us. The constable told me privately that he wished to heaven he could go back to Sydney with us, and shook hands.

Almost, I was sorry to leave. Seated in the side-car with George straddled across me, I wondered how long I would survive the machinations of Woggo Slatter's gang in Sydney. As we rushed along the road, we were leaving behind us a place of quietness and peace where the cows browsed placidly on the footpaths and even the flies buzzed in a minor key. And for what were we leaving it? For a roar and a shriek and the sound of hurrying feet. Back to the smoke and the clatter and the pale faces. Back to the place of lightning shaves, half-eaten breakfasts, bundy clocks, and stand-up luncheons.

Progress we call it, this manifestation of group lunacy. What is the use of all this vaunted progress? Jones builds a bungalow with a sliding roof, rotary floors, disappearing gate, electric window-wipers and an automatic bath-room and thinks he has said the last word. But he hasn't.

Smith comes to light with an aeroplane catapult on the roof, escalators to the front door, a revolving porch, illuminated keyholes and a verse from the Koran inscribed on his doormat. So determined are we to live as close as possible to the stench of business that we live on top of each other in flats and have to wait our turn to cross the road. What is the use of it all? How much deader than a dead stockbroker is a dead potato-grower, when all is said and done?

Had it not been for the fact that I cannot bear the dullness of the country, I would have ordered Stanley to turn around and go back.

We travelled along in a conversationless silence which, though partly enforced by the noise of the cycle and the disposition of its passengers, was, for my part, both voluntary and welcome. The three of us were tired. My body ached from the jolting of the side-car and it was an effort to keep my head from wobbling as we bounded over the ruts. I longed for home and a bath and rest.

It was six o'clock before we rounded Flannery's corner and came in sight of the house.

"The door's open," said Stanley, accelerating.

We swept around in a curve opposite the house, leapt the kerb, clattered over the flattened fence and jolted on to the veranda. George fell out and the engine stopped.

"Dammit!" cursed Stanley. "We could have gone straight in through the door. We'll have to push the thing now."

I clambered out and together we lifted it over the step and pushed it into the front bedroom.

"Cup of tea," suggested George in a tired voice.

We trailed dejectedly out to the kitchen.

Agatha and Gertrude were seated at the table, their hats on, their hand-bags in their laps.

"We were just going, when we heard you," said Agatha.

"Don't let us stop you," I replied.

I was too weary to be even mildly surprised at their presence.

"How are you, George?" said Gertrude, coldly.

"All right. How are you?"

"All right."

"How are you, Agatha?" said George.

"All right."

Conversation lapsed.

Stanley groaned loudly.

"What's the matter, Stanley?" queried Agatha, anxiously.

"Tea!" he murmured piteously. "Make me some tea."

He subsided on the floor, moaning softly.

Agatha rose hastily to her feet.

"Is he sick?"

"He will be if he doesn't soon have some tea and something to eat," I replied, kneeling and patting Stanley on the shoulder.

"Where's the kettle?" demanded Agatha, removing her hat.

"In the bath-room," murmured Stanley weakly. "The teapot is on top of the wardrobe in my room."

"Go and get them, Gertrude," she requested.

"Let that great, useless hulk go and get them," snapped Gertrude, jerking her head at me.

"Go on, dad," pleaded Stanley.

I put my hand over my eyes, tottered a few steps and fell into George's arms. Gertrude sniffed.

"You'd better go and get them, Gert," said Agatha. "The other one is getting ready to swoon too."

George lowered me gently to the floor.

"I'll go," he said, and trudged off up the stairs.

"The pair of you can get up now," snapped Gertrude. "Agatha will get your tea ready and there is no necessity for the theatricals. No one will ask you to do anything."

George returned with the kettle and teapot and Agatha set about preparing a meal. In utter silence she prepared it, while we watched her. She was enjoying herself. Pottering about with the kettle gave her an opportunity to display her sweet, forgiving disposition. I have noticed this in women, that they positively glory in displaying a long-suffering meekness in the face of imagined wrongs. They do it in the hopes of embarrassing the male. They wail of their sacrifices, they write about it in books, one sees it on the screen—"the woman always pays".

Yet there is not a woman of them who wouldn't walk miles to be in at a sacrifice. The woman who can't get an opportunity to sacrifice herself, is a woman thwarted. She will start an argument with a man just so she may tell her women friends what a hell of a time she has with her husband, and act the downtrodden martyr generally. I have heard of a woman living in Woolloomooloo who, on viewing the bruises of the other wives in the terrace, assaulted her husband in the hopes of getting bruised. The husband was a man of forgiving temperament and in desperation she pinched herself all over and emerged triumphantly the next morning before an admiring crowd of other female martyrs.

I was able to watch Agatha at work without any of the qualms which less experienced men might have felt. I know women. Know one of them and you know all of them. Of course, there are remarkable differences in women, but they can be likened to motor-cars. Different models, different qualities, but they all work by means of internal combustion. The principle is the same.

We ate the meal in silence. Neither Gertrude nor Agatha spoke a word. I was puzzled by their restraint and astonished at this display of will power. The fox gnawing at the bosom of the Spartan boy could not have been more painful than the unspoken questions clawing for utterance in the minds of the two women. I could see in their faces that they were burning with curiosity. Where had we been? What was George doing with us? Had we been out all night? Who were the two men who had laid out their private detectives? Who were the two women?

The mental agony must have been excruciating, yet they sat tight-lipped until we had finished.

Stanley went to his room, sick, as usual in cases like this.

George, making sure of things, said he had an appointment and went out. I was left alone.

"Well," I said, taking my towel and soap out of the stove, "I suppose you people can amuse yourselves somehow until I get back. I must get cleaned now. I have very important business in town.

"As a matter of fact," I added, glancing at the clock, "I'm late now."

"Of course," said Agatha, "it is not for me to inquire your destination, nor to be acquainted of your comings and goings. Being merely your wife—ha-ha—I do not, of course, expect any consideration from you. It is not for me to complain that my life has been wrecked by a lazy, lying, drunken, good-for-nothing brute. Ha-ha—do not for a moment think that I have forgotten my position in your scheme of things. Far be it from me that I should even dream of accusing you of poisoning Stanley's mind against me and dragging him with you into a cesspool of vice. Ha-ha—no! But still, if you could spare me a few minutes of your valuable time, I am sure you will not find me lacking in gratitude. I am fully aware that your time must be taken up with your lady friends and your drinking orgies. That, of course, is none of my business. Ha-ha—no. Never has been. But if you will condescend to listen to me for a few moments…"

She paused for breath.

"What's that you were saying?" I asked, turning away from the stove.

Her nostrils lifted slowly like the wings of a bat and her eyeballs bulged. Round one had gone to me.

"You might have known, Agatha," said Gertrude, "that it would be quite useless to expect the smallest courtesy from this thing calling itself your husband. How you can bear to speak to him, I do not know. His very presence is repulsive to me."

She shrugged her shoulders in a realistic shudder.

I filled my pipe slowly and carefully. I know of nothing more maddening to a woman than the spectacle of a man filling his pipe while she is attempting to goad him.

"You carry your forbearance too far, dearie," she said, patting Agatha who had covered her face with her handkerchief and was heaving her shoulders up and down.

I lit my pipe and leaned back in my chair with my feet up on the table.

"Poor dear," she went on, "to think that he should have taken you from your mother's home when you were an innocent girl, and brought you . . ."

"Here!" I cried. "Who did this? Tell me!" I demanded, taking my feet off the table.

"Did what?" snapped Gertrude.

"Took her when she was an innocent girl," I replied.

Gertrude leapt to her feet.

"Give me that filthy pipe!" she panted, and snatched it from my mouth.

"There!" she said, throwing it out the window.

I searched the mantelpiece, found another pipe, and sat down.

"You will have your little joke," I sighed, "but I wish you would remember that I am a busy man. What is it you wanted to see me about? Of course, it is not for me—ha-ha—no, not for me to...."

"Shut up!" screamed Agatha.

I could see that the pair of them were at the end of their tethers and looked like dragging their mooring-posts down, so I commenced once more to fill my pipe, whistling softly the while.

"Listen to me," muttered Gertrude in a low, harsh voice. "Agatha, as you perhaps know, intends to divorce you. We have decided on that."

"Have we?" I queried.

"I have advised Agatha to free herself of you," she explained in a voice that trembled. "Having been brought up in a good family she considers it beneath her to spy on you, although, heaven knows, she has accumulated sufficient evidence during her married life to secure a hundred divorces."

I nodded pleasantly.

"However, we have thought it advisable, in order that there may be no hitch in the divorce proceedings, to give you the opportunity of providing indubitable grounds for divorce."

"And then you can carry on to your heart's content," sobbed Agatha.

"I'm speaking," said Gertrude coldly. "Please allow me to deal with this."

"Oh, go on," I pleaded, "let her have a say."

"Mother has agreed to pay all legal expenses," continued Gertrude, "and has even given Agatha five pounds to give to you so that you will not stint yourself in supplying the evidence."

"Five pounds!" I exclaimed. "Why, I couldn't even get started on five pounds!"

"You managed very well on your pocket-money when I was living with you," whimpered Agatha.

"Please!" cried Gertrude sternly.

"I will say something if I want to!" declared Agatha, glaring defiantly over the top of her handkerchief.

"Now, now," I admonished. "No fighting. Let one have it."

"Anyone would think it was she who was getting the divorce," said Agatha indignantly.

"Quite right, my love," I replied. "You tell Jackie all about it."

Gertrude sniffed like a suddenly cut off steam jet.

"That is all I have to say," she snapped. "I put myself to great inconvenience, thinking to help a certain person and this is how I am treated."

She rose from her chair.

"One moment before you both hurry away to your—er—appointments," I said. "I regard your suggestion favourably, but there are one or two little drawbacks. First, there is the matter of alimony."

"Your generosity will not be imposed upon," replied Gertrude coldly.

"I would find it hard indeed to accept maintenance money from you," put in Agatha in a haughty voice.

"I'd find it very hard to give it to you," I replied.

"What is the other drawback?" demanded Gertrude.

"The five pounds."

"What about it?"

"Make it ten," I replied. "It's no use half-doing the thing."

"Very well," she consented with another shudder.

"I must go," she added. "The air is tainted. Come, Agatha."

"Well, where is it?" I asked, following them up the hallway.

"Where is what?"

"The tenner."

"It will be posted to you, you low beast," hissed Gertrude.

"Ho!" I cried. "Nice pair of high-souled beings, you are! You come here asking a man to barter his honour away for ten pounds, to steep his blameless life in sin, to submit to having the name of a proud family dragged in the mire for ten pounds—and then you won't hand over the money!"

I was astounded and disgusted at their total lack of ordinary decency. It was driven into my mind at the time, that one never knows to what despicable trickery a woman will resort, until some occurrence like this one lays bare her paltry soul in all its hideousness.

They hastened to the door as though I were a viper.

"Very well," I called after them, "I will take no action until I receive the money—and remember, the more the money, the better the action."

The door slammed and I walked back to the kitchen, suddenly aware that I was tired to the point of exhaustion.

A footstep sounded softly on the stairs.

"Have they gone?" came a low whisper.

"Yes, Stanley, they have gone, after making the most dishonourable suggestion I have ever heard."

"Yes, I heard it," said Stanley, emerging into the light.

"I was sitting at the top of the stairs."

"For ten pounds!" I exclaimed bitterly.

"By gee, yes!" said Stanley in a hushed voice. "I didn't think ma was like that. A miserable ten pounds!"

I shook my head. I was disillusioned.

"Where's Uncle George?" inquired Stanley. "That'll be him," he added as a low knock sounded at the door.

I went and let George in.

"Have they gone?" he whispered.

I nodded.

"I thought I saw them going up the road but I wasn't sure. I was standing in that little lane at the side of Flannery's and I couldn't see very well from there. My crikeys, how did you get on?"

I gave him the gist of the discussion.

"Fancy them having the nerve to offer you ten pounds!" he exclaimed.

"That's what hurts," I complained bitterly.

"Why, I wouldn't take it if they offered me a thousand," he declared. "They must think you've got no principle."

Stanley smiled at me, and patted George on the shoulder.

"Come on, uncle," he said. "Come to bed."

Chapter 21

Days passed, during which I waited in vain for a registered letter from Agatha. I even went up the street and peered down the drain, thinking that perhaps the postman may have thoughtlessly disposed of it.

I was not actually in need of money, thanks to my own thrift and George's generosity, but ten pounds is ten pounds. Although, as I explained to George after three or four days had elapsed, I would rather have died than accept it. One has one's honour to consider and as I have said before, the Gudgeons are a proud family. We are a noble family. The name, Gudgeon, is a corruption, or rather, a modernization of the original Good John or John the Good. I am not sure whether the original John the Good was really King John, or John the Baptist. Suffice it to say that the Gudgeons were nobles when William the Conqueror and his gang were still in short pants. It would ill become a descendant of such a family to lower his standard of conduct by even so little as an inch. I told Stanley that if they did send me the ten pounds I would immediately send it back, and he agreed that this was the best thing to do. As he remarked, we could hold out for twenty.

We were practically in a state of siege. Twice, Woggo had called at the house, leaving five or six retired pugilists to wait for him on the pavement while he knocked and kicked at the door and invited us to come outside. The human detectophones in the opposite terrace enjoyed the spectacle immensely, some of them tearing their window-curtains down in order to get a better view. The situation was most humiliating. Stanley had discovered some secret route whereby he could escape from the house unseen and he, I think, spent most of his time with the girl Estelle.

George fretted a great deal at his confinement and despite my frequent warnings that he was a marked man, sneaked off whenever he could to the local picture-show. He had a passion for pictures, especially the highly emotional kind. His chief complaint was that out of the seventy-four scenes in which the villain struggled with the virtuous heroine, not one had been satisfactory. In each case the hero arrived after the heroine had lost a single shoulder-strap. Nothing worse ever happened. He could not understand why the hero should burst into the lonely cabin after the girl and the villain had been struggling for hours, and why the girl always leaned against the wall with her hair over her eyes, holding one shoulder-strap up. He declared that anyone who could get no farther than a mere tearing of blouses was no villain. Hope springs eternal, and George continued to patronize the motion-picture theatres in the hope of seeing a real villain with pep in him who would batter the heroine into insensibility and then tear the cabin apart.

I was left alone a great deal and except for occasional furtive visits to Flannery's, life for me was bounded by the four walls of the house. In such circumstances it was inevitable that I should brood. I am particularly subject to melancholia. Left alone, misery romps all over me. My thoughts had been with Agatha during the past few days, and I had begun to think kindly of her. It is curious how a man can think his way into these moods. In my earlier days, I have, with all the wily enthusiasm of youth, told women that they were wonderful and that I loved them. Kept on telling them and tried hard to look as if I meant it. And if the affair lasted the requisite number of weeks—behold! I did love them! Practically talked myself into it! How many, many liars have convinced themselves! That's how I came to marry Agatha, anyhow. Perhaps it was by this auto-suggestive method that I had become more kindly disposed toward her; looking back, I can see that it must have been. George and Stanley should not have left me so much alone. Though I will say this much for Agatha, she is a *good* woman. That is, of course, as far as I know. I don't think she has that pioneer spirit that is always blazing new trails. Although it's hard to say whether she has or she hasn't. One never knows. I am something of a pioneer myself, but I don't know about Agatha. Men will be men but women take some time to make up their minds.

Agatha is somewhere about thirty-eight. Not an unattractive age. Not at all unattractive.

I thought a lot about that.

My mind hovered balefully around Gertrude. She had always been the hair in the soup. She pushed her way into my married life when Stanley was born. His mother bore him then and I have borne him ever since, but that is beside the point. Gertrude it was who took charge of Stanley when he was a baby. She took charge of the house and Agatha after a while; she is that sort of woman—ears, tongue and advice. She tried to take charge of me. That was the beginning of the hatred that still rankles beneath her brassière. She "washed her hands" of me then and I have been washed off her hands ever since. She cultivated the habit of taking Agatha aside and advising her, pointing out various odds and ends that might be worthy of suspicion. It was she who taught Agatha to suspect me. I'd have been safe only for her.

Still, if it had not been for Gertrude I should not have known Flannery half so well as I do. Agatha would have been a contented wife if it had not been for Gertrude, I thought. She really was a good wife, in a way. She could make pea-soup to a degree of excellence that has never been surpassed on land or sea. I like pea-soup. Then she always kept the house clean and tidy, there was always a clean collar for me when I wanted it and she managed Stanley somehow without bloodshed.

When Stanley and George were home they continually urged me to go ahead with the divorce; Stanley especially. He saw, or thought he did, an opportunity for indulgence in a celebratory saturnalia in my company, with my permission and at my expense.

It may have been obstinacy, or perhaps I resented their interference in my affairs, anyhow I decided to visit Agatha and try to make it up with her. I mentioned it to neither of them but waited until they were both out and then phoned for a closed-in car and with all blinds drawn, proceeded to Chatswood. It was the silliest thing I have ever done in my life.

Chapter 22

Chatswood is one of those places that are a stone's throw from some other place, and is mainly given over to the earnestly genteel. Here, respectability stalks abroad adorned with starched linen and surrounded by mortgages. The clatter of lawn-mowers can be heard for miles on any sunny Saturday. Sunday evenings, the stillness of death descends on the place, but if one listens very attentively one may hear the scraping of hundreds of chewed pens as they travel the weary road of principal and interest and pay-off-as-rent.

Agatha's mother's home tucked its lawns about its feet and withdrew somewhat from the regular line of houses in the street. It had been paid for. My mother-in-law's chief occupations were writing letters of complaint to the municipal council, and calling upon God to look at our so-called democratic government and blight it. She also laid a few baits for the neighbours' dogs, kept a strict eye on the morals of the whole street, and lopped off any branch, twig or tendril which thrust itself from the next-door garden over the fence and so trespassed on her property. What spare time she had left was used up by various communings with God about the water-rates, and the only really light work she indulged in was when she seated herself behind the window-curtain and watched for small boys who might be tempted to rattle sticks along the front fence. Altogether, she was a busy woman. And then, of course, there was the parrot. The parrot was also an opponent of governments, cursed the municipal council, squawked miserably over the water-rates and was withal highly religious. Whether this spiritless subservience to local opinion was due to force of example or merely a desire for a quiet life, I do not know. In this description of my mother-in-law's mode of life I think I have written with a certain amount of tolerant restraint. She is an old lady and the age of chivalry is not dead while a Gudgeon lives. Perhaps a different son-in-law might have described her as a senseless, whining, nagging, leather-faced old whitlow not fit to cohabit with a rhinoceros beetle. But I wouldn't.

Arriving at the house, I paused. The lawn needed mowing. I crossed the road and stood regarding the place. That the grass of the front lawn needed mowing may seem a very little thing and not sufficient to make any one pause, but I had bitter memories of my infrequent visits to this place in my earlier days. I would enter and be given a cup of tea, then—"Ha! Now we have a man in the house."

In other words: "Ha! Here is a work-beast. Let him paint the tool-shed; let him mend the wheelbarrow; bring out the hedge-clippers and the lawn-mower and point out to him the location of the axe and the woodheap."

That, of course, would be when I was comparatively welcome.

And now?

As I gazed across at the place, a window-curtain quivered. I had been seen. I could not now retreat with dignity so I crossed the road, took a deep breath, and knocked at the door. Wiping my feet industriously on the mat, I waited. I could imagine the scurrying and the whisperings that were going on inside. I knocked again. I had expected this sort of thing, and after waiting a few moments longer I turned and made for the gate as though about to leave. The strategy was successful. The door opened a few inches and the hideous beak of my mother-in-law protruded from the gap.

"Well," she snapped, "what do *you* want?"

I doffed my bowler.

"I've come to see my wife."

"You've come to see your wife, have you?"

"Yes, ma."

"S'nmmph!"

Just like Gertrude.

"Supposing I don't allow you to see her? Supposing I forbid you to enter my house. Supposing I set the dog on you!"

"In that case," I replied, taking another step toward the gate, "I think I'll go."

"You just come inside here!" she whinnied, flinging the door open.

"Come inside at once, my fine gentleman!"

I went in, like the fool that I was.

"Sit there," she commanded, pointing to a chair at the drawing-room table.

"Now then," she said, seating herself opposite me, "explain to me, please, if you can—*if* you can, why my daughter comes to me in tears for my protection. Who are these low women whose company you prefer and why is it that after being drunk for practically every day of your life and ill-treating and starving Agatha, my daughter—my daughter, mind you, who has had a better upbringing than the whole of your common Gudgeon relations put together and the Lord God on high who watches over His lambs knows what it cost me to bring up my girls, the sacrifices I have made, the money I've spent; me, a poor lone old woman who has had to struggle and pinch to keep a roof over my head and paying for this and for that, and the council wanting me to pay for the drain—me, mind you; an old woman who has hardly enough to keep body and soul together, paying for their filthy drains. I never asked for drains. Why should I? What do I want with drains at my time of life? Calling themselves aldermen——"

"They'll never get a penny out of me! They'll never get a penny out of me!" shrieked the parrot, scuttling into the room excitedly. I sank back into my chair and fumbled in a hopeless manner for my pipe as the bird fluttered on to the table.

"And you," continued my mother-in-law, recovering from the interruption. "*You* have the audacity, the impudence, the—the——"

"Hyperbollicality?" I suggested. It was the best I could think of at the time.

"The brazen impertinence to come here and ask to see my daughter. I'd rather see her dead and in her grave!"

The parrot scuffled feverishly up and down the table.

"Call this a government!" it demanded hoarsely.

"Look here, ma," I said. "It's this way——"

"Don't 'ma' me! Don't try any of your soft snivelling ways with me, my soft-soaping gentleman!"

"But listen——"

"Listen! Oh, yes, listen to him! Just listen to him!"

"I came here to see Agatha!" I shouted, thumping the table. I was becoming annoyed.

"Don't you raise your voice to me!" squeaked the old lady, clawing the air.

The parrot was almost frantic with excitement. It staggered drunkenly up and down the table between us, shrieking of governments, of municipal councils, of poor, lone women, and the mercy of God.

"Where is Agatha?" I shouted, rising and jamming my hat over one eye.

"Not a penny!" shrieked the parrot. "Call this a government! Take that back, I won't have it! This is your council for you! Milko! Call this——"

I swiped it off the table and it struck the floor and lay prone, frothing at the beak.

"Gertrude!" screamed the old woman. "Police! Gertrude! Unchain the dog! He's killed my parrot!"

She picked the parrot up, and it croaked weakly, "This is your council for you," and ceased to flutter.

"You drunken beast!" hissed my mother-in-law.

"That's all right," I replied. "You like your little drop, you old sponge."

"Get out of my house!"

"I'm going," I said.

As I made for the door I noticed for the first time that Agatha was in the room, regarding me with horrified amazement.

" 'Lo Agatha," I said, nodding pleasantly.

She covered her face with her hands and dashed out of the room.

Almost immediately after, a dog dashed in with Gertrude bringing up the rear. I decided that it was best to leave and would have managed it easily only for getting caught on the front fence. I vaulted it all right but my coat caught on one of the pickets. The dog leapt the gate and came at me with all external appendages streamlined and its teeth bared for business. Just in time, I wrenched the picket off the fence and swiped it in mid-leap. It never yelped but fell back on the pavement, breathing calmly. The three women screamed on the front lawn. I threw the picket through the largest pane of the front window and hurried away. One dead parrot, one unconscious dog, one busted fence, one broken window. Not bad for one visit I thought as I bounded into the waiting taxi.

I was calm, but I felt sickened with life. With the very best intentions I had come, and in a shower of broken glass and dead parrot I had gone. And not through any fault of mine had the sweet spirit of forgiveness turned to ashes in the mouth. The proffered hand of friendship had been spurned, and Charity was even now feeling her bruises and sobbing in the arms of her disillusioned sisters, Faith and Hope. I am a man of vast experience and worldly knowledge and perhaps I should have passed over this rebuff with a shrug and a smile; but my better nature had been wounded. The iron had entered my soul and no faith-healer could help me unless he was also a blacksmith.

As I jolted along in the taxi, too dashed in spirits to smoke, I felt that I understood why men burned their boats behind them, sold up their homes and went to Africa to hunt elephants.

It is the last defiance of a manly soul to quaff the bitter cup of fate and fling the dregs in its face. How have I sometimes yearned to stand on a peak where the wind howled, and bare my teeth and laugh. Laugh! Or drive a ship through whistling spray into the very jaws of a gale while the splintered rigging thrashed on the heaving deck. And all that. To fling aside the petty considerations, the conventions, the saving, the sordid cares, and hoist myself to a seat beside the gods in one wild, glorious burst.

I pulled up the blinds of the car and looked out. We were nearing home.

"Driver," I said, "do you know Flannery's?"

"Dance-hall, pub, or——"

"Pub," I replied hastily.

"Can't say as I do."

"Don't know Bill Flannery's Crown and Anchor!"

"Oh! That's the place that supplies the beer for Gudgeon's parties?"

"Yes," I replied, puzzled. "What do you know about Gudgeon?"

"Eh? Everybody knows about him. There's been letters in the papers about it and the Woollahra Council held a special meeting about it. The Citizens' Reform League want him removed. He must be in with the police or that last party would have settled him."

"But, damn it all, man; we only ever had one party!"

"Are you Gudgeon?" he asked, twisting his head right around.

"Look out for the footpath!" I cautioned him. "Yes, I'm Gudgeon. What about it?"

"Ain't you frightened to be seen out?" he asked admiringly. "Struth!" he went on, "when I read in the paper about your son holdin' off a gang of thugs while you got away, I said to meself, 'That's the finish of the pair of 'em; the gang'll get 'em sooner or later.' I wondered why you wanted the blinds pulled down," he mused. "No doubt about it, us taxi blokes pick up some queer birds."

"Explain yourself," I demanded, commencing to climb over into the front seat. "No. Hold her! Stop!"

We had arrived at Flannery's corner.

"Care for a little gastronomic diversion?" I inquired, nodding toward the hotel.

"No," he replied. "I never touch the stuff; but I'll have a dot of whisky with you."

"Same thing," I assured him.

"Oh, no it ain't. You wouldn't call drinkin' whisky a diversion, would you?"

"What is it then?" I asked, pushing the bar door open. "An exercise?"

"It's a duty," he replied sternly. "Me father was Scotch."

"Hello, Jack," cried Flannery. "Go through into the saloon bar. Stanley is in there with his uncle."

We continued on to the private bar and seated ourselves at a little round table, opposite Stanley and George. We greeted each other and ordered our drinks.

"Stanley," I said, "do you know anything of certain reports that have appeared in the press of late? Have you heard of a certain Stanley Gudgeon who heroically held off a gang of thugs while his father fled to safety?"

Stanley blushed.

"Aw, well——" he commenced.

"Say no more," I put in wearily. "I understand."

"You see, dad. It was this way. This reporter feller comes up to me and says—he knows I'm well known at the Blue Garter—he says, 'Things are very dull today.' So of course, as the poor chap was only trying to earn a living I might as well——"

"*All* right. *All* right. Have you been enjoying yourself, George?"

George giggled, made a few rings on the table with his glass, and looked away.

"He's got a girl," explained Stanley.

"That reminds me!" exclaimed the taxi-driver. "I gotter get away.' He rose and shook hands with me.

"Any time you've got a party on, let me know and I'll bring a carload of girls for you. All sports. Be glad to come meself. That's the phone number."

He flung a card down on the table, waved his hand, and left us.

"Handy sort of chap to know," remarked Stanley. "Not that I'm short of a girl or two, but there are occasions when one hasn't time to round them up. Better give me that card."

"You've become very sophisticated in the last few weeks, Stanley," I said.

"My youth is past," he replied with a sigh. "Look at Uncle George."

George was gazing into his glass with a soft sheep-grin on his face, oblivious to everything.

"Who chose that suit for you, George?" I asked, shaking his shoulder.

"Eh? Oh, she did. She bought me this shirt, too."

"Bought you a shirt, eh? Well, I'll admit you've avoided the Split Rock motif in your dress this time. It's a great improvement. What's she like, George?"

I always think that in humouring a man who has made the Great Mistake, one should adopt the tone usually applied to children and half-wits. A man properly in love would be quite satisfied to sit on a log sucking a pencil and thinking of the price of furniture.

"She's got yellow hair," stammered George reluctantly.

"That all?" I inquired, encouraging him.

"Blue eyes," he added. "She bought me a shirt. She sewed a button on for me."

I shook my head sadly.

"Tell me, George. Does she catch hold of your coat lapels and look up at you? Does she pick little threads off your suit in a motherly kind of way, and straighten your tie? Does she catch hold of your hand when she crosses the road?"

George stared at me and nodded wonderingly.

I slid down into my chair and smirked bitterly at my finger-nails.

Here and now I would like to say that of all the refinements of female technique there is none to approach the subtlety of "picking the thread". The reason for the infallible success of this method is deep-rooted in psychology, and it is not for me to go into it. It is a combination of the "motherly" and "clinging vine" that has led more men to a one-suit-for-life existence than any other of the legitimate holds.

I felt sorry for George.

"And you, Stanley; what have you done?" I asked. "How is little Whatsername?"

"We're engaged," said Stanley calmly.

I sighed. There they were, self-sufficient, happy in their ignorance and blind to the horrible example before them. I rose and, leaving them, strolled into the other bar to talk to Flannery.

I felt like a lone passenger on a sinking ship, who had played "Nearer My God to Thee" three or four times, SOS'd till the batteries had run out, shot off his last rocket, and was now preparing to dance the Charleston on the top of the wheel-house. Too many sorrows and calamities defeat their own ends and tend to make one divinely careless and callously flippant.

"Flannery," I said, "a mug of whisky, and have one yourself."

"Well—if you don't mind, Jack—a mug, you know——"

"All right. Please yourself. I have no friends."

"Aw, but I was real bad the last time, Jack——"

"Go on. Have your fiddling nobbler. Don't consider me."

"Oh, all right then. I'll have a mug," he assented miserably.

Time passed.

Stanley and George came in as Flannery and I were leaning over the counter, harmonizing softly in "Sweet Adeline".

"George," I said, knocking his hat off, "have a mug of whisky."

"I would, Jack, only I've got to go out tonight," he replied apologetically.

"Ah! So I've lost another friend." I sighed. "I ask you, George, for the last time, will you have a mug of whisky?"

"Aw, all right," said George.

"Stanley?" I questioned, raising one eyebrow.

"Absolutely," said Stanley.

How that word "absolutely" reminded me of Daisy!

Dear Daisy. The only woman who ever understood me—partly. Daisy Slatter....I wondered what her name was before she married Woggo, and if I would ever see her again. I think I almost cried a little.

"Come on," I said, "let's sing 'Sweet Adeline' again."

We sang it, the old song. The song we used to sing when I was a boy. The song we used to sing around the fire at the week-end camp. We sang it, I remember, on the beach in the moonlight, and sitting on the kerb at two o'clock in the morning. When we were blue, when we were drunk, when we were broke and the night before I got married we sang it—the old song—"Sweet Adeline".

"Ah, don't sing it any more," blubbered Flannery, and fell behind the counter.

It was half-past nine. The doors were locked and only the four of us were in the bar.

"Come home, daddy," whimpered Stanley. "Li'l Stanley feels sick."

"Come on, George," I said.

I forget what happened after that. Nothing of any importance. I know we got home all right because I woke up underneath the dining-room table the next morning. Stanley showed up about four in the afternoon. George seemed to be all right physically, but filled with remorse. He had promised the yellow-haired thread-picker that he would never touch another drop.

Such is the frailty of human nature.

Taking it all round, it was a pretty dreadful day.

Chapter 23

Late in the afternoon things were very bad. Both Stanley and George were acting like the beasts of the fields and woods. They dragged themselves about the house, kicking things about and bumping into things and cursing me. It has always been my opinion that if a man cannot drink without making a beast of himself, he should not drink at all and seeing that nearly twenty-four hours had elapsed since they'd had anything to drink—or eat—I could find no excuse for their boorishness. I can understand a man feeling a little off colour after a few mugs of whisky. I felt a bit leadenish myself, but to keep it up all day! Disgusting. It practically amounted to a mutiny. When I say a mutiny, I mean that I have always been recognized as the head and leader in any company. I am not a domineering man, but there is something about me, some innate air of authority that has always made men look up to me and respect me. I remember, when I was a small boy, my mother took me to a phrenologist. After examining me, he said, "Madam, your son is a remarkable type; his bump of philosophy is enormous while the authoritative region of his cranium is abnormal. He is a born leader." Unfortunately, my mother, who was a simple soul and not versed in the phrenological jargon got the idea that a born leader was a man who walked in front of a road-roller carrying a red flag, or Number One in a chain-gang, so my talents were never exploited or encouraged. Despite this lack of opportunity to display my gifts as a leader of men I have always been respected and looked up to, as I have said before. It therefore came as a blow to me when Stanley, speaking to George in an undertone, said, "He's mad!" I knew he meant me.

George agreed with him.

"Mugs of whisky!" he said contemptuously. "Practically forced me to have them. Forced me. You know that, Stanley! And after promising her not to touch another drop. I wouldn't mind so much if I didn't feel so crook. He hasn't the slightest consideration for any one but himself. He *is* mad, Stanley. He must be mad."

"Of course he is!" replied Stanley. "Why, do you know what he did a little while back? Chased me up on the roof with a meat chopper!"

"Diddy!" exclaimed George.

"He did. You saw how the door of the front bedroom is bashed in? He did that. I tell you, Uncle George, it's a wonder I'm alive today. And yet I stick to him and help him," he added in a tone that would have made Agatha envious.

All this, mind you, while I'm sitting in the same room reading the paper!

"It's the drink," said George, continuing the discussion. "No wonder Agatha left him. Gertrude too. It beats me how they stood him as long as they did."

"Aunt Gertrude would never have been as she is, only for him," said Stanley, shaking his head.

"Fine woman, Gertrude," agreed George. "Just listen to him rustling that paper! Wouldn't it get on your nerves? No consideration at all!"

"Every time he rustles it, the noise goes right through me," replied Stanley, shuddering.

I flung the paper down.

"What the hell's wrong with the pair of you?" I cried. "Can't a man read a paper without you two prawns moaning about it?"

"Who's a prawn?" demanded George, standing up.

"Stanley."

"That's all right then," he mumbled, sitting down again.

The pair of them started to whisper together again.

I could easily understand their sudden close friendship.

Sympathy bound them together. George with his thread-picker, and Stanley with Estelle the giggler, were both in the same scuttled boat. They were suffering from the effects of their own intemperance, and I, the outsider, had been marked down as a scapegoat for their bad feelings. I have often noticed this clannishness among men who have capitulated to women. The married men collect into little cliques, and the next grade, single but earnestly in love, collect into other cliques, and so on. They know damn well they've made fools of themselves and they think by consorting with similar fools to blur the realization.

It annoyed and saddened me to see the two of them mumbling into each other's ears, and after putting up with a whole day of slights and grumblings, I think I had just cause to be annoyed. But kind hearts are more than coronets, and a soft answer turneth away wrath even if it does invite suspicion. Walking softly as evidence of my consideration for them, I left the room and went into the kitchen. I mixed them a pick-me-up and took it to them.

I'm rather proud of my reviver. It's made from a recipe of my own and consists mainly of Worcester sauce, with a little lemon juice and two or three other odds and ends.

"The trouble with you is that you've had nothing to eat all day," I told them. "You're too highly strung. Cultivated people always are. The higher the civilization, the higher the stringing. What you both want is something to eat and a walk in the fresh air in congenial company. I've not had very much to eat myself today, so as soon as that reviver has soaked into you we'll have a meal. Stanley can lay the table and get things ready while you do the cooking, George. I'll soon have a meal ready for you that way."

They sipped at their glasses and grunted.

It was time for a supreme effort.

"I'll get the meal ready, myself," I said, and made for the kitchen.

"He *must* be mad!" whispered Stanley. "He's going to get the tea ready!"

"About time he did his share," grumbled George.

Patience and forbearance are not so much virtues as a sort of stultification of the intellect. I stulted about and got the meal ready. "Come on, you chaps," I called jovially.

It hurt me to the bone to have to be jovial and pander to the miserable cows, but having gone so far I was determined to get them into a good mood so that I could tell them what I thought of them.

They ate their food in a languid way that implied that they were merely humouring me in their good-natured way and that they would have much preferred to starve. In the same way they accompanied me out of the house and up the street, when I suggested a little fresh air. Stanley kept up his beastly grumbling just to annoy me, I know, but George's peevishness had its roots in remorse. There was only one way to bring him back to normal and I loathed the idea and shrank from the thought of what the conversational possibilities might be, but I tried it.

"George," I said, "this little girl you've got—is she nice?"

"Orright," he answered grudgingly.

"How old is she, George?"

"Couldn't say. About twenty-five."

"Mother and father living?"

"No. Poor little devil, she hasn't got a mother or a father."

"Lucky," said Stanley, flinging his cigarette past my face.

"It's a terrible thing for a poor girl to be left alone in the world," I muttered. "There are so many snares and pitfalls. Dance-halls, two-seater cars, and things—unsafe. Unsafe."

"She doesn't go to dance-halls or anything like that. She's a good quiet girl."

"I couldn't imagine you being acquainted with any other kind of girl, George," I replied, putting my hand on his sleeve.

Stanley giggled. "Neither could I," he said.

"You speak when you're spoken to," growled George, glaring at him.

"She is a good girl."

"When did you find out?"

I reached around George's back and hit Stanley in the back of the neck.

"Shut up," I commanded, "or you'll be sent home."

"Yes," continued George, "she's a good girl, all right, and real nice besides. Do you know what she did?"

"No."

"Bought me a shirt."

"That's nothing," said Stanley. "I know a girl who——"

"Shut up!" I snapped. "Bought you a shirt, eh, George? That was nice of her wasn't it?"

"Mmm...She sewed a button on for me."

"Where was the button off?" inquired Stanley.

"Off me trousers."

"How——" He paused. "Hmph!" he grunted.

"If you don't mind, George, I'll walk in the middle," I said, stepping in between them.

"Funny, the way her eyes look at you," mused George, dreamily. "Sort of bright looking. Blue eyes she's got. Blue like—like—you know the back of a match-box? Well, like that, only not so dark."

"Striking," I commented.

"Do they match?" asked Stanley.

"We shall laugh at that little joke later on," I put in. "Remind us that we owe you a laugh. But for the present, be silent when a lady is being spoken of."

"Good enough for him," agreed George.

We walked along in silence for a while.

George had his half-cow smile draped over his face and a vision before his eyes and had to be helped up the kerbs and jerked away from passing cars.

"Mary, her name is," he muttered as we reached a quieter thoroughfare.

"What's her other name, George?"

"Smith. Mary Smith."

"Mary Smith," he repeated, chewing it over like old brandy.

"Gee!" exclaimed Stanley, chuckling derisively.

"What's wrong with it!" demanded George. "You're

such a smart young feller! What's wrong with it?"

"Nothing, uncle, nothing. I just happened to have heard of someone by the name of Smith and I was wondering if it was the same. Seems funny, her name being Smith and I having heard of someone by the name of Smith somewhere——"

"Aw, you get on my nerves," drawled George.

"Y'know, Jack," he said, turning to me, "the very first time we saw each other, we kind of liked each other. And the last time I saw her, I said, 'D'you love me, Mary?' and she said——"

"Hold on," interrupted Stanley. "I know what she said. She said, 'You know I do.' You can't tell me she didn't, because that's what they all say. And then, of course, you asked her to prove it, and she said——"

"Stanley!" I said, grasping him by the shoulder. "Go straight home."

"Aw, leave him alone," drawled George. "He doesn't understand; he's only a boy. Mary's different to other girls."

He maundered on.

I sighed and listened and Stanley chewed his finger-nails disgustedly. If he ever had any respect for his uncle, it fled that night.

As for me, I was bored and appalled, if such a combination is possible. The man seemed to think that he had discovered something entirely new in the way of women. Even if by some joke of nature, half of what he said about her was true, her very perfection would have had an ordinary man in the lunatic asylum within a week. I bitterly regretted my introduction of the topic. Coming back, it was Stanley's turn.

I happened to ask him why he became engaged to

Estelle when he was not yet twenty-one.

Stanley packs a vocabulary of remarkable range and can shoot it from the hip when the occasion demands. He has introduced to me eleven entirely new curses at odd times, and if there was anything hanging to it, he could talk his Aunt Gertrude to sleep, but never have I heard him run on as he did about this bony-kneed chocolate receptacle. For a start, he said, age made no difference to him. The girl had experience, and as regards the possible withholding of my consent to his marriage, he hadn't really thought of marriage. If two people suited each other to such an extent that they could live together, well, by all means let them live together. As for the girl herself, she was the best dance partner he had ever had, and also she was very economical to run. She dressed well, and told a good story, was broad-minded about the problems of life and though she took her spot with the rest of them, she could take it or leave it. On top of that, she could cook and played the banjo by ear.

There were details.

She was a homely girl. Washed her own stockings occasionally. Knitted her father half a sock once. Let her mother go for an outing every Sunday afternoon, while she stayed at home. That would be, of course, if it was raining. Washed and combed the Pomeranian herself. She had sold a pair of her father's boots to a dealer with a cart and bought Stanley a tie with the proceeds. He had tied it on his motor-cycle to keep the mudguard from rattling and would show it to me when we got home.

I was dazed by the time we reached the house. Even George, a fellow victim with a more or less sympathetic ear, bore a stunned expression.

Tired in body and mind, I sat in the kitchen and

sipped a cup of tea George poured out for me. We were friendly again, but at what a cost! But I had my little say before we retired for the night. They gave me the opportunity and I pulled the stopper out of the vials of wrath and splashed the wrath around like ginger-beer at a Sunday-school picnic.

George had said, "You've cheered us up all right, Jack. I don't know what we'd do without you."

"Yes," I replied. "I've cheered you up. I've listened to your gibberings, I've prostituted my intellect and degraded my powers of reasoning, listening to you mumbling of your paltry love affairs. You, with your thread-pickers and sundae tanks! You, who have no more than glimpsed the cup which I have drained to the last insipid drop! You prate to me of love. Look at Agatha—and, my God," I cried, pointing to him, "look at Stanley! I was a fool as you are now, and look at the result!"

"Aw, cut it out," protested Stanley.

"Love!" I sneered. "You think it is the door to the palace of romance, when it is only the fire-escape exit leading out to a back lane. A fork in the road leading to the divorce court or the giggle-house. You'll come to me one of these days, bored, baggy-kneed and broke and ask my advice. I give it to you now. Forget it! Go in for fretwork or stamp collecting. Join a domino club, do anything you damn well like but leave love to the furniture-dealers who invented it. Never utter the word in my presence again. I've finished. I'm through. I'll show you how a man should live in the next few days...you mawky pair of fools, you prospective perambulator-pushers, you lip-salve soaks! Good night!"

And I strode away and left them sitting in the kitchen, looking at each other.

Chapter 24

I rose early the next morning, breakfasted at Flannery's and returned home to don my new suit. While I was dressing, Stanley was hanging around, walking in and out of the room pretending to look for something. I did not speak to him, and at last he asked me the question he could contain no longer.

"What are you going to do?"

"So you can see that I intend to do something, eh? I'm going out, my boy."

"Where to, dad?"

I finished lacing my boot and turned to him.

"Listen to me, boy. Yesterday I went to see your mother."

"Oh!" exclaimed Stanley. "Now I understand. That explains everything. I thought you had gone a bit wonky in the melon. Last night, you know."

"I have been a good father to you, Stanley," I continued quietly. "I have tried to be a good husband to your mother. I have done my duty. I have done my best. I can do no more. I have, up till now, led a quiet and practically entirely respectable life. All that is finished now—and I am going out."

"May I come?" he asked.

"Please yourself," I replied carelessly.

"Me too?" put in George, who had been standing outside the door.

I shrugged my shoulders.

"If your Marys and your Estelles will allow you to accompany me, I have no objections—providing," I added, "that George doesn't wear that damned yellow tie."

"Orright," agreed George meekly, "but where are we going? What are we going to do?"

"The first thing we are going to do is to find Woggo Slatter," I curtly informed him.

"Gee!" gasped Stanley, "I'm coming! Just wait till I get my rompers on."

"What tie shall I wear?" said George, stepping aside as Stanley hurried past him.

"Black," called Stanley from the stairs.

George hesitated in the doorway for a moment, gazing at my unresponsive back.

"Aw, I dunno what tie to wear," he said miserably.

"Go and get dressed," I snapped.

He shuffled away.

My little lecture of the previous night had evidently brought home to them that I was something more than a mere third member of the household. I was getting my rightful due: respect and civility.

I telephoned for the taxi-driver, whom on account of the frequency of our patronage I had come to regard almost as an old family retainer. By the time he arrived we were ready, and we entered the car and seated ourselves.

"Where to?" asked the driver, looking at George.

"I dunno," replied George.

"Where are we going, dad?" asked Stanley.

"Damned if I know," I replied. "Get a move on, driver, we'll think of some place presently."

"I suppose Slatter wouldn't be at the Blue Garter now?" I asked Stanley.

"I don't think so. After lunch he may be. He works in the morning I think; he has to make a living somehow when things are slack. Lots of favourites been getting pipped off lately."

"Where does he work?" I asked.

"Down at the Forty Tables in Pitt Street. He's generally at the end table they tell me."

"Billiard marking?"

"Gee, no! Playing pool. He's the best pool player there."

"Hmph," I grunted. "I'd like to have him on for a small wager."

I wield a crafty cue at pool.

We called at the Forty Tables and made inquiries. We were told that Woggo had been barred by the management and that he was usually to be found in the Blue Garter, where he did a little training in the basement. We thanked the marker and went to luncheon.

I dislike idling about town. I seem to meet everyone I don't wish to meet and by some strange coincidence I always seem to have forgotten to pay them some minor debt. We therefore arrived at the Blue Garter only an hour or two after luncheon.

There was no one in the place, but the manager remembered me, and after a little talk directed us to Slatter's basement training quarters. "I hope, gentlemen, that there will be no—er—disturbance, so to speak. We are—er—persecuted by the police already, and it would be—er—most—er——"

"That's all right, old chap," I assured him. "There will be no outcry."

I had brought a small length of lead piping with me and felt fairly confident that there would be no scuffling. But I was mistaken. I never even had a chance to use it. The manager left us at the door of a room from whence came the quick, rhythmic thudding of a belaboured punching-ball.

"Stanley," I directed, "bend down and let your uncle stand on your back. George, you get up on Stanley and look through the fanlight. Tell me the exact position of Slatter in that room. Then jump out of the way and I'll rush in and bash him to a pulp."

Stanley, grumbling a bit, allowed George to stand on his back. I gripped my piece of pipe.

"Gee, dad! You're not going to use that?" gasped Stanley.

"I won't hurt him. I'll just—I'll just show him, that's all. Don't rock about so much; think of your uncle."

"I'm going," whimpered Stanley. "I won't be mixed up in a murder! You're mad. I'm sorry I came. Get off me, uncle!"

"There's six of 'em," whispered George, glancing down at me. "They got muscles on 'em like workin' bullocks. One bloke just got hit under the chin with an Indian club, and he laughed!"

"Get off me!" wailed Stanley, sagging at the knees.

"My crickeys!" yelled George. "He's seen me!"

Stanley collapsed, with George on top of him. The door was jerked open and Woggo in shorts and rubber shoes stared down at the scrambling figures on the floor. They got up as three or four half-naked athletes strolled up behind him.

"Ar!" growled Woggo, reaching out for George, "it's you, is it!"

I led the way up the stairs.

The most casual student of strategy knows that surprise is the most important factor in an attack of any sort, and as our plans for surprising the enemy had gone astray, the obvious thing to do was to retreat. Just an ordinary matter of move and counter-move.

Of course, I never thought of all this before I decided to go. I thought of it afterwards, but at the time, I acted on instinct. If a few more of our so-called generals had possessed the same kind of strategic instinct and acted upon it, the Great War would have been over a lot earlier.

It seemed to be a lot farther up the stairs than it had been coming down. Stanley and George passed me on the second flight, and had it not been for this foolishness, what followed might never have occurred. Instead of making for the door at the street level, they kept going on up the stairs. Perhaps it was because Woggo and his ball-punching friends were so close behind us. I don't know why I followed them, but I did. Thinking it over now, I think it must have been instinct again that urged me to stay with them to protect them if possible.

Four strides in front of me on the landing of the first floor, George and Stanley dived through the doorway of the lounge-room and slammed the door in my face. A filthy trick to play on a man who was doing his best to get them out of trouble. I jerked the door open just in time to slam it again on the foremost of my pursuers. Stanley's head showed for a moment above a window-sill. He was outside, on the roof of the veranda. George had one leg through the window, struggling clumsily. I bounded to the window and pushed him through. He fell on the roof with a crash. I felt a hand grasp at my coat as I leapt after him. I had no idea how far down the veranda was, but, judging by the noise George made, it must have been quite a few feet. Marvellous the risks one takes in times of stress. Fortunately, I landed on George.

I glanced hurriedly about me. The veranda, at slightly varying heights, stretched unbroken for nearly a block. Already a dense crowd had formed on the opposite pavement, for we were in the centre of a busy spot. Stanley had removed his coat, or had it torn off him, and stood clasping an electric-light pole that jutted up through the roof. The crowds shouted as Woggo and one of his friends became jammed in the window-frame in their anxiety to get at us.

Stanley commenced to ascend the pole as George staggered to his feet. The pole seemed to be the only way off the roof, so I made for it.

"Go on, damn you!" I shouted, pinching Stanley on the leg. "What the hell's keeping you?"

A wire, from which depended an electric light, stretched across the narrow street. He grasped it and swung out on it. I reached the top of the pole and was standing on the cross-bars when Woggo bounded out on to the roof. George clattered over the iron, seemingly at a loss for inspiration. Hand over hand, I swung out over the centre of the street and stopped next to Stanley.

"Go on, you fool!" I cried, swinging one foot at him. "What are you dawdling for?"

"There's a policeman on the roof at the other side and one at the foot of each pole," he panted. "Go on if you like. Don't mind me."

My arms were beginning to feel the strain. I looked down at the street. All traffic was blocked, and in a little space cleared of the multitude of cheering spectators, the police-wagon waited.

"Slick, eh?" remarked Stanley, nodding toward it.

"Gee," he added, "if Uncle George doesn't get picked for the next International Rugby team, the game's not fair. They haven't got him yet! Look at him side-stepping! Gee, dad! Here comes a copper out of the window. He's a gonner!"

"Damn your Uncle George!" I replied, shifting my aching hands. "I can't hang here all day like a side of blasted bacon!"

"Boiled bacon," amended Stanley. "Drop off if you want to but stop wriggling about or you'll snap the cable. Here comes uncle!"

I looked around. George was on top of the pole with Slatter hanging on to his leg.

"Don't come here!" I shouted. "It won't hold three of us. Get off!"

"Get a wire of your own," shouted Stanley, angrily. "This is ours!"

George, despite his many qualities, has one trait in his character which I do not admire. He is absolutely selfish. Thinks of nothing else but his own comfort and safety. Despite our warnings, he kicked Woggo in the face and swung out on the cable. He looked haggard.

When he was about five feet from us, the cable snapped. I knew the confounded thing would snap. It broke away from the Blue Garter end and we swooped through the air, all hanging on. It struck the edge of the veranda on the opposite side of the street. Luckily, we had just the right length, otherwise we would have been plastered all over the edge of the roof. As it was, we swung under the veranda and Stanley shot through a plate-glass shop-window without touching anything else. My feet mowed a swath in the crowd on the pavement and in the confusion I rushed through the splintered window after Stanley.

George had the way practically cleared for him. I heard moaning and screaming and curses, and the sound of his footsteps crunching behind me as I bounded through the hole Stanley had made in the back of the window. I felt that it was a time when each man must act for himself. Stanley evidently thought so too. The crowd impeded the efforts of the police to a great extent and the maimed and injured created a certain amount of diversion in the front of the shop, but there was no time to waste. And, really, we hadn't wasted any. It was only about thirty seconds since the cable had snapped, and Stanley had already disappeared. I leapt forward and dashed through an archway.

It was a big store and crowded, yet my escape was easy. An automatic lift took me to the third floor. I straightened my tie and made myself presentable with the aid of a mirror so thoughtfully provided in elevators presumably for people who like to see themselves going up. Then I stepped out.

In a critical situation, mere calmness will not always save one, but the man who keeps cool when hundreds are excited will come out on top as regularly as the head's hair. I had no hat and that fact gave me an idea which was nothing less than a stroke of genius. I put my pencil behind my ear, expanded my chest, and with a grave demeanour paced the length of the department.

The shoppers who had flocked to the windows overlooking the street, the spectators, the what I have heard called fickle public were already returning to their normal blasé state of mind.

Someone touched me on the elbow, and I turned slowly and gracefully toward an old lady.

"Now that all the excitement is over," she said pleasantly, "I want to see some hand-bags. Not expensive ones; it's for my daughter. You have some advertised at six and eleven, marked down from five guineas."

"Oh, yes, madam," I replied suavely. "Take elevator, eighth floor, first counter on right."

"Eighth floor! But there are only six floors in the building!"

"I said the sixth floor, madam."

"You didn't, you said the eighth floor!"

"Oh, go to blazes!" I said, and walked away.

I hate arguing with old ladies, and I don't know how a man can degrade himself to such a position as shop-walker.

"Check, please!" called a salesman from behind a nearby counter.

I drew a lightning sketch of a dog fight in his sales-book, that being as near as I could get to the usual checker's signature, and replacing the pencil behind my ear, strolled away.

I could feel his gaze boring into my back and looked around suddenly to see him staring suspiciously at me. It struck me that I had made a mistake in snapping at the old lady as she was almost certain to complain about it and cause trouble. I decided to try my luck on the second floor, and descended the stairs. I was at least one floor nearer the street and safety if nothing else.

I was walking slowly toward the front of the building in order to see how things were getting on in the street, when I was stopped by another confounded customer.

"Can't I get any attention?" he snapped. "I've been standing here for the past hour or so, waiting to be served!"

I put my hand on his shoulder.

"Now," I said gently, "that's a lie, about your standing here for an hour or so. However, we'll let it pass. What do you want?"

He went red in the face and sat down in a chair beside the counter.

"I want a beastly hat," he exclaimed at last.

I stepped behind the counter and took a hat off a little pedestal.

"Is that beastly enough?" I asked, handing it to him.

"Don't you want to know the size or anything?" he asked querulously.

"Lord, no!" I exclaimed. "What's it to do with me? Have a go at that one."

"It's too small," he objected.

"They're wearing them small now," I assured him.

"Let me have a look at that one."

I passed him the hat he pointed to.

"It fits," he mumbled, "but I don't like the colour."

"*I* like the colour," I said. "That's all right. Don't be so finicky. Now, listen to me," I continued, raising my hand to silence him. "As a sensible man, you must admit that you only buy a hat to cover your head. But as a man of fashion, you want a hat that looks well, don't you?"

He swallowed, and nodded.

"Well, then, you only want it to look well so people will admire you in it. I admire you in that hat. What more do you want. I'm a good judge."

"How much is it?" he mumbled, twisting it about on his head.

"Aw—let me see. Say about two shillings?"

"I'll take it!" he exclaimed eagerly.

"Kick in with the cash," I said, holding out my hand.

He gave me the two shillings.

"There are some paper and string if you want to wrap it up. Sing out if you want anything else."

I left him and walked away. I've heard about this art of salesmanship as they call it, but it seems to me that any fool can sell things if he goes the right way about it. I was two shillings better off, anyway, and I had satisfied the customer, and that's the whole essence of salesmanship. I was enjoying myself, in a way.

There were so many people in the place that I ran very little risk of detection while I kept walking about. I had absent-mindedly brought a hat away with me from the hat counter. It didn't fit, but I decided to keep it for a while. If it had not been for seeing a short, stout man being marched off between two massive plain-clothes detectives I might have stopped for hours, but the sight of an innocent man being bundled along to the police-van reminded me that until I got out of the building I was in danger all the time. I noticed for the first time that big men in civilian clothes, obviously policemen, were roaming all about the place, peering suspiciously at everyone.

I turned once again to the stairs and descended to the ground floor. It was risky, but I felt that if I did not soon leave, something might happen.

I gazed around me and my eyes bulged as they sighted Stanley. He was standing behind a counter in his shirt-sleeves, folding up a travelling-rug.

Astonished, I walked over to him.

"Yessir? What can I do for you?" he inquired pleasantly.

"Lord, you've got a nerve!" I exclaimed.

"So have you," he whispered. "Where's Uncle George?"

"Pinched, I suppose," I murmured.

"This is a very good quality rug, sir," babbled Stanley, as a man paused at the counter. "Best camel wool, hollow ground with side flaps and hot stripes."

"Yes," I replied, "I'll take that."

"Anything else, sir?"

I looked round as the man walked away.

"Yes," I said, "I'll have that overcoat there, and a suit-case."

"Hey! Cut it out!" whispered Stanley, hoarsely.

"Make it snappy!" I replied.

He hesitated a moment and then handed me the overcoat.

"Now the suit-case," I said, draping the coat over my arm.

Mumbling to himself we went to the end of the counter and removed a leather case from a display stand. I pretended to examine it while I spoke to him.

"I know this looks very much like dishonesty, Stanley," I said softly, "but don't let it trouble your conscience. You know me for a man of honour and integrity and that though I may have my faults, petty dishonesty is not one of them. I will explain everything later. Have you got anything else that you could put into the case?"

"We've only got travel goods here," he replied sulkily. "I don't know whose overcoat you've got."

"All right, all right. There is no need for you to get sulky. I'll pay for the stuff just to set your mind at rest. How much is it?"

He brightened up.

"We'll let it go at a pound. The stuff is worth more, but I don't know the price of anything, so we'll say a pound, eh?"

"Yes," I replied, "we'll just say it. Here's two shillings."

"That's not enough," he said, putting it in his pocket.

"Do you mean to keep that money yourself!" I demanded. "Why, boy, that is theft! Haven't you got a streak of decency somewhere in you?"

I was astounded. I had never suspected my own son. What father would?

"You're coming out of it all right," he mumbled.

"Give me back that two shillings!"

He walked away and I picked up the suit-case and went after him.

"Remember, you bandit, that's two shillings you owe me," I hissed and passed on, donning the overcoat as I went. With the coat on, the suit-case in my hand, the rug over my shoulder and my new hat tilted over my forehead, I hurried away to another exit and left the place.

Chapter 25

When I am in one of my reckless moods it takes a lot to surprise me. Reckless but calm, that's me. I remember when Agatha's grandfather, who had become increasingly absent-minded as he grew older, explained to me his reasons for going to sleep with his head in the gas-stove. He had intended to suicide, but had forgotten to turn the gas on. Another man might have telephoned for the police or the ambulance or a straightjacket. It *is* rather surprising when one comes to think of it, to find an old man asleep on the floor with his head in the gas-stove and the door squeezing his neck. But it takes more than that to surprise me. I just turned the gas on for the old chap and left him. It sent my gas account up enormously, but I was never a man to quibble over a little expense. And I am calm at all times. Still I could not help the slight raising of one eyebrow when, on arriving home, I found George sitting on the doorstep.

"Hullo," he said. "Where did you get that hat?"

"What's wrong with it?" I queried.

"It looks silly."

"How did you manage to get away?" I asked curtly. A man who wears ties like George has no right to criticize.

"I dunno, exactly," he replied, scratching his head. "I was standing there, just inside the window, when in comes two detectives and about nine policemen. So I starts to get back into the window and one of the detectives says, 'Eh!' So I looks round and he says, 'Oh, all right. You watch the stuff in the window, will you?' So I says, 'Righto,' and off they went and left me."

It was plain to me that on account of his build and the way his clothes didn't fit him, the detectives had mistaken him for one of their own kind.

"What did you do then?" I inquired.

"Well, I stood there and watched the window for a while, and then a policeman comes up to me and says, 'I'll take your place here. O'Halloran wants you.' So I went off and had a look round but I couldn't find any one by the name of O'Halloran, so I thought I might as well come home—and here I am."

"Oh," I said.

What else could I say? Fools rush in where angels wouldn't go in an armoured tank, and they stroll out again in safety with a silly grin on their faces. I stepped past George and entered the house to rid myself of the overcoat and suit-case. Looking myself over in the mirror, I had to admit that the hat was a bit on the small side, but by wearing it over my forehead or tilted on to the back of my head it did not look so bad. Beside, a man with the right air and bearing can wear practically anything.

I had washed, and was putting on a clean collar when George shouted from the doorstep that Stanley was coming.

I went to the doorway.

"Hullo," he said, kicking the gate open. "Nice damn mess you've got us into. I had terrible trouble getting away. I sold out everything at my counter and just as I was going, they came looking for me. I was lucky to get away. I suppose you think that sort of thing funny——"

"I did not ask you to come," I put in. "You came of your own free will."

"You've ruined me at the Blue Garter," he grumbled. "That's the second time you've gone there and caused a disturbance and I'll be barred from the place now. You've taken my living away from me, that's what you've done. As for you, you'll be sand-bagged on sight if you ever go near the place again."

"Nevertheless, I'm going back there as soon as I've had something to eat."

"What for?" gasped George. "Tired of life?"

"Something like that," I replied.

Stanley looked at George and tapped his forehead.

"Yes," agreed George emphatically. "And my crikeys, he looks it with that silly hat on!"

"Never mind my hat," I snapped. "Take that rotten tie off. If you must know my reasons for returning to the Blue Garter, I'll tell you. I intend from now on to get the last ounce out of life. While Slatter remains out of hospital, my activities will be hampered. That is all."

"Well," declared Stanley, "I'm not going to be in it."

"Neither am I," said George.

"Stand out of the way then," I cried. "I'm going."

"Straightaway!" exclaimed Stanley.

"Flannery's first."

"Oh, we'll go that far with you," said George.

Stanley brushed past me.

"Wait till I get another coat and hat."

He was ready in a few minutes and the three of us strolled up to Flannery's. Flannery looked hard at me and then shook his head vigorously.

"I know it by the look of your face, and I'm not having any. Not even one, so it's no use asking me."

"What are you talking about?" I asked him.

"Mugs of whisky," he replied tersely.

"Neither am I," I assured him. "I have a busy night before me."

We ordered our drinks.

"Where did you get that boy-size egg-boiler?" asked Flannery. "It looks funny."

"To say the least of it, Flannery, your criticism of the hat of a good customer is impolitic. I'll say nothing of your lack of taste."

He apologized, but kept glancing at the hat in a way that annoyed me greatly.

As time went on, Stanley became silent, and George increasingly voluble. Stanley came and shook hands with me.

"You're game, dad," he whispered. "I've a good mind to go with you tonight."

"It is no expedition for boys," I replied gently.

"Oh, isn't it!" he exclaimed. "I'd like to see any one try to stop me if I wanted to go. I'd be of more use than that big slump over there."

"What's that?" inquired George.

"Stanley was just announcing his intention of coming with me to the Blue Garter as you seemed to be a little too nervous to accompany me and he does not like to see me go alone."

"Nervous!" shouted George.

George was coming too.

At half-past six we left Flannery's by the back entrance and entered the taxi which had been waiting for us since six o'clock. "Blue Garter," I directed.

"My God!" exclaimed the taxi-driver, and we started off.

"I should be seeing Mary tonight," mumbled George.

"It's not too late to withdraw if you want to," I replied.

"Oh, I'm coming. I didn't make an appointment, but was thinking of calling on her.... Ah, well!"

An aura of gloom hung about George and Stanley and I could not help being affected. The car was comfortably upholstered and we rolled along without the slightest jolt. The driver, having by this time got used to my ideas, had hung a tin flap over the face of the taximeter. We travelled in luxury and on pleasure bent, more or less, and yet the expression on the faces of Stanley and George could not have been worse if we had been travelling in a hearse. They sat stiffly, gazing sadly at the driver's neck. After enduring it for about six minutes, I tried to cheer them up.

"What's wrong with you totem-poles!" I snapped. "Look as if you're enjoying yourselves. This isn't a tumbrel!"

"I was wondering," said Stanley in a toneless voice, "I was just wondering whether we would take our next ride in the police car or the ambulance wagon."

"I should have gone to see Mary," mumbled George.

"What's the rush?" I queried. "Frightened she'll escape? Don't you believe it. Plenty of time. She'll keep; they all do."

"I've had 'em go bad," said Stanley.

"Anyhow, George," I continued, "what do you intend to do about her? You'll have to get rid of her sooner or later before she gathers too much evidence."

"I'm going to marry her," he replied stolidly.

"Don't start, dad!" exclaimed Stanley. "I'm not in the mood for it."

"I wasn't going to say anything," I replied, "only that

speaking as a man of experience, if ever I got married again it would have to be under an anaesthetic."

"None of them new fangled ideas for me," said George, sternly. "Anaesthetics! When I get married, I'll get married raw—with me eyes open."

The car eased to a stop.

"Blue Garter," said the driver.

"Already!" exclaimed Stanley.

"You'd better wait," I said, after we had alighted.

"Not me!" the driver exclaimed. "And I want me money now. I might never see you again—unless I have to identify yer," he added thoughtfully.

"Do you want to lose my custom, or will you wait?" I snapped.

"Oh, all right," he replied sulkily. "I'll wait on the corner of the next block."

I turned my back on the cowardly fool and we entered the doorway of the Blue Garter and ascended the stairs. There was a little altercation as to who should go first. Courtesy prompted me to request Stanley and George to go on ahead but they were equally decided that I should lead the way. After a few minutes, I acceded to their requests and went in front.

Seen from the landing, the place was crowded. I could see neither Woggo nor the manager and I beckoned to George and Stanley who had hung back on the stairs. Together we entered the room.

"See any one you know?" I asked, turning to George.

He shook his head.

"Hard to tell in this crowd," said Stanley dubiously. "I don't suppose he'd be in here and it's no use hanging around. Let's go."

A waiter paused in front of us and eyed me suspiciously.

"We want a table," I said, nodding to him.

"What for?" demanded George.

"To sit down at," I explained patiently.

Very grudgingly, the waiter secured us a table. We had just seated ourselves when a glad cry welled from afar down the crowded room.

"Oo-oo! George!"

We looked around.

"Mary!" whinnied George.

"Stone the crows," gasped Stanley. "It's Eggs!"

And it was. There she stood, a triumph of chemical science, waving her plump white arm above her blonde head.

"George!" I commanded, "sit down!"

But it was no use. Grinning from ear to ear he lumbered toward her like a dray-horse just turned out of harness straight into the lion's mouth. Stanley and I stood up on the table to watch the impact. Out of the corner of my eye, I saw the manager enter the room. His face blanched as his gaze alighted upon us. "Oh, my God, they're in!" he cried.

"Har!" came a deep-throated growl from the other end of the room. I saw Woggo get up, I heard Eggs scream, "Leave him alone!" I saw Steak hanging on to the drunken Simpson as he strove to get to Slatter's side. And then Stanley pushed me off the table.

In his excitement he elbowed me off, or that was his subsequent excuse. He may have done it deliberately, but anyhow, I don't think I lay on the floor for more than half a minute, although I was a bit stunned. Supposing that it took me a minute to fall to the floor and get up again, one could hardly expect much to happen in such a short time, but when next I could see Slatter's end of the café, it was a wreck. As I watched, tables flopped over, flower vases sped glittering through the air and smashed against the walls. Women stood on chairs and were swept off. Men, catching a sauce bottle in the ear, rose with a howl of rage and cast themselves into the fray with the abandon of open-air eurhythmicists. Meanwhile, George demonstrated the importance of being earnest while Eggs clawed those nearest. Steak quietly collected the spoons.

"Isn't it great!" exclaimed Stanley.

"Go in and help Uncle George," I commanded.

"I can help him from here. Watch this," he said, swinging a chair around his head. He let go and it rose in a gentle curve above the heads of the mob and then fell into the thick of it.

"You've hit your Uncle George!" I exclaimed.

"Ah, well. I'll try another one, a little more to the right. Watch this one."

I left him and crawled on my hands and knees under cover of the tables to the farther end of the room where it was quieter. Someone had locked the door leading out to the street and around it a sweating mob milled in their endeavour to escape. Hunched up in a corner behind a table, I found the manager. His face was buried in his hands. He looked the very dregs of dejection.

"Bear up, old man," I said, patting him on the head. "Try to smile."

He looked up.

"Hur-r-r-rgh!" he screamed and leapt to his feet like a maniac. I rushed down the room from the ungrateful beast. I could feel him at my back. He was mad! With a last despairing leap, I flung myself into the tumult and the wreckage. Divine Providence must have guided me, for I struck Slatter in the back with such force that he shot forward, hit the floor with his forehead, and lay still. Someone kicked me in the stomach. A sudden feeling of disinterest swept over me and I crawled behind an upturned table holding myself together. But my luck had not altogether deserted me. Through eyelids half-closed in anguish, I saw a waiter grasp a palm in its earthen pot, raise it above his head and hand it to the manager in the back of the neck. He dropped, covered with dirt. The waiter caught my eye and grinned.

"I owed him that one," he panted.

Weakly I pointed to another palm, but he shook his head.

I closed my eyes. The din had subsided a little. There was more panting and less shouting.

The queue at the exit had broken the door down and got away.

I felt a soft hand on my forehead.

"How are you, Jack?" said Steak.

"All right, Daisy," I replied feebly, gazing up at her. "Got all the spoons?"

"Absolutely. Did you see Stanley?"

"No. What's the matter with him?"

"I think he's dead."

"Good!" I exclaimed, and closed my eyes again.

"You won't leave me, Daisy?" I whispered.

"No, Syrup," she crooned, kissing me on the ear.

"Police!" yelled someone from the doorway.

I sat up.

Daisy gripped my hand tensely, and then relaxed.

"They always get you in the end," she said sadly. "The only thing to think of, is which end they'll get you in."

"Stop Stanley!" I cried as I saw him rushing past. She tipped the table over, bounded across it and tripped him up, while I scrambled to my feet.

"He knows a way out, if any one does!" I exclaimed. "George!"

"Maureen!" screamed Steak.

"Mary!" bellowed George.

"Come on! Come on!" shrieked Stanley, struggling to get loose from my grip.

"Yer not goin' ter leave Woggo, are yer!" cried the drunken Simpson, dragging the unconscious Slatter toward us.

A crowd stampeded past us and swooped, jostling, down the stairway.

They met the police coming in.

"This way!" shouted Stanley, breaking loose.

George hoisted Slatter on to his back and we dashed after Stanley.

Down steps. Flights of them. Wooden ones. Stone ones. Through doors. Past barred basement windows. Over crates and barrels. Then out into a little dark lane. I leaned against the wall, breathless. George put Woggo down on the pavement.

"My crikeys!" he panted.

"Stanley," I said hoarsely, "run up to the next block and get the taxi."

"And get pinched!" he ejaculated scornfully.

"I'll go," said Steak. "They won't take any notice of me. Hold these spoons."

I told her where to go and sat down on the kerb to wait.

"My crikeys!" said George, squatting beside me.

"Heard you the first time," snapped Stanley. "What the devil made you start all that uproar?"

"My... Gee!" muttered George dazedly.

"Woggo seems to be comin' round," said the drunken Simpson.

"Knock him again," said Stanley callously.

Maureen stooped in front of George and patted him on the cheek.

"Mary," he bleated.

"Ah, George, you're wonderful!" she sighed.

I got up and walked away. Stanley strolled after me.

"You know," he muttered, "we're just as likely to be pinched here. The police are bound to search the basement and find the place where we got out."

"What the blazes did you bring us here for then?" I exclaimed.

"Not to camp in the gutter for the night," he replied hotly.

"You wait till I get you home, my boy! I'll teach you to be continually getting your father into trouble!"

"Ar!" he growled.

The car rolled up in time to save any active unpleasantness.

"Say!" grumbled the taxi-man as we flocked toward it, "this ain't a omnibus."

"That's all right," I rejoined. "We'll fit in all right. George, you get in and let Maureen—Mary—sit on your knees. Daisy can sit on Slatter. Arrange yourselves."

Somehow, we squeezed in.

"Let her go," I said, slamming the door.

"Where to?" queried the driver.

"Just go," I snapped.

We went.

Chapter 26

My grandfather used to say, when in the throes of his rheumatism and casting his mind back to his courting days when the grass was damp, "Great oaks from little acorns grow." And I well remember my grandmother's description of the vagaries of life. "First it's one thing and then it's another, and something leads up to something else and this and that, and before you know where you are—there you are!" It is wonderful what trouble one's little mistakes will engender. The Creator carelessly leaves a speck of protoplasm on a quiet world, and, damn it all, there's Stanley! I do not usually make mistakes and I very seldom misunderstand people, but I had made a terrible mistake about Slatter—with Stanley's assistance.

We had stopped in a quiet street to allow of some readjustment of the passengers. Slatter had regained consciousness and objected to Daisy sitting on him, explaining that he had lost money that way before.

"I'm sure," I said, "that Mrs Slatter would never think of such a thing."

"'Oo?" said Woggo.

"Mrs Slatter!" giggled Steak. "Don't be scandalous!"

"You didn't get married to me while I was unconscious?" cried Woggo anxiously. 'You wouldn't do a dirty trick like that on a man!"

"Blow in your ear and wake yourself up," exclaimed Daisy contemptuously. "I wouldn't send in the coupon if you were a free sample. What put that horrible idea into your nut, Jack?"

"Stanley said—Hey, Stanley!" I growled, grasping him by the collar, "what made you tell that despicable lie?"

"You said that Maureen's brother, One-hit Mulligan was after me for tipping her out of the side-car, and tried to frighten me....."

"I haven't got a brother," interrupted Maureen.

"There you are!" cried Stanley gloatingly. "Who's a liar now?"

"Strikes me you both are," said George loftily. "Up at Split Rock..."

"Ah, don't give us any more about Split Rock," moaned Stanley.

"Tell me some more about Split Rock, dear," cooed Maureen, patting George's cheek.

"What did you run away for, that time at the races?" demanded Woggo gruffly. "And 'oo started the brilliant idea of chasin' me round and hittin' me on the face every time they seen me?"

"Now let's get this straight," said Stanley.

"You shut up," I snapped. "You've caused enough trouble. It's a pity you weren't born dumb."

" 'E was," put in Simpson sleepily.

"Now, first of all, Woggo," I said, "there was the incident at the races. I thought you were annoyed when you saw me cuddling Daisy, and you looked so belligerent that I thought it best to leave."

"I——"

"Wait a minute. Then you chased me. After that, you came round to my home and tried to waylay me. Then

Stanley took Maureen out in his motor-cycle and crashed with her. She came with you, Simpson, and Daisy to the house to get her revenge on the pair of us——"

"Revenge, nothing," interrupted Eggs. "You've got bees!"

"We were hiding in the wardrobe when you were in the room. I distinctly heard you say, 'We came here to get them, and we're going to get them.' "

"Me false teeth!" she shrieked. "Me false teeth, you fool! They got jolted into the side-car when we crashed. You don't think I'm going to pay nine guineas for a top set for Stanley to cart round in his side-car?"

"Well——" I mumbled, stroking my ear as I do when puzzled.

"Now, listen ter me," said Woggo, clutching at my tie and gazing earnestly into my face. "I done me roll on that ——Useless Annie. I comes up to the stand for the sole purpose of bitin' yer ear for a few quid, and yer bolts! 'Ow was I ter know y' was broke? I runs after yer and loses y' in the crowd. Daisy tells me that yer broke too, so I calls round to your joint later on ter see 'ow yer gettin' on and——"

" 'S all a mistake," interrupted Simpson. " 'S all a bloomy mistake. An' all I get out of it is a black eye. Look at it!"

"What a beaut!" exclaimed Stanley admiringly.

"Nobody 'it me, mind yer! Some dirty cow threw a chair."

"What a thing to do!" Stanley exclaimed.

"Yes. I wouldn't 'a' minded if it had been one o' them sorta brawls, but it was just a nice, quiet, fren'ly fight, an' open to everybody—an' the dirty cow must go an' throw a chair!"

"Well," said Steak, "are you all set now? I'm so dry I'm beginning to break out in little cracks. What about shaking hands all round and calling it a draw?"

"Good idea, my love," I agreed, leaning toward her.

"Shake, Rocky," said Woggo, offering his hand to George.

"You don't mind me left hand, Woggo, do you?" replied George, blushing.

"Of course he doesn't," put in Maureen, hurriedly.

They shook. We all shook.

"Have you finished?" inquired the driver sarcastically.

"On with the cattle-truck, slave," ordered Daisy.

"Home, James!" cried Stanley.

"Step on it, Comet."

"Look here!" he exclaimed angrily. "If you think you can pile into my car like it was an ambulance and insult me and——"

"Move yer cart along or I'll push yer face in," growled Woggo, sticking his chin out.

We moved.

"What's the name of that friend of yours?" inquired Steak.

"You don't mean Flannery?"

"That's him."

"Driver!"

"Oh, I know," he snapped. "No need to tell me."

I became silent after this. Steak sat on my knee, with her cheek against mine, and smoked. The rest talked. Wild talk, for the most part, like that which might have been heard in the inns of Port Royal when pirates forgathered to tell of bloodshed and pillage in the bad old days when rum was rum. George told tales of dreadful doings in Split Rock to Maureen who listened with the light of wonder in her eyes and the slump of utter boredom in her body.

Stanley listened to Slatter and Simpson, with his mouth open, like the little boy whose uncles have returned from the Barracoons with green parrots and knife wounds. They told of "dongings" of policemen, of the fight at the Butchers' Picnic at Neilsen Park, of raids escaped, and "good things" successfully negotiated.

They may have been bad company for the boy, but they were healthy. Time has shed a glow of romance over the old buccaneers, the pirates, the smugglers, the gamesters and the blades who ran each other through in a sporting spirit in the days that are dead. When our police administration has become so ineffective that there is no longer the lure of the spice of danger in crime, the bad men will die out, and future novelists will beguile our chinless descendants with tales of Benny the Blower, who blew the front out of the National Bank because he didn't like the architecture.

I fully realize, as a good citizen, that private property is sacred and that no man should be robbed except by the proper business methods, but somehow the sporting malefactors of this world appeal to me more as men than people like my rotten landlord, who goes to church on Sunday and has the damned hide to call for the rent on Monday.

The driver took advantage of our preoccupation and took us about eight miles farther than was necessary before he at last found Flannery's. I felt at peace with the world, otherwise I might have refused to pay him. But I am no man to muzzle the ox that treadeth out the corn.

Flannery was in bed with his wife, a toothache, and

other minor complaints but he came to the back door and let us in.

"Surprise party, Flannery!" I informed him.

"Is it going to be mugs?" he inquired testily.

I nodded.

"Well, I'm going to bed!"

"Be yourself, Flannery!" I protested. "A mug of whisky will banish your toothache and put you in good with the wife."

We got in after a little argument.

It was rather disappointing. Maureen whispered in horrified tones that she never touched it, and craved lemonade. George looked uncomfortable and said he'd have a lemonade too. Steak kicked Slatter on the leg and said that they very seldom drank but would have one weeney little one for friendship's sake. All this for Maureen's and George's benefit.

"George," I said, "take Mary down to our place and sit on the gas-box till we come."

Eagerly and obediently they left with their bottles of lemonade.

"Now then," I said, gazing around. "First of all, a mug of whisky for the taxi-driver, to mellow him."

"Don't want any," he replied curtly.

"Bowl him and hold him," said Stanley.

Woggo pushed him in the face, Stanley sat on his chest, Simpson held his legs and I held the mug.

"Will you accept my hospitality?" I asked.

"No, damn you!" he shouted.

"Not so loud!" whispered Flannery. "It's late!"

"Screw his ear," suggested Stanley.

Woggo screwed it. Simpson pinched his leg.

"All right," he muttered at last. "Let me up."

We allowed him to get up and stood around the bar and watched him sip it while we sipped our own.

He finished it in half an hour, and then stumbling to Woggo, leaned with both hands on his chest, and looking up into his eyes pleadingly, said "Bowl me again."

We put him out the side door and draped him over the radiator of his car where he would be warm.

"A man who gesh drunk li' that shouldn't be 'lowed to drive carsh," said Simpson.

We put him out alongside the taxi-driver.

" 'E 'ad a bit of a start on us at the Blue Garter," said Woggo, apologizing for his friend. "Is that Flannery's brother?" he asked, pointing to Flannery who had fallen asleep on the counter.

"Who?" asked Steak.

"The bloke sleepin' next to him."

Steak and I led him out and sat him in the taxi, and stood glumly on the pavement.

"Jack," she said, "this is very unsatisfactory. You ought to break open a shivoo."

"A party?"

"Absolutely. George can announce his engagement to Mary."

"You don't mean it," I gasped.

"It's a fact. Mary's never seen any one so soft in all her life and she's fallen for him. She likes him. Truly."

"Well I'll be damned—and so will George," I exclaimed.

"Mary's all right, Jack. What about a shivoo?"

"Righto," I sighed. "Tomorrow night."

I felt sorry for George.

We stood for a while in silence, facing each other.

I liked Daisy. I still like her.

"Well, I suppose we'd better break up," she sighed at last.

"What about George and Mary? Better go and get them."

"Oh, they'll last out the night on the gas-box. Don't worry them. What are you going to do?"

"Go home, I suppose."

She leaned against me and fumbled with the lobe of my ear. The wail of a steamer siren came floating eerily up from the distant harbour.

"Mary's lucky," she said softly.

I had nothing to say and didn't answer.

"Well," she said after a long pause, "better go."

She kissed me.

"It's too late to go. Come home with me," I said, feeling tired and miserable.

She patted my cheek.

"Sorry, honey," she said, "but I'm not....I suppose you've got your own little opinions, but I drink and smoke a bit and take what I can get. I have my fun but.... I like you, Jack. You understand, Jack?"

I nodded. My head was aching and the night air seemed to be cold.

"But you can't go home with them," I said listlessly, nodding toward the figures around the car. "Let me take you home. Here's a car now!"

I hailed it.

"Thanks, Jack I'll go by myself. I'd rather go by myself. I'm a bit ratty tonight, I suppose. Kiss me, Jack."

I kissed her, while the taxi-man opened the door.

"Good night, Syrup!" she called gaily.

I waved my little hat which after all *was* too small.

I watched the tail-light of the car dwindle away in the

distance, and then went home to bed. Stanley had gone home before me. Woggo, Simpson, and the taxi-driver would wake up in the morning and I left George and Mary whispering on the gas-box.

For a long time before I undressed I sat on the edge of my bed and nursed my aching head, and thought.

I'm getting no younger. A man has to face it sooner or later.

A man's a fool to drink mugs of whisky.

I'm old...

I wonder if Solomon sat on the edge of his bed when he said "All is vanity."

Chapter 27

When the day broke George was up to observe the fracture. Somewhere about 4 a.m. he came to my room and shook me. I could not, at the time, understand what he was saying but at last sleep ebbed reluctantly away, my eyelids came unglued, and I sat up.

"What's Stanley done now?" I inquired sleepily.

"Nothing. Come and see the sun rise, Jack."

"Where's it rising this morning?" I asked.

"Same place—what do you mean?"

"Go away," I growled. "A rising sun is nothing new to me. See one, you've seen the lot. I saw one years ago. It can rise without any help from me. If it can't let it sink."

I lay back and shut my eyes. I was so tired that I had almost fallen asleep when he spoke to me again.

"Jack," he whispered, "Mary and me are engaged."

"Who's the promoter?"

"Engaged to be married."

"Same thing. Don't come to me with your troubles. I warned you and you took no heed, so it serves you damn well right."

I kept my eyelids closed.

"I don't think I'm worthy of her, Jack."

"You needn't think you can get out of it that way," I muttered feebly. "You've done it now. I wish you'd go away. I thought I'd got you out of this Split Rock habit of getting up in the middle of the night practically, and stamping about the place like a wardsman in an Old Men's Home."

I dragged myself up to a sitting position again.

"I'm awake now, you fiend, if that's any consolation to you. Why the devil didn't you pick on Stanley? Strike me pink, you're childish! When Stanley was a baby he used to wake at this very hour every morning, and sit up and crow and 'Goo' and crawl all over me and put his foot in my mouth until I felt like sending him to an orphanage. Pity I didn't. Sunday morning, the only morning when I could lie in bed and read the paper, he'd wake an hour earlier. What the devil's wrong with you, man! Go to bed and stay there till you feel civilized."

"But, Jack, how can I stay in bed..." he paused. "Love's a funny thing," he said softly.

"Ah, go away!" I snorted disgustedly. "Love must be a blasted funny thing if it gets you up at four o'clock in the morning to come and sit on my bed looking like a sheep with rickets and complaining about your engagement."

"I'm not complaining. I'm glad!" he remonstrated.

"Be glad while you can," I replied wearily. "I'd like to see Eggs getting up at four o'clock in the morning."

"What do you call her Eggs for?"

"Because you don't see the yolk at first sight. Go away. Go and talk to Stanley. Talk to him about Estelle. Ask him to tell you what he knows about Eggs."

"I will," he replied, getting up from the bed. "I'd like to know how a bad-mannered old nark like you ever got to know her."

He shut the door and I punched a dent in my pillow and curled up again.

Bad-mannered old nark! I'd get even with him. There

are always plenty of ways to work off a grudge on a man who is getting married.

I remembered when I was coming out of the church with Agatha on my arm, after receiving my life sentence. The junior clerk from the office, who had tried to borrow a pound from me and failed, hit me fair in the back of the neck with an old boot. It had a hobnailed sole and was bought specially for the occasion. He then wished me all possible happiness, stressing the word "possible".

Thinking of my own wedding and Stanley's babyhood set my mind wandering along the cobwebbed years. I remembered the day we bought the furniture. And the day Stanley was born. I thought it was great, I remember. Went up to Flannery's and shouted all hands.

Haw! What a fool a man is! And yet—I had some good times with Agatha before Gertrude arrived on the scene. Married life is not so bad for a man with the right outlook on life. You need a sort of baggy-kneed temperament. I haven't got it. Very few have, but they either acquire it, or get divorced, or suicide.

My thoughts were becoming blurred and mingled with dozey dreams when the door flew open and Stanley burst into the room and pulled up against the bed.

"What's up!" I exclaimed.

"Look, dad! Look what that damned brother-in-law of yours did to me!"

I looked. His eye was swollen. The shades of eventide were drawing over it and it would soon be black.

"What did you get it for?"

"Nothing, dad!" he cried.

"Cheap," I said. "Sit on the bed and tell me all about it. I'm the target this morning, I can see. Spit it out."

"He came up to me and woke me as if I was a fowl

hanging back a bit on the perch. The sun's only just up! He started to talk and then asked me how we came to know Daisy and Mary, and asked me what I knew about his Mary."

"Yes."

"Well—I told him."

"*Hinc illae lacrimae*," I murmured.

"What's 'at?"

"Another name for a black eye. You may go now. If there are any more of the afflicted that want to sit on my bed, tell them to wait outside. I'm getting up now. Go and apologize to your Uncle George."

He went away, cursing.

I was staring at the bed-rail, thinking about getting up, when George entered with a cup of tea, a nobbler of rum, and a plate of prawns.

"Breakfast, Jack," he said, pulling a table up to the bed. "I'm sorry I said you were an old nark. Not cranky are you, Jack?"

"Go and apologize to Stanley," I said, peeling a prawn.

"I'm going to take him up some breakfast. I'm sorry. He's only a boy. I'll go and get him a piece of steak for his eye as soon as the butcher's is open. I'll apologize to him, too. I didn't think I hit him so hard—only a tap."

"All right. Where's the rest of the rum? I've drunk that sample you brought in."

He closed the door softly and lumbered back to the kitchen.

Wonderful, the difference a woman will make in a man. Poor George!

I imagined him apologizing to Stanley. And I thought of Stanley borrowing a few pounds from him on the strength of it.

At lunch-time I rose, bathed, dressed, and dined. There was much to be done. Stanley and George cleared away the dishes, I handed a pencil and a sheet of paper to Stanley and we seated ourselves.

"Now then," I said. "About this party."

"What party?" they queried.

"I'm giving a party tonight. Sort of reunion. I thought you knew about it. Steak is coming, and Slatter and the rest of them."

"Who else?" asked George.

Stanley reached for the telephone directory.

"We'll start from the A's," he said.

"We'll do nothing of the sort," I snapped. "I had a taste of your methods at our last party. This is *my* party, and it's going to be a quiet, respectable turn-out. George is going to announce his engagement to Mary."

"Aw, gee!" exclaimed George feebly.

"Now as regards the expenses," I continued, "I think we'd better share them."

"Oh, well it's *our* party," said Stanley.

I raised the eyebrow.

"I'll do the managing," I said quietly.

"The list of guests must be carefully compiled. We want no roughnecks—and none of the Boys," I said, glancing meaningly at Stanley. "Put these names down, Stanley. First of all, Steak and the gang—Flannery."

"Yes."

"Flannery's chucker-out, the two barmen and the girl from the private bar."

"Go on. This is going to be select, all right."

"The milkman—he kept up well last time—the postman, McLavish..."

"Who's McLavish?"

"He works at the bakery. He's Scotch, so they let him put the currants in the buns. Then we'd better invite Temple from next door. 'Hokum' Kennedy, he's the second-best poker player at the lodge, and...."

"Hold on," said Stanley. "Aren't there any women at all?"

"We-e-ell," I said, rubbing my ear, "the only women I know would charge a small fee for being present, unless—what about the taxi-driver?"

"Good," said Stanley. "He'll get some. Will two carloads be enough?"

"Hm. I suppose so. Put it down, anyhow. Two carloads of women."

"I don't think we need bother about all this," put in George. "What about the refreshments?"

"Ah!" said Stanley. "Five cases of lager, five..."

"Stop!" I cried, "I'll arrange about that with Flannery."

Stanley's ideas of hospitality belong to the days when they roasted whole bullocks on spits and the guests rode in in battalions with spurs on, and the villagers danced on the green. I'm not niggardly but at the same time I'm no feudal baron.

After long discussion we had our plans complete.

Stanley went out in the highways and the byways issuing oral invitations. George tidied the house and after cleaning the laundry laid down a few bags on the floor in case any of the guests should want to settle a dispute. I went into town and bought cigarettes and spittoons. Somehow, I could not feel enthusiastic about the party.

As a matter of fact, if Daisy had not mentioned it I would never have thought of it. I felt depressed. The old worries were returning like homing pigeons. Stanley; I had to start him off in life somehow. As for myself, I would have to go to work again soon—or perhaps I wouldn't. What did it matter? Then Agatha. Where would all that rotten business end? Misery piled upon me like compound interest. The bluer I got, the bluer I got.

As the afternoon wore on I tried to brighten up and smile but I felt like a washing-machine salesman knocking at his hundred and ninety-eighth door, and the nearest I could get to a smile was to pucker up the corners of my mouth and show my teeth.

The milkman, our first guest, rolled up at seven o'clock. He left his cart outside and turned the horse loose on the front lawn. He explained that he had to start work at an early hour in the morning and it would save him trouble to have his cart and horse handy.

There was room enough on the lawn for the horse to lie down, provided he lay down lengthways, so we threw a carpet over him and left him contentedly browsing.

Next came McLavish, looking eager but worn. Anticipating, he had not eaten during the day, and he offered me fourpence of the eightpence he had saved. The Scotch are a proud people and he did not wish to be under any obligation to us. We gave him a sandwich and something to drink and sat him on the gas-box to mind the horse until the rest of the guests arrived. Knees, chest and back, clad here and there in some pink curtain-looking stuff with beads on, arrived and was hailed loudly as Estelle and taken into the drawing-room.

George and I stood at the gate and waited long.

"Mary hasn't come yet," murmured George, peevishly.

"She'll come, if she has to do it on a stretcher," I assured him. "This is her last chance to retire from the ranks of the Gimmes, and she knows it."

"What do you mean?"

"See me in six months' time. Here comes somebody."

A Rolls-Royce guided by Woggo slid gently to the kerb, with eight men inside.

" 'Ow she go?" he called cheerily.

"All out!" he bawled to the other occupants. "Toss up to see 'oo takes the bus back."

"Take her back! What for?"

"We can't leave it here, Brains. S'posin' the owner seen it?"

There was a deal of grumbling.

"Aw'right," said Woggo. "Just run 'er up to the corner and leave 'er. Toss two at a time. The last bloke in, loses."

He strolled over to us.

"Brought along a few friends," he said. "All pretty 'andy with their mitts. Keep the party respectable. Decent mob, they are." He turned as a huge negro with a mouth like a squashed inner-tube and what looked like a tartan suit touched him on the elbow.

"Ah's been illuminated from de composition," he drawled.

"This is me sparrin' partner, Cocoa Collins," said Woggo. "One er the mob."

We passed him on to McLavish.

"This is Smacker," continued Woggo, as another of the eliminated ones strolled up. " 'E's a fireman at the Crematorium."

We shook hands and sent him in to Stanley.

"'E's the bloke wot invented the sayin', 'Do you know Fat Burns?' " whispered Woggo. "Very clever bloke but a 'orrible liar."

The car purred softly and swung out from the kerb.

"The little bloke what's drivin' the car is a bit of a

mug. 'E was a certainty to take the car back but 'e don't know it. Forgit 'is name. Y'know Dogsbody," he added as Simpson came to the gate in front of five more men. "The big bloke with the chewed ear is the ex-'eavyweight champeen of Tasmania," he continued, pointing them out one by one, "Bung Thomas, 'is name is."

"This is Mickey, the door-keeper at Watson's two-up school. 'E's only little but 'e's all there. The other three is Johnno, Corpsey, and Splinter. Preliminary boys. Ten rounders, and none of 'em work. Any'ow you'll know 'em all before the night's out."

"Glad to meet you, boys," I said. "George, go inside and give the boys a gargle."

"Where's Mary?" asked George dolefully.

"She's comin' with Daisy, later on. Gotter get 'er 'air curled or 'er face lifted, or somethink," put in Woggo. "'Ullo! 'Oo's this?"

"Carload, number one," I informed him.

Our taxi-driver honked loudly on his horn, and drew up at the gate.

"Seven," he called. "Back in ten minutes with another bunch."

"Sheilas!" gasped Woggo as the girls clambered out of the car.

"Take them inside and introduce yourselves," I said. "George, go inside and make them at home."

Flannery appeared, carrying two suit-cases.

"The boys are bringin' the rest," he panted, "and there's plenty more when that's gone. Let me in."

George came out again and peered up the street.

"Where's Mary?"

"She'll be here," I said patiently. "Go and start the gramophone."

He hovered about fretfully for a while and then went inside.

I heard a crash and the tinkle of falling glass; one of the dining-room windows. The party had started.

Temple leaned over his gate and waved both hands excitedly.

"She's gone out!" he shouted hoarsely. "Taken the kids with her!"

"Right inside," I directed, opening the gate.

Two men walked slowly past the house and then turned back.

"Is this the Gudgeons' place?" inquired the younger of the two.

I told him that it was.

"Is Stanley at home?"

"Stanley!" I yelled. "You're wanted!"

He came to the door with his sleeves rolled up and a corkscrew in his hand.

"Who wants me? Oh, it's you!" he cried, advancing. "Dad, this is Mr Wills of the *Daily Herald*."

"How do y'do," I said coldly as the young man put out his hand. This was the man who had dragged my name into print and notoriety.

"Mr Sloove," he said, indicating his companion. "Meet Mr Gudgeon. Mr Sloove is putting up for this district in the coming elections," he added.

"Come inside," invited Stanley.

They followed him into the house and collided with George coming out.

"Where's Mary?" he whined.

"Ar, go away!" I growled.

A touring-car, with Maureen and Daisy in the back seat, rounded the corner.

"Mary!" bawled George. "Mary!" he bleated, and started to climb the fence.

"You'll find it easier to use the gate," I advised him, "or wait till she gets here."

The car pulled up as he leapt the fence. Mary stepped out and was engulfed, and I hastened to welcome Daisy.

"Step right inside, driver," she said. "Hello, Sweetness!" she cried, turning to me. "How's the body?"

"Come inside," I said. "Leave those fools to fate and the horse."

I conducted her through the hallway.

Inside, the folding doors which separated the bedroom from the dining-room had been wrenched off their hinges by the heavyweight champion of Tasmania. There was nothing wrong with the doors only they wouldn't fold, and although it seemed a drastic method of securing additional space, it was necessary. Most of the guests were sitting on the floor and the place looked like the steerage of a coolie migrant ship. The taxi-driver's girls were quite at home. One of them was playing the piano I had bought for Stanley—he had learnt a few scales on it and then decided that music was not in his line—while she played, another one of the carload did a new sort of step on the top of it.

"They haven't warmed up yet," said Daisy, surveying the scene with an expert eye. "What they want is an excuse to start warming. I know all about parties. Better let George make his announcement now. That'll be a start."

While I was looking for George and Mary, the taxi-driver landed his second consignment, and Flannery's staff entered with more suit-cases.

George and Mary were sitting on the wash-tubs in the laundry.

"Come out of that," I commanded. "This is where you make your first false step in public, George. Take Mary inside and tell the company you've been trapped."

"Aw...crickey! Jack...."

"Go on!" I urged. "Drag him in, Mary! You roped him, don't let him get away unbranded."

Mary dragged him in. I heard him painfully stuttering, "Ladies and gentlemen," and a silence descended on the assembly.

I walked out into the back-yard.

Cheering and stamping, mingled with a little hissing and hooting told me that George had made the announcement and I hurried in to drink the fool's health. Woggo was proposing the toast.

"Well," he said. "This is the first time I ever seen a bloke slip and then come and skite about it. 'Owever, I wishes the pair of 'em good luck fer as long as they can stand each other. I dare say if Split Rock passes Mary a belt in the face every time she comes 'ome after midnight —things'll be pretty jake. 'Ere's luck. You'll need it."

A moment's silence, and then the party broke out. Somewhere a ukulele thrummed. The Boys had got in despite my precautions.

Estelle plonked a few notes on her banjo. One of the carload spread herself out in front of the piano. The milkman got out his saxophone, and hell broke loose to the tune of "I got 'em—She's lost 'em".

The party had been going an hour when I strolled to the front door to see if the police were about. Someone standing outside the gate called me. It was Agatha.

"It's me, Jack," she said.

"Oh, it's you!" I replied. It was one of the rare

occasions when I have been lost for words.

I went to the gate and we looked at each other for a while.

"I just thought I'd come along and see you," she said hesitatingly. "I didn't know....I didn't think....is it a party?"

"Stanley's," I said, delving for my pipe. My fingers were shaking. She picked a flake of paint off the gate and crumbled it.

"Looks like rain," I said.

She looked up. "Yes. Doesn't it?"

At last I found my tobacco-pouch. It was empty.

"Well, I suppose I'd better be going," she sighed, fooling around with her gloves.

"What did you want to see me for?" I asked after another pause.

"Oh...well...nothing, Jack. It doesn't matter now. Are you keeping well? You look thinner."

I opened the gate.

"Come inside and sit on the gas-box for a while."

"I think I'd better go, Jack."

I pulled her inside and shut the gate. We sat on the gas-box and she cried on my new suit. Between sobs, she told me her troubles. She had had a row with her mother and Gertrude. They had said some dreadful things about me—and it wasn't true—she knew it wasn't true. She had left the place. She hated Gertrude. She hated everybody.

"Oh...Jack!" she sobbed.

I put my arm around her. After all is said and done, it's nice to put your arm around the same old waist—after a holiday away from it; and to find when you kiss that you get quite a kick out of it.

Funny thing, married life. You get to know each other.

For instance, Agatha has a mole on her left hip. I hoped that it was still there. I earnestly hoped that it was still there. Looking at that mole, I could say, "There's Agatha. That's my wife."

Then again, she has a funny little habit of wrinkling up her forehead before she smiles. Of course, any one who isn't married wouldn't understand. There are little mannerisms and tricks of speech that one gets used to. They become part of your life, somehow. Queer. It's hard to explain....

After about an hour we went inside. No one noticed us. They were playing Postman's Knock. They had to run three games at once because it was so long between knocks. Flannery had brought up the reserves.

I had a look round for Stanley but he had disappeared.

We were sitting in a little space on the floor near the piano when Daisy found us.

"Hullo, Johnny! Who's the lady friend?" she asked, pointing a sandwich at me accusingly.

"Squeeze in next to us if you can," I said, "and meet the wife."

"I think we've met before," said Daisy doubtfully.

"Do sit down, Miss—er——"

"Slatter, is the lady's name, Agatha."

There was no fight. They just sat together and talked. That's the sort of woman Daisy was. Hard as nails, a woman of the world, and a good sport. She had tact. It is the tactful ones of the earth who keep it from flying apart.

Woggo came and stood over us.

"This 'ere Postman's Knock game gets on my nerves," he growled.

"It'll peter out presently," I said, "then you can start something."

"If it doesn't peter, it'll pall," said Agatha.

She was trying her best to enter into the spirit of the party, but I didn't see why she should drag the Apostles into it. Gradually we gathered a little party of our own around us. George and Mary came and sat opposite us. Bung Thomas, the Tasmanian champion, squatted with his back against the piano. McLavish came stumbling over the almost countless legs of the guests with a small keg of beer clasped to his chest.

"All the sensible people are here," he grunted, dumping it on the floor, "and it's here that I'll stay, and did y' see that feller Simpson? What's the matter with the puir chap?"

"Yes," put in George, "he looks sick."

"He's sober," explained Woggo. "First time for three years. Been savin' his thirst for tonight. 'E'll be all right presently. 'Ere's Smacker."

Smacker leaned across George and whispered huskily to Woggo. "Cocoa Collins just threw three young fellers over the next-door fence because they arst 'im if 'e was black all over. 'E's gettin' a bit out of 'and."

Woggo turned to the ex-champion. "Bung, go and bowl 'im and chuck 'im out."

"Will one be enough, do y' think?" queried Smacker. " 'E's pretty wild."

"Stand outer the way," growled the big man. " 'E's a lime soda for me. Jammed in between two lions, 'e wouldn't make a decent sandwich for me."

"Cocoa goes like that when 'e's elephants," explained Woggo. "We gen'rally dongs 'im and chucks 'im out."

"Elephants?" queried Agatha in a puzzled voice.

"Elephant's trunk," said Steak.

"Drunk, missus," explained Woggo, "only we don't

mention it in front of ladies."

It is a little humiliating to have one's wife display her ignorance in public, but I said nothing to Agatha. She always was like that.

It was becoming difficult to converse without shouting, and the noise was increasing every minute. Smacker and Bung returned quietly and announced that the negro had been thrown out on the footpath and that the milkman's horse was sound asleep.

"Sleepin' like a little baby," said Smacker, "and talkin' of babies reminds me of the time I was firin' on the *Homostole* before I signed on at the Crematorium."

He squatted down next to us.

"I just come off watch and I'm leanin' over the rail talkin' to the bosun."

"I told yer 'e was a liar," whispered Slatter, warningly.

"And while I'm talkin' to 'im, 'e starts cryin'. I says, 'Wot's the matter, Bill?'—Bill, we useter call 'im—and 'e tells me. It appears when 'e got 'ome trip before last, 'e found 'e'ad a little son and 'is wife dunno wot to call it. So 'e says, call it Arethusa after the ship 'e was a 'prentice on, and when the christenin' party is on, and Bill cracks the bottle of champagne over the baby's forehead, the poor kid rolls over bows first, and sinks. Snuffs it. 'E was that cut up, I felt sorry for 'im, but all the same, the kid couldn't 'a' been too strong in the first place, and wot I says is——"

"Sing us a song, George," interrupted Slatter in a disgusted tone.

"Oo, yes, George!" cried Mary. "Do sing. I didn't know you could sing."

"Neither does anyone else," I remarked.

"Go on, George!"

"Aw, don't be silly!" gasped George.

"Mary, make him sing," said Steak. "Make him recite 'Gunga Din' or something."

"I can't sing and I can't recite," gabbled George, growing panicky. "But I'll tell you what I'll do," he added brightly, "I'll show you the muscles on me back."

Feverishly he peeled off his shirt.

"Isn't he lovely?" said Mary.

"Put yer shirt on, quick!" growled Woggo. "The mob'll think y' want to start something."

"I think," muttered McLavish, "I think—I think I'll start the gramophone."

He kicked the empty keg away and stumbled off.

We had just rearranged ourselves when he returned.

"They won't let me have the gramophone," he growled sullenly.

" 'Oo won't let yer 'ave it?" asked the heavyweight.

McLavish pointed solemnly into the crowd.

"Them."

"Come with me."

"There'll be a fight 'ere before long," said Smacker as the pair wandered away together.

"I suppose so," agreed Woggo, taking off his coat.

"Oh, Jack! Don't let them fight!" pleaded Agatha.

"All right," I assured her. "I'll stop them. Wait for me, Woggo. Coming, George?"

George dragged himself unwillingly to his feet and we picked our way through the crowd. I had expected a fight. It is my opinion that if there is no fight at a party, the party isn't a success. Parties have degenerated these days. The old time shivoos and picnics where there was tea and scandal for the women, and ginger-beer and sticky toffee for the kids, and beer and fights for the men, were better than the modern version. In those days, the young man who didn't come to work on Monday morning with either a black eye or a headache, must have spent the week-end in jail or in bed. A fight livens up the evening and weeds out the undesirables, and if modern hostesses only had the enterprise to arrange a brawl among the guests, the present boredom of the social round would not exist.

It was not much of a fight, being practically finished at the end of five minutes, but the gramophone was torn in halves during the struggle and a few of the girls got trampled on. Three men including McLavish were knocked out and were subsequently stacked in the laundry to regain consciousness. I went back to where I had left Agatha to tell her about the fight being only a trivial disagreement, but she had gone. Stanley caught hold of me as I was going upstairs to look for her.

"Gee, dad! You've had a narrow escape!" he whispered hoarsely.

"Oh, it never had any glass in it," I replied, referring to the picture-frame someone had hit me with.

"I don't mean that," he said impatiently. "I've just got you out of a lot of trouble, and you can thank me and the Boys for it."

"Thanks," I said. "What was the trouble?"

"Why, ma was here! Sitting next to the piano as large as life!"

"I——"

"It's all right, dad. She's gone now. I asked her to come outside and I and the Boys helped her into a car and Fussy's driving her back to Chatswood. Didn't want to go either!"

"Damn it all!" I roared. "Who's Fussy?"

"One of the Boys."

"Spare me days!" I yelled. "What have you done now. I invited your mother in here!"

"Ar," he grumbled disgustedly. "Call yourself a father! Here I go and do you a good turn and go to a lot of trouble—what with ma struggling and all that—and all I get for it is abuse."

I sat down on the bottom step of the stairs and sighed.

"I thought I was doing the right thing, dad," he protested.

"All right, son. All right. I suppose you meant well. Leave me now."

He brushed past me and ascended the stairs. Had I known what his crowning act of the night was to be I would have felled him with a blow and requested his deportation of the government. As it was, I just cupped my chin in my hands and thought. Fate pokes its stubby interfering finger into everything. I have lived a full life and I have learnt that it is useless to protest. Things will happen. Man, rough-hewing his destiny with the blunt axe of Reason, sees the head fly off his axe and his destiny bashed into a shapeless lump. When this happens a few times, as it has happened to me, one feels inclined to drop the axe, sit on a log, and say to Fate: "Hew it yourself."

During the hour prior to her enforced departure I had made up my mind to forgive Agatha and take her back. She had returned to me chastened, submissive, and repentant; with those qualities renewed which I had once admired. When a man has been married for twenty years and is past the forty mark he cannot afford to lose his wife. Wireless sets, footwarmers, and a seat on the club committee are not enough and, furthermore, if he has been able to tolerate the woman for twenty years, he may as well see it out to the bitter end. It was only in the last two or three days that I had begun to realize how I missed Agatha. For instance, she always knew where I had left my pipe and somehow or other she could always find my studs. During the whole period of her absence I hadn't had a decent bowl of pea-soup. Just when I realized my necessity, she came back.

And just as she came back, Fate had stepped in and taken her away again. I wondered why Fate seemed to inhabit Stanley's body almost continuously.

The party had quietened down considerably. There was a strip-poker party in the dining-room and a drinking party in the bedroom adjoining. Couples whispered here and there in corners, a few stupid ones sang determinedly around the piano and the weaker vessels slept and mumbled in strange attitudes. I strolled past the strip-poker table, noticing as I passed that most of the girls evidently could not play poker and that Smacker was sitting behind a routine flush. I watched him see a bet of one camisole and raise it a pair of suspenders and a singlet, and then joined the other party.

I found myself a couple of bottles of whisky and sat down. "You're not going to drink that on your own?" exclaimed Temple, who was lying on the floor next to me with his head propped up on his elbow.

"There's plenty over there for you," I replied, pointing to the stack.

"But, man, you'll kill yourself!"

"I'm not worrying about that," I said, putting the bottle to my mouth.

"He's drinking it out of the bottle!" he shouted to the company.

"Etiquette, mon!" said McLavish, shaking his finger at me.

" 'Member yer etti-hic!"

"Leave 'im alone," growled Woggo, thickly.

"Am I to sit here and watch a man drink himself to death!" shouted Temple. "I say nothing against a man drinking, but to drink like that...I regard it as my duty and as the duty of all of you, to stop this man, in his own interests."

"Talk sense!"

"I am talking sense. It is for his own good and the good of those associated with him. I've seen this man, Gudgeon, chasing his own son all over the roof of this very house with a meat-chopper."

"Was 'e drunk?" inquired Woggo.

"Of course he was!"

"Well, there may be something in wot you say. P'raps if 'e hadn't been drunk 'e might've caught 'im."

"Why, you're drunk yourself!" cried Temple. "You're all drunk. Mr Sloove," he said, pointing to the politician, "and myself are the only two sober men here!"

"Bung," said Woggo, nudging the heavyweight. "Bowl 'im and stack 'im."

Bung Thomas rose unsteadily to his feet and rolled toward Temple.

"Erpologize, or I'll breathe on yer," he growled.

Temple mumbled a sullen apology and subsided, glaring at me.

"Gentlemen," announced Mr Sloove. "Mr Temple has just mentioned my name to you and accused me of being sober. I must admit the charge while not agreeing with his opinions of our worthy host."

I bowed as well as I could, lying on the floor.

"As a matter of fact," he continued, "my presence here tonight is mainly due to my young friend from the *Daily Herald*, Mr Wills. Knowing that Mr Gudgeon is a gentleman well liked and respected in the locality, and an old resident of the district, I thought to seize the opportunity of combining business with pleasure by addressing a few remarks——"

"Siddown!"

"I will not weary you with——"

"Chuck 'im out!"

"Briefly, the position——"

Woggo rose to his feet.

"Bung," he called.

Mr Sloove sat down.

"Yes, Corpsey? Wot do you want?" said Slatter belligerently as a head poked around the door.

"Sling me a coupla them sheets," said Corpsey, nodding toward the bed.

The sheets were passed out and presently he appeared among us wrapped up like a Roman emperor.

"Toughest game I ever played in," he muttered, dragging the rest of the bedclothes off the bed. "If Smacker was playing poker in Klondike 'e'd 'ave been shot as soon as he shuffled."

He threw the bedclothes into the adjoining room.

"Give one of them sheets to the fair 'aired sheila," he cried. "She's got a cold."

Another loser strolled in, barefooted and holding his trousers up, and brought his banjo with him. McLavish sang "Annie Laurie" and cried bitterly. The milkman sang "The Star Spangled Banner", "O Heart Bowed Down", "Paddy McGinty's Goat", finished up with a little yodelling, and then went to sleep. We had "Sweet

Adeline" three or four times and we were all feeling pleasantly sad and comradely when Mr Sloove rose for the second time. His face was flushed and he mounted the only chair in the room and stood swaying uncertainly.

"Gentlemen," he said, speaking with painstaking distinctness, "with Mr Gudgeon's permission and in the distinguished presence of Mr Bung Thomas, the greatest heavyweight Tasmania has ever produced, and also that well-known sporting man, Mr Woggo Slatter, I would like to say a few words."

" 'Ear! 'Ear!" cried Thomas and Slatter.

"Our respected friend, Mr Temple, who has just been carried outside, saw fit to make a few remarks with which I entirely disagree. It is on the subject of drink and drinkers that I wish to speak."

At this moment Simpson came swaying happily into the room and collapsed beside me.

"Don't make a noise," I whispered. "We're having a speech. Where have you been?"

"Owside with horsh," he gurgled. "Like horsh. Had a horsh once."

"Sh-hh!"

Mr Sloove seemed to have captured the interest of the assembly.

"Of course," he was saying, "there are people who will never drink. Subnormal freaks, or misguided in their early youth."

Stanley came in.

"Dad," he whispered.

"Hush!"

"But, dad——"

"Shut up!"

"There are others who may be converted," continued

Mr Sloove. "I have to my eternal credit one outstanding case. He was a miserable man for whom life held but little interest——"

"Dad!"

"Will you be silent!" I hissed at him. "Have you no manners——"

"But it's important——"

"Go away from me," I cried, pushing him away. "I'm sick of the sight of you. I don't care what you've got to say, I don't want to hear it."

He slouched out of the room, mumbling as usual.

"...Taciturn and morose, he was," continued the speaker. "Wrapped in his petty ideas of life and pleasure. In fact, gentlemen, he had never had a proper drink in his life."

There was a mutter of amazement from the audience. I noticed the young man from the *Daily Herald* taking shorthand notes.

(Our party was described as an orgy and a saturnalia in the next evening's paper. The hound! I got a copy of Mr Sloove's speech from him, though. Best speech I ever heard.)

"I persuaded this man," continued Sloove, "to taste —just taste my fine old brandy, two cases of which comprised my late father's estate. He was run over by a bus and couldn't finish it. He died a broken-hearted man. Sometimes I think he haunts the cellar—spirit calling to spirit—but I digress.

"I offered this poor, water-logged waif the brandy.

"He smelt it. He sipped it. He sipped again, eagerly. He tossed it off. Then turning to me, he clasped my hand, a look of reverent wonder in his eyes. 'To think . . .' he said, 'all these years. And I never knew. I never knew!... *Fill it up again!*"

A burst of cheers awoke Simpson, who started to clap.

Stanley came in.

"Now, any night, I can go to his flat and find him lying under the table—happy."

The speaker waved his hand.

"Alcohol! The last gift of the relenting gods. The simple word that makes life's crossword puzzle easier to elucidate."

"Listen, Stanley," I said. "If you come near me again, I'll brain you."

"But, dad, the——"

"Ord'r!" growled Woggo.

Bung Thomas glared meaningly at Stanley who went into a far corner of the room and stood there making unintelligible signs to me. Mr Sloove was holding a glass of lager out before him.

"How many paltry figures have ranted against it, shrieked their censure," he cried, "and faded back to the earth from which they come—to fertilize the vines."

"Gaze on your glass of beer."

We gazed.

"See how the lambent, lazy bubbles drift to the top, as men drift through life; linger a while in the froth, and burst of old age, or are cut off in their prime in Fate's thirsty gulp. This scourge, this shame, this liquid degradation—what is it?"

" 'Ere!" protested Simpson, angrily.

"It links the extremes of mankind in one common friendly girdle. The labourer disturbing the rocks of ages with his pick, and Shakespeare in his favourite inn—and Attila, the Scourge of God, who died of too much mead."

"What's this mead? Where c'n it be got?"

"Look here, Simpson," I whispered. "Don't interrupt again. This man's a genius. Listen to him."

"Noah," shouted Sloove, "the greatest navigator of all times; cooped in the ark with his relations and a lot of other wild animals, drifting in a landless world. Chosen from countless teetotallers drowned in their favourite drink; he landed at last on the lonely peak of Ararat. When the awful responsibility of beginning a new world had eased—what happened?"

Woggo shook his head vigorously.

"The Bible says that his son found him lying in the vineyard, his back teeth awash and a happy, boozed smile on his face."

Stanley had sidled up to me and touched me on the shoulder. I quelled him with a look.

"Scots!"

McLavish looked up.

"Behold your Bobbie Burns. He died. Certainly, who doesn't? He drank himself to death! What of it? For every man who dies of drink, a thousand die of dinner-distended stomachs. Ask the man who owns one."

"What the hell are you looking at me for?" I demanded, as Stanley eyed my vest with a silly grin on his face.

"Aw, nothing. Listen."

"Says the earnest reformer," continued Sloove, "supposing that, instead of drinking whisky, you drank milk. Look at the benefits to your health, your pocket, and the race in general. Against this horrible suggestion there is, thank heaven, a stone-wall fact, a gesture in granite, one great unshakable answer, 'I don't like milk.'

"It is an axiom of economists that supply follows demand like the blood follows a punch on the nose. We want beer. Therefore there is beer. Peer into the murky mystery of your orange phosphate. What do you see? A chemical laboratory. A bit of this being added, a bit of that tipped in. And in the translucent depths of booze? Hop-fields, rippling acres of barley, and whistling boys in the sunshine, picking grapes. You would have me drink this coloured eye-lotion? Consider, then, this awful possibility.

"Two old friends meet.

" 'Bill! Why, you old son of a gun!'

" 'Where've you been? Haven't seen you for years!'

"A moment of happy grins, of surging happy memories, of hand-shakes truly meant.

" 'Well—well—well!'

"Glad. Awkward. Lost for words.

" 'Come and have an *orangeade*!' "

He paused, while a wave of horror swept over the company.

"I *ask* you!" he exclaimed passionately.

Stanley sprang to his feet and took advantage of the momentary silence.

"Gentlemen!" he yelled. "I have a very important announcement to make...."

I hurled myself at him and grabbed him by the throat.

"Out!" I shouted, pushing him towards the door.

" 'Ear! 'Ear!" cried Woggo. "If yer interrupt again Bung'll bowl yer. Won't yer, Bung?"

"Too right, I will," muttered Bung, savagely. "'E's spoilin' a good speech."

I returned to my seat on the floor.

Sloove cleared his throat.

"Alcohol is a necessity," he said. "The craving for food is recognized as legitimate, even though the rabid vegetarian seeks to snatch the chop from his brother's mouth. Yet I am asked to satisfy my desire for a drink with water! Water! Empty jam-tins are all right for goats but a hungry dog wants meat. We are but dust, add water and we are mud.

"Why, when the world was first made it was all water, until the mistake was seen and rectified, and land made available for hop-growing."

"A course," agreed Simpson.

"I don't want to disparage water. It is an excellent medium for sailing boats in, washing, cooking, and irrigation. It is an ingredient of most liquors. But to drink it in its raw state! Watch a drinking fountain in Pitt Street. You'll stand for hours and see it undisturbed, save for the mooning messenger boy who stamps on the button to see the water squirt."

Stanley had come in again and was standing next to me fidgeting nervously with his fingers.

"As to those who have tasted liquor and liked it not, well, they do exist; but about them we need not bother. They are akin to the horse that drinks water and the calf that guzzles milk. Evolution will weed them out. Lack of the booze taste is lack of virility and they cannot survive. Is there any more expressive word in our language than 'Milksop'? And what is it but a weak sopper of milk, a lemonade lapper, a cocoa gargler?

" 'Yo! Ho! And a bottle of Raspberry!' Absurd, isn't it?"

"My oath, it is."

"Despite our modern education there are fools who have never tasted drink, lunatics who have, and don't like it, and plague-spots—positive menaces—who seek to abolish it!"

There was a general movement of uneasiness.

"Ah, friends. If you would learn, come with me beneath the bough. I'll bring the bread and the thou. I can't bear all the expense. We shall transform that wilderness and people it with pink lizards and blue monkeys with hats on. Be saved while the thirst is still on you and you shall have access to a land where every prospect pleases, and only closing time is vile.

"And I—when I have sunk my last pot, when my foot no more rests on the rail, and old Time calls, 'Six o'clock, sir!' then carry me to the strains of the Little Brown Jug and lay me on my bier...'And in a winding-sheet of vine-leaf wrapt, so bury me by some sweet garden-side.'

"Till then...Here's luck!"

There was a moment's silence, a silence that was only marred by a curious sound coming from somewhere upstairs. Then suddenly the assembly burst into a roar of delighted applause. They stamped their feet, whistled piercingly, and cheered and clapped.

Mr Sloove smiled, and attempting to bow, fell off the chair. There were a dozen hands to help him rise.

"Dad!"

"Well, what is it?" I snapped.

"The house is on fire."

"Eh!"

"Upstairs, dad. I was showing Estelle my photograph album up in my room and I must have dropped a cigarette on the bed. We were so busy looking at the album and all that, I didn't notice——"

I pushed him aside and elbowed my way through the crowd to the foot of the stairs. A long arm of black smoke stretched lazily down to me as I stood gazing up, and a belch of flame showed for an instant on the upper landing. It dawned on me that I had heard this crackling noise fully a quarter of an hour ago, I had smelt this odour of things burning and attached no importance to it. I had seen the wisps of smoke crawling along the ceiling and had thought it to be just more tobacco-smoke with which the lower part of the house was hazy.

Someone called me and I returned to the bedroom. Slatter handed me a glass of wine.

"Drink this to the 'ealth of Mr Sloove," he cried, slapping me on the back. I raised my glass and drank with the rest to Mr Sloove's very good health. Then I raised both arms above my head and called for silence.

"Gentlemen," I said. "It is my unpleasant duty to inform you that the party must terminate at once. The upper portion of the house is on fire, but please do not rush away. There are a number of our friends asleep in these two rooms and I would like you to carry outside those who are incapable of walking and wake the others. Thank you, gentlemen."

For a few seconds they hesitated, on the verge of panic, until the harsh voice of Woggo Slatter brought them to their senses.

"Any one wot tries to bunk out the door gets donged by Bung. Don't 'e, Bung?"

"Too right, 'e does."

"Each bloke will carry a body with 'im as 'e goes out and it wouldn't be a bad idea if 'e took a bottle or two with 'im as well. We can't let everything burn."

There was a rush to secure the stricken ones.

"Smacker!" shouted Woggo. "Go out to the laundry and see if there is anybody there that ain't recovered yet. "If there is, lump 'em out."

"Aye, aye, sir!"

Like the captain of a sinking ship, I waited till all the

rest had gone and then, in a dazed condition, walked slowly out.

I remember I locked the front door and put the key under the mat.

I felt ill. About fifty of the guests were sitting in a row on the kerb on the opposite side of the road, chatting excitedly, and as I turned from the door and made toward the gate they fell silent and each one of them stared at me curiously. I felt like some great tragedian walking on before a hushed and crowded house. A crowd of spectators was gathering quickly and the windows and balconies of the opposite terrace were festooned with faces.

The crowd on the kerb cleared a little space for me and I sat down. I heard dimly a quick patter of footsteps coming along the road, I felt the crowd give way and step aside, and then Agatha flung herself down beside me, with her arms about my neck.

"Johnny! Johnny! What have they done?"

I tried to push her away.

"Leave me alone," I muttered.

"They carried me out of the house—they took me away—my own son—and now the house is on fire. Oh! My poor Johnny!"

Woggo patted her gently on the arm.

"Don't worry 'im. 'E looks as if 'e's sick. Sit quiet."

I felt her arm tense about my shoulders.

"Is everyone out of the house, Jack?" she whispered tremulously.

I staggered to my feet and gazed around while she stood beside me and supported me.

"Where's George and Mary?" she cried.

George and Mary were not there.

"I'll go and look for them," I said.

"I'll go," growled Woggo.

"*I'll* go," I replied shortly and, crossing the road, entered the house. A cloud of dense smoke rolled over me as I opened the door and I clung weakly to the door handle before going in.

I felt feeble and ill and my knees seemed as if they were no longer dependable.

"George!" I called. "George!"

I made my way into the dining-room and the smoke curled around me as I opened the door. George and Mary were sitting in the little corner the piano made with the wall. George was nursing her and their faces were close together.

I shook him by the shoulder.

"What's the matter?" he snapped gruffly.

"The house is on fire."

"Well, why didn't you tell us before!" he muttered peevishly.

He kissed Mary on the forehead.

"We'll have to go, love," he crooned.

"Oh, George! Must we?"

I got them out at last.

Stanley met me at the gate.

"What a gorgeous blaze, dad!" he exclaimed enthusiastically. "The whole top of the house is alight."

I tottered on past him and he followed me.

"Gee! There's ma back again! Can you beat it!"

He dodged away and stood by Slatter and I called out to them.

"Slatter," I said wearily, "why doesn't the fire brigade come?"

"Gee, I never thought of that!" exclaimed Stanley. "I'll go and put in an alarm now."

He gazed around excitedly and then spying the milkman's horse, stamping nervously near by, he bounded to it, leapt on its back, and clattered up the roadway, shouting "Fire! Fire!" in a voice of hilarious enjoyment.

I staggered back to my seat beside Agatha.

"Hadn't we better try to save something while there's still time?" she asked anxiously. "There are plenty of men here."

"Let it burn," I replied. "It's all insured."

I did not discover until later that the policy had lapsed and forfeited its usefulness for want of monetary encouragement.

The faces around me were lit up by the rosy glow of the burning house. Cracklings and loud reports, showers of sparks and wreaths of cavorting smoke issued from the dully roaring flames. A window burst outwards and the glass tinkled across the road. A piece of it lodged at my feet and I picked it up. It was hot.

Three fire-engines swept, clanging, around Flannery's corner and scattered us from the kerb. Brass helmets glistened, orders were shouted, the quick pulsing of the pump motors set up their rhythmic throb and the first jet of water burst spitting from the nozzle and hissed through a flame-lit window.

"Get back there! Right back!" shouted a policeman.

We crowded back on to the verandas of the opposite terrace.

"You too!" he commanded, pushing Stanley in the chest.

Stanley edged back reluctantly and stood beside me on the veranda.

"Clothed in a little brief authority," he shouted bitterly. "It's coming to something when a man can't look at his own fire that he started himself."

Five jets were playing on the front of the house. The wet street glistened and the gutters gurgled with a burden of water. Lines of bloated hoses sprawled across the roadway like great, grey, torpid snakes. The smoke rolled above the house-tops and screened the moon.

"Looks as if they're too late to save the joint," said Woggo, who was standing behind me. "The roof'll go any minute now."

"The balcony will come down before the roof," said Stanley.

"I'll bet it don't!"

"What'll you bet?"

"I'll bet two to one on the roof," snapped Slatter.

"You're on!" said Stanley eagerly. "Ten pounds to five."

"Put yer money up—give it to yer father."

They handed me the money.

"Roof's a certainty," said Woggo gloatingly. "Yer throwin' yer money away."

"Oh, am I! Look at that balcony. There's only one wooden joist that's not burnt through. The balcony will romp home!"

"We'll see," grumbled Woggo, gazing tensely at the roof.

Stanley patted me on the head.

"Hang on to that money, dad. I'll be back presently."

"Where's 'e going?" queried Slatter, his gaze still fixed on the roof.

I sat down. I was too weak to stand. Little bright specks danced before my eyes when I closed them. I was shivering continuously and my hands shook so that I could scarcely hold the glass that Simpson offered me.

Agatha found me and sat next to me.

"I've been talking to George," she whispered. "He's going to take you to a little ham and beef shop in the suburbs. Isn't he a dear?"

I nodded feebly.

"Mary and he will be married as soon as they can arrange it and George is going back to his farm. They'll spend their honeymoon on the farm. Won't that be lovely?"

Mary, the Gimme! On a farm!

"Don't look so dreadful, Jack. Try to cheer up, there's a good boy. Things could be worse. When we get the ham and beef shop we can be together—what are you trembling for?"

"I'm not well," I moaned.

She rambled on. Trying to cheer me, I suppose.

I seemed to be sliding into unconsciousness when Stanley put his foot on my hand and stepped on to the veranda.

"Har!" exulted Woggo. "Now wot d'yer think of yer chances?"

"I'm game to double the bet," replied Stanley coldly.

"Give it to yer father."

More money changed hands.

I gazed once again on the fire. The roof was shot through with flames. The upper floor had burnt through and fallen, and the balcony was a centre of flame. A fireman on a ladder was pouring water on to the roof. As I watched, the back wall of the house crashed inwards and the roof subsided a foot.

"Roof!" shouted Woggo.

The balcony cracked ominously and leaned outwards.

"Balcony! You beauty!" shrieked Stanley.

"Roof! Roof! Roof!" roared Slatter.

"Balcony! Balcony! Come on, balcony!" screamed Stanley, jumping up and down.

"Roof! Roof! She wins!" bawled Woggo as the roof tottered before its downfall.

The roof hung. Both of them were silent, staring intently into the flames.

"Balcony! Balcony! Balc—balc—balc—balcony! *She's home!*"

Crash went the balcony. The roof disappeared with a roar and in a storm of sparks.

"Beaten by a—neck!" cursed Slatter.

"It was fair, wasn't it!" demanded Stanley.

"Ar, yes. I ain't whinin'. You'll 'ave to lend me me fare 'ome, but."

"That's all right. Give me the money, dad."

I felt in my pockets. It was gone.

"It was in my pocket a minute ago," I mumbled. "Simpson will tell you that."

"Simpson's not here!"

"Ar, well that's where it's gone," chuckled Woggo. "'Ard luck, son."

"Stone the crows!" stormed Stanley. "What——"

"Stanley!" snapped Agatha. "Not another word out of you!"

He mumbled viciously. "How am I going to pay the fireman?" he demanded sullenly.

"Did you square the fireman to squirt my roof!" yelled Woggo. "I thought there was some dirty work."

Stanley bounded toward the street.

"Come 'ere!" shouted Slatter.

I remember seeing Stanley sprint up the street, and leap into the saddle of his motor-cycle, and then an enormous green elephant seemed to walk from out the very centre of the flickering ruins of the gutted house. I screamed and swooned....

I've been out of hospital a week now. My life was despaired of and I suffered frightfully. The doctors told me that I had alcoholic poisoning but I know that it was something entirely different and far more serious. Something to do with a nervous breakdown. I suppose they didn't want to frighten me with the truth.

Simpson recommended me to this sanatorium I'm in now. It is all right and they treat me well, but it seems that every man here is suffering from the effects of continued over-indulgence in intoxicants. I am the only genuine case of nervous prostration in the place. I was annoyed at first, but as my health improves I become more tolerant of other people's mistakes. Just to please Agatha I signed the pledge while I was in the hospital.

I'd have signed anything.

Agatha has taken Mary's place and is sharing Steak's flat until I am well enough to take over the ham and beef shop. They promised to visit me today. So did Flannery.

I hope Flannery doesn't fail me.

Stanley has not been sighted since the fire, but Agatha had a letter from him in which he asked if it would be safe to come back, now that I am recovering my strength.

I have decided on a career for him. I've just written this letter:

To the Secretary,
Department of Navigation.

Dear Sir, —

I should be greatly obliged if you would put this request before the proper authorities.

It is my wish to place my son, Stanley Gudgeon, in a position for which he is fitted, and I think your department may be able to do something for him in that respect. He is going on for twenty years of age and is a bright, smart boy and fairly well educated, having been studying for the Public Service examinations for some time. Mr Sloove, M.P., will vouch for his character.

If there is any possibility of a vacancy occurring on the staff of some fairly remote lighthouse I shall be deeply grateful if you would remember my son.

Thanking you in anticipation,
I am, sir,
Yours faithfully,
J. GUDGEON.

That's that…

Here comes Flannery! Thank God!

PRION HUMOUR

IF YOU ARE INTERESTED IN RECEIVING DETAILS about Prion's continuing humour publishing programme, including the Humour Classics series (details of other available titles overleaf), please write to the freepost address below, with the details of your name and address. You will receive a regular newsletter containing forthcoming title information, reviews, extracts and special offers. Please note that the Freepost address only applies to correspondents within the United Kingdom, when no stamp is required. Overseas readers should please use our full address, given after the Freepost address, using the correct postage stamp.

FOR UK CORRESPONDENTS:
PRION HUMOUR
FREEPOST LON12574
LONDON NW5 1YR

FOR OVERSEAS CORRESPONDENTS:
PRION HUMOUR
IMPERIAL WORKS
PERREN STREET
LONDON NW5 3ED
UNITED KINGDOM

OR EMAIL YOUR DETAILS TO: humour@prion.co.uk

A SELECTION OF PRION HUMOUR CLASSICS

AUGUSTUS CARP ESQ
Henry Howarth Bashford
introduced by Robert Robinson
"much funnier and darker than *Diary of a Nobody*, with which it is often compared" *Independent on Sunday*
1-85375-411-0

SEVEN MEN AND TWO OTHERS
Max Beerbohm
introduced by Nigel Williams
"the funniest book about literature ever written" Nigel Williams
1-85375-415-3

HOW TO TRAVEL INCOGNITO
Ludwig Bemelmans
introduced by Robert Wernick
"a complete original" *Saturday Review*
1-85375-419-6

MAPP AND LUCIA
E F Benson
introduced by Stephen Pile
"a wonderously bitchy caricature of upper class
English manners" *The Scotsman*
1-85375-390-4

THE FREAKS OF MAYFAIR
E F Benson
introduced by Brian Masters
"acid-tongued… peerless" *Kirkus Review*
1-85375-429-3

HOW STEEPLE SINDERBY WANDERERS WON THE FA CUP
J L Carr
introduced by D J Taylor
"a wonderful book" *The Observer*
1-85375-363-7

Diary of a Provincial Lady *
E M Delafield
introduced by Jilly Cooper
"an incredibly funny social satire... the natural predecessor to Bridget Jones" *The Times*
1-85375-368-8

The Papers of A J Wentworth, BA
H F Ellis
introduced by Miles Kington
"a gloriously funny account of the day-to-day life of an earnest, humourless and largely ineffective school master" *The Daily Mail*
1-85375-398-X

Squire Haggard's Journal
Michael Green
introduced by the author
"marvellously funny spoof of the 18th-century diarists" *The Times*
1-85375-399-8

The Diary of a Nobody
George and Weedon Grossmith
introduced by William Trevor
"a kind of Victorian Victor Meldrew" *The Guardian*
1-85375-364-5

Three Men in a Boat
Jerome K Jerome
introduced by Nigel Williams
"the only book I've fallen off a chair laughing at"
Vic Reeves
1-85375-371-8

Mrs Caudle's Curtain Lectures
Douglas Jerrold
introduced by Peter Ackroyd
"one of the funniest books in the language"
Anthony Burgess
1-85375-400-5

SUNSHINE SKETCHES OF A LITTLE TOWN
Stephen Leacock
introduced by Mordecai Richler
"there is no-one quite like Leacock, and no-one quite so good"
Tatler
1-85375-367-X

NO MOTHER TO GUIDE HER
Anita Loos
introduced by Kathy Lette
"classic and even funnier than Loos's *Gentlemen Prefer Blondes*"
The Independent
1-85375-366-1

HERE'S LUCK
Lennie Lower
"Australia's funniest book" Cyril Pearl
1-85375-428-5

THE AUTOBIOGRAPHY OF A CAD
A G Macdonell
introduced by Simon Hoggart
"wonderfully sharp, clever, funny and cutting"
Simon Hoggart
1-85375-414-5

THE SERIAL *
Cyra McFadden
introduced by the author
"an American comic masterpiece" *The Spectator*
1-85375-383-1

THE WORLD OF S J PERELMAN *
S J Perelman
introduced by Woody Allen
"the funniest writer in America" Gore Vidal
1-85375-384-X

* for copyright reasons these titles are not available in the USA or Canada in the Prion edition.